# YOU CAN DO MAGIC

## CARNIVAL OF MYSTERIES

R. L. MERRILL

Published By: Celie Bay Publications, LLC
Edited By: Kelli Collins – Edit Me This
Cover Design By: Lyrical Lines Design

❀ Created with Vellum

*To those struggling with addiction, and seeking a second chance at happiness...I see you. You are worthy. You matter.*

*If you or someone you know is struggling, please reach out.*

*In the U.S. dial 988.*

*In the U.K. dial 0800 689 5652*
*In Canada, try one of these services*

*For My Fellow Music Lovers*

*A Playlist For You...*

# CHAPTER 1

**Kal**

*A new day breaks*
*Under the blue skies above*
*A new crowd waits*
*All they need is a little shove*
*The Carnival is here*
*With mysteries galore*
*To satisfy your cravings*
*To leave you wanting more*
*We're here today, gone the next,*
*Taking along our magic and song.*
*Come inside, take a peek*
*Surprises like these won't wait long*
*Here we have the fantastical calliope,*
*come dance with our talented Kal*
*His music will delight and seduce you*
*With the power of the siren's call*

*So step right up, and don't be shy*
*For his time is coming to a close*
*Come shimmy and shake with this talented guy*
*And celebrate the last of his shows...*

I'd memorized the ringmaster's introduction, though it was more sensational than I deserved. And last night's version had a new ending, one I'd been expecting, but hearing it brought a sliver of anxiety to my bones.

The instrument I played was actually a calliaphone—a more efficient and portable version of the forced-air organ—and I'd built it myself, that much I knew. It was my voice. It spoke all I knew to say, my own words lacking. I possessed the ability to speak, but I'd mostly forgotten how, therefore I preferred to let my music speak for me. I played for the crowds. I smiled for them, but I was transparent to the onlooker.

One year had passed in this way, one year of my life, and I had nothing of my own. No friends to help, no family to love, and no safe place to lay my head away from the carnival. What would I do, where would I go, and would someone see me for me?

The boss, Mr. Ame, told me soon it would be time to move on to the next phase. I'd no clue what that meant other than I would no longer travel with the carnival. There was nothing to pack, nothing to carry, only the clothes—and the scars—I wore on my body. I would miss my calliaphone and the crowds, but I knew it was time. My stay had been healing, educational. My time taught me plenty. The carnival would go on without me and my music, on to the next place to entertain...and seduce the locals. They'd fall under the spell of my fellow travelers. Some might even be chosen to come along.

I remembered little from my time before I, too, had joined the carnival. Humiliation and regret reverberated within the structures of my cells, but I didn't recall more than that, much less the reason for the debt that forced me into servitude. The boss took me away from the darkness, and promised to set me free one day. But what was free, what would it mean, who would I be? A musician, a man, alone? I'd forgotten my past. I'd learned all I could in this place. Would I survive what lay ahead?

I took my questions to the man in charge, the one they call Errante Ame, and he confirmed that my time with the carnival was at an end.

"My dear, Kallos," the boss said to me. "The world has done you wrong, not the other way around. You have been a part of something important here, and we shall never forget the joy your music has brought to our clan and our guests. But now it is time for you to move on, as all in the crew must do. It is your choice where you'll go once you leave the perimeter, what you will do with the time you have left.

"You have been invisible to our guests for so long, adored for your playing, of course, but who you *are* remains unseen, unspoken. A blank canvas, a puzzle. Only you can solve the riddle of your life. The time is near when you will set out on your greatest adventure, the journey to find your purpose. Being reborn can be frightening. You will have questions, but the answers you seek can be found within yourself. All you must do is follow your instincts, and your heart's desire. Do what you feel is right and true. Be good to yourself and your fellow creatures, and walk the path of least harm.

"When the next sun rises, you will step outside the bounds of the carnival. You will have all that you need to begin anew. By the following sunrise, our carnival will have moved on. A traveling music festival will share these grounds with us tomorrow. Perhaps you can start there."

I knew down deep in my bones that he was correct, that something momentous was about to occur.

That night I slept soundly, tucked into the trailer that housed my calliaphone, where I'd slept for the past year, but when I woke before dawn, my body trembled and my skin was clammy.

I sat up and exhaled, glancing around my tiny space. Fresh water was delivered to my trailer each morning, and I cleaned up the best I could. I made my bed as neatly as possible, as I didn't know who might be there next. There were fresh clothes laid out for me. Strange clothes. A plain white sleeveless undershirt and a short-sleeved checkered button-up, a pair of denim trousers that felt scratchy to the touch, a handkerchief—in fact, there was a stack of them—and a pair of black canvas lace-up shoes.

Next to that pile was a coat made of some sort of fabric that made swishy noises when you ran your finger over it. There was also a billfold. I'd never seen one like it. It had a chain with a hook on either end, I supposed so you could hook it to your belt loops. Seemed like a smart idea. I'd seen people lift billfolds from unsuspecting visitors at the carnival before.

Inside the billfold were more surprises.

A little card had a picture on it that looked remarkably like me. It said Kallos Alexandrou, born January 1, 1997. The address listed was somewhere in a town called Muscatine, Iowa. The back of my neck itched as I read the card, like a bug had landed on my skin, making enough of a distraction that I felt I needed to swat it. My hand came away empty.

I put the new clothes on. They felt right, as if I'd always worn clothes such as these.

I knew that I'd come here with the organ, but my memory

of its origin was hazy. What would happen to my only friend when I left? Would someone else play it, care for it? Would it be abandoned? What would life be without my fingers on its keys? I played so many of the standard tunes, as those were what folks mostly wanted to hear, but I also played my own compositions in between. Visitors to the carnival applauded them just as often.

I ran a loving hand over the keys. *If we are meant to be together, I'll find you again.*

Before I lost my courage, I climbed down to the grass below and moved toward the exit. The sky was the same as every morning since I could remember; the brightest blue with puffy white clouds here and there to accentuate the promise of a whimsical day. I had another itch on my neck and reflexively smacked at it, thinking there was a time before when the sky hadn't looked like this. It had been something to…fear?

My stomach clenched and I caught a chill as my feet carried me closer to the boundary. The banner at the entrance that welcomed travelers had a different message on the side facing the carnival. "Enjoy Your Journey."

Before me was an expanse of black asphalt. Several rows of enormous, shiny metal tubes on wheels lined one side of the space and workers rushed around setting up colorful tents. They were smaller than ours and were open-faced, displaying colorful items of clothing, rather than our tents that contained bits of the mysterious to titillate guests young and old.

I stood at the threshold for some time, glancing back toward my trailer and then looking forward, intrigued by all of the activity before me. Black and white checkered flags adorned poles throughout the space and someone was setting up a giant inflatable screen of some sort, like one you'd see at a moving picture house.

*Where had that thought come from?*

Every so often, I would make a connection between something I saw and something I remembered but I couldn't tell you the how or why or even the *when* of it! I'd had more of them the past few weeks. Perhaps it was the fact that I was coming up on a year of service. Maybe the magic of the carnival was wearing off.

It had to be magic, whatever made me forget my life before. The boss said I'd been hurt something awful, but you'd think I'd recall something like that. My body was adorned with visible physical scars, but it was the ones that lie beneath the surface of my consciousness that terrified me the most. I wasn't sure I wanted to remember them.

A breeze tickled my face and I inhaled—and nearly coughed up a lung. Some sort of burning smell permeated the air. It seemed to be coming from the big rumbling metal tubes. Reminded me of the coal used to power the old calliope the carnival kept around. I preferred to play my calliaphone rather than that old thing. It was much easier on the ears and didn't require coal to function.

There were other scents though that were familiar. Tobacco, fried food, and something sweet floated on the breeze, like cotton candy.

Loud, echoey voices rang out through the early morning like some sort of announcer. I couldn't quite make out the words from where I was but it sounded important.

"It's almost time."

I hadn't heard Mr. Ame approach, but that was his way.

He held out a hand, and I shook it.

"Things are vastly different now than they were when you left their world. You need to take care who you trust, with whom you share your truth. The cards in your billfold will help you acquire what you need. The currency will replenish as necessary. If you want answers, go to the address on the identification card. Keep it safe. Remember to follow your heart."

A crackling sound ripped through the air, and I covered my ears as a screeching and pounding sound bounced off every surface.

"Good luck, Kallos."

Mr. Ame nodded and walked back toward our row of tents.

*His* row.

None of this belonged to me, nor I to it any longer.

I lifted my right foot, closed my eyes, and stepped over the threshold.

# CHAPTER 2

**Ryan**

The morning brought with it the schedule reveal, and my brothers in Backdrop Silhouette were not pleased with our time slot.

"Another early set? Damn. It's like they want us to suck."

I stood in the bathroom of my band's tour bus applying the day's sunscreen, foundation, and eyeliner while I listened to the new guy bitch.

Getting ready for a performance, putting on makeup, was a ritual that helped me focus. I liked to get a little creative with the corners of my eyes and tops of my cheekbones, but I wasn't good at makeup like Brains from Hush, or Chris Motionless from Motionless in White. I was more old school, like Scott Weiland maybe. He'd been one of my role models growing up. Same with Chester Bennington, Chris Cornell, Layne Staley. Notice anything those guys had in common?

Yeah, me too.

Every day I woke up was a gift. I had to remember that, especially when I was trapped on a tour bus with my closest friends and biggest detractors. Those two characterizations fit all the members of my band at one point or another. Over the course of a day they'd love or hate me within minutes. This was our fifth Warped Tour, and though I was sad it was going to be the last one, I was also ready for a break from touring. We'd only been on the road together about six weeks at this point, but that was enough.

They were all on my last nerve, and I wasn't their favorite person either.

That should all be par for the course in a rock band, but we had some extra baggage thrown in there, namely my prison term, my parole requirements, oh, and my sobriety.

I guess it was fair to say I was the baggage in this scenario.

Someone pounded much louder than was called for on the bathroom door. "You almost done in there?"

I opened the door to find TJ, one of the two newest members of Backdrop Silhouette. When I got locked up, our previous rhythm guitarist and bass player quit the band. They weren't original members either.

Burke, Parker, and I founded the band seven years ago and were used to each other's quirks. We didn't have a lot of tolerance for assholes, and yet we kept ending up with them on the payroll. After my little "fuck up," I guess I'd become one of them myself. Parker and Burke hadn't come out and said it, but there was a deep, dark crevice between us that hadn't existed previously. They'd tried to have me fired, but the label assured them they could hang up their instruments if they chose to do so. My face, my ass, my sparkling personality, my stage antics, and my voice were our moneymakers. Probably those five traits could be a band on their own.

That thought had me chuckling to the point that I forgot TJ wanted something.

"What's so fucking funny?"

TJ was four years younger than me, and damn he had a chip on his shoulder bigger than he had any right to have. I don't think he'd always hated me this much, but lately he looked as if he wanted to throat punch me every other minute. For that reason, I delighted in fucking with him.

"Your face. Oh, come on. What did you think I was going to say?" I pushed past him, being sure to knock him off his unplanted feet. Dude should have been on his toes. I was always on mine. Prison will do that to you.

He stumbled over his words, scoffed, and told me to fuck off before slamming the door.

"You're going to pay for that when it breaks," I said in my sing-songiest voice.

"Do you have to start with him every morning?" Parker sat at the booth in the kitchen drinking coffee with Burke. My other big fan, Oscar, was out jogging. He ran every morning, which I admired. Fitness was important in this life we led, a fact some of the guys could stand to get on board with. I had my own routine that I'd done every day for the past three years save two days: the first full day I had out of Soledad, and the day my best friend died.

"I think I do. It's more fulfilling than morning yoga. More potent than that shit coffee."

Parker looked down at his coffee and frowned. "It kinda is shit coffee. Maybe The Ricker can get us some better coffee."

Rick Costa, aka The Ricker, was our tour manager. The kid was such a hard worker, earnest, always looking out for hacks to make the tour more bearable, and he could make a dollar go far. We didn't have quite the budget some of our peers did so we tried to be frugal.

I pulled a sugar-free Monster energy drink out of the bus fridge and guzzled half of it down. They gave us the shit for free and I'd rather pound it down than hot, shitty coffee when it was going to be hot and shitty outside all day.

"How was your field trip yesterday?" I asked Burke. He had disappeared for a few hours and gone off to visit his grandparents' place outside Nashville. He thought no one noticed.

Burke was a stoic dude. Long straight brown hair covered his face a lot of the time. He hid behind it rather than deal with folks. There was a lot about him he wanted to keep private, like the little affair he had going on with a guy connected to our tour mates, the band Hush. I only knew about it because the guys in Hush were friends of mine, sort of. As friendly as I got. I cared because I didn't want there to be any trouble between us. That, and I wanted Burke to find something positive in life. He worried me sometimes.

"Fine."

"Didn't sound like it was fine," Parker said, curling his lip. "Sounds like there was some drama."

I knew exactly what the drama was about. Burke was as closeted as they came, and an old flame of his had come fluttering back into his stratosphere. One look at his forlorn expression let me know the dude was in a bad way.

I recognized that emotion all too well.

I'd been in a self-imposed exile for over two years now, and I often wondered if I'd ever feel that spark, that magic of finding that one soul who complemented mine, one who could look past the dirty exterior and see the jewel inside.

Damn, I needed to quit reading poetry before bed.

"Yeah, well, I got your back if you need anything." The words came out awkward. It was a sentiment we used to throw around freely with each other, but since my fuckup, they hadn't given it, and I hadn't given it often.

Making amends was hard as fuck.

Burke stared at me for a long minute, and then he gave a quick nod and looked down at his hands around his cup of shit coffee.

"Awesome. Okay, I'm going to get in a workout before Hades ascends to reclaim this circle of hell."

"But you just did your makeup," Parker said.

"Yeah. I like it to look authentic. Cheap and used, like me."

I winked at him and he laughed, just once, but it sounded like the laugh I used to be able to count on from him, not my best, but my oldest friend. I'd take it.

I stepped off the bus and the heat flared up from the asphalt even at nine in the morning. *Lord.* It was going to be miserable. And we were on at 11:45. Maybe the temps wouldn't peak until later.

There was no shade at the Tennessee State Fairgrounds outside Nashville. The kids were in for a scorcher. I didn't mind it too much. Hell, I didn't mind any sort of discomfort if it meant I could be doing the job I loved. I was grateful for every damn day I got to get up in front of people and sing. Even if it meant sweating pools of funk into my black leather pants.

Maybe it was time the band had a makeover. Wonder if the guys would go for speedos and safari hats? Sundresses? Something loose and cool to give the balls some air?

"Hey, Ryan." The Ricker was great about making sure the road crew set up my weight bench each morning. We even had a canopy for the stops with hellfire raining down like this place.

"Ricker, my man. Appreciate the setup."

His cheeks reddened from more than the heat. Kid had a crush on me. It happened. There'd been a time when I would have had him help me work out, if you follow, but the last employee of the band I screwed was now in a wheelchair thanks to my dumb ass. Part of my legally binding agreement with the band was I wouldn't shit where I ate. Fine. At 30 years old, I supposed it was time to learn some impulse control.

Rick stood there gaping at me as I pulled off my t-shirt, leaving me in a pair of ripped-up gray sweatpants I'd torn the bottom half of the legs off of. They were pretty threadbare but I couldn't find soft ones like these anywhere. Not like I had time to shop. Not for twenty-seven more days.

This last cross-country Warped Tour would hit thirty-eight stops before all was said and done. We had very few days off during the two months-ish that it lasted. Life was truly on hold.

Honestly, I'd felt like my life had been on pause since my last relapse. Like I was holding my breath for something nebulous that still hadn't presented itself.

"You need anything else, Ryan? Some water?"

"That'd be great." I hadn't realized Rick was still there. He scurried off and I got to work adjusting the weights on the bar, adding ten pounds to each side for a total of a hundred eighty pounds. I probably should have had a spotter but I preferred to do my workouts alone.

Bench press, squats, kettlebells, and resistance bands. I finished up with some core work. I was nearly done when Rick ran up with my water.

"Sorry it took me so long." He was totally out of breath and his shirt was soaked with sweat.

"Maybe *you* need it more than I do."

"I'm okay, but I'm helping out Just Like Love. They can't find their laptops. Roxanne thinks they may have been left behind in Houston."

"Shit. Their backing tracks. That sucks. Tell her to let me

know. Maybe we've got a laptop they can use? I hope their stuff is in the cloud."

He nodded and took off, leaving me with my thoughts. There were a lot of folks who disagreed with bands using pre-recorded tracks when they performed live. Those folks were around back in the day before computers were a thing in music. I didn't really pay any attention to that bullshit. Using tracks in a limited capacity meant that you could have a fuller sound on the road. It meant cutting back on the amount of backup vocalists and organ players and all that shit that makes songs that much more powerful. I felt for Roxanne and the guys.

Movement to my left caught my attention. The roadies for Just Like Love had set up their trailer next to ours and they were standing around having a cigarette while their gear was half unloaded. *Probably why they were missing laptops.* I was grateful that we had really responsible techs now. In the past we hadn't been so lucky. Mo and Jimmy were likely supervising getting our shit over to the left foot stage since we were on so fucking early.

The roadies walked away leaving Just Like Love's stuff unattended, which wasn't unusual. Security was usually good about keeping folks out of the band areas, but shit still happened. Explained why their laptops went missing perhaps.

I packed up my equipment into the trunk Rick had gotten for me to keep it all organized when I heard…a keyboard being played?

I turned to find a big blond white kid bent over keyboardist Dane Mitchell's equipment. I'd never seen this kid before, and I'd remember if I did. He looked like something out of an early Americana coffee table picture book. His short-sleeved shirt was buttoned up to his neck, and his nearly platinum hair was cut short and combed neatly back.

And what he was playing took me back.

*"Come on, you guys." I'd dragged Josh, Tyler, and Tara along with me on my bucket list trip to the Santa Cruz Boardwalk. "We still have time to hit the carousel before they close."*

*We'd been running from ride to ride in the freezing cold, and my captives were wishing they'd never agreed to come with me. Not that I'd given them much of a choice. It was more fun to have company when tying one on than drinking alone.*

*"Rye, we gotta get back, dude," Josh had tried to convince me. As our tour manager, I'd given him a run for the money. He was supposed to keep me in line. Funny. No one did that, not back then. Plus, he was pretty. I didn't want to keep my hands off of him.*

*"Yeah yeah, after this, I swear." Of course, I'd planned to drag them to a bar before we got back to the hotel, where I'd sneak Josh into my room and have my way with him again. He was eager, and I was insatiable. I loved the way he looked at me with those dreamy eyes. It was nice to have someone not see the bullshit.*

*The place had three intricately designed antique organs playing the same kind of music as they'd had at a carnival I tried to forget from my childhood. I stood in front of that damn thing watching all of the gears, the xylophones, the little angels with their drums, the pretty ladies hitting the bells. The music was so intense it shook my insides and made my teeth rattle.*

*I leaned my forehead on the Plexiglas that enclosed the cabinet and the kid working the ride yelled at me not to touch. I ignored him and let the vibrations take over. I had a nice buzz going and the sensation was almost enough to lull me into a pleasant state. But then I heard my uncle's voice in my head and—*

*"Rye? Are we doing this?" Josh put his hand on my back and I jerked away from the glass. Josh's eyes were wide when I turned to face him.*

*"Yeah, baby. Let's ride."*

*His smile was hesitant, as if he knew I'd been somewhere else.*

*We rode the carousel until Tara had to hop off and puke. Tyler held her hair as she leaned over the garbage can. I pulled rings from the holder at the wall and pelted them at the clown's face until the holder was empty and the organs shut down. I remember complaining but the kid said the whole boardwalk was closing. I was about to pull a wad of cash out of my wallet when Josh put a hand on mine.*

*"We need to go."*

*He was right but I was in such a weird state, like on the cusp of remembering something important, and the music had a hold of me. He tugged on my arm.*

*"Please, Ryan?" he whispered close to my ear. "I promise I'll take care of you when we get back." He licked his lips, and I knew he would.*

*The four of us stumbled out to the car I'd rented, my ears still ringing from the organ, me arguing I was fine to drive.*

"'Buttons and Bows.'"

The kid looked up from what he was playing, and I discovered he was no kid. He was probably in his twenties, but dressed like a kid in a picture from a century ago. His innocent blue eyes were wide, though, and when he swallowed, my eyes tracked the movement of his throat. He was of strong build, and *tall*. He didn't give off any sort of aggressive vibe. No. This man was a wallflower, he avoided the spotlight though his talent was unbelievable. And his beauty was off the charts.

"That song you were playing. It's called 'Buttons and Bows,' right?" I'd listened to a ton of music while at Salinas Valley State Prison in Soledad, Monterey County. I spent about three months strictly listening to Americana and the like and teaching myself how to play piano in the chapel when they'd let me. The songs were all stored in my mind like some sort of Rolodex. Everything about that time was.

The man nodded, then he looked down at his hands. He had the longest fingers I'd ever seen, the tips turned up slightly, and each hand had quite the wingspan. He ran his hands over the keyboard and then stood from the bench.

"No, sit," I said, placing a hand on his shoulder.

And time stopped.

No, that's not right. It tilted, whirled, spun, and he grabbed onto my arm to avoid toppling over. He was close to my height; a tad taller and a smidge thicker. But his giant blue eyes held me mesmerized as I guided him back down to the bench.

"Play something else."

He kept his gaze on me and his lips twitched as if he wanted to smile but had forgotten how. He turned his body toward the keys and let his fingertips hover above them. He closed his eyes for a moment, and then blew out a breath as he began to play another tune.

"I know this one." I squished onto the bench next to him and began to play alongside his hands for a few bars, and then I cleared my throat. "It won't be a happy marriage, I can't afford a mortgage, but you'll look sweet da da da da—"

The man hit an off note and I turned to see him looking at me strangely.

"Oh, yeah, I like to make up lyrics to these old tunes. Makes it more realistic. I mean, who buys a carriage anymore?"

He raised an eyebrow and launched into another tune, this one faster. It was "The Entertainer," and I stumbled through it right along with him. I kept sneaking looks at him and he was grinning as I struggled.

"You play fast. I can't keep up."

He sped up even more until I bumped him with my shoulder, and then he started to hit random keys while laughing soundlessly.

"Hey, where'd you come from, man? I've never seen you before. You play beautifully."

He glanced at me and stood so fast he almost knocked the bench backward. He shoved his hands in his pockets, and with curved shoulders, he walked away at a fast clip.

"Hey, wait up," I called out, but then I heard my name being called.

"Ryan?" The Ricker was trotting over from our bus. "Hey, Ryan, Roxanne does want to talk to you. She wants to see if you can help with their set."

I checked my watch and saw it was nearing ten o'clock in the morning. Gates would be opening soon.

"Yeah, I'll help. Hey, you see that guy? You know who he is?"

# CHAPTER 3

**Kal**

I'd been so overwhelmed with the amount of instruments strewn about this strange place that I hadn't thought twice about sitting down to play. I certainly hadn't thought I would be noticed, not by someone like *him*.

The other man had called him Ryan. A classic name for a not-quite classically beautiful human being. I'd never seen someone wear as much ink on their skin, not even the Tattooed Man at Mr. Ame's carnival had that many pictures etched onto his skin.

His playing showed he was not classically trained on the piano. His finger placement wasn't correct and the way he used brute force on the keys gave that away. He was most definitely a tremendous vocalist, though. Even the few bars he'd sang of "Daisy's Bell" had given me goose bumps. There was a musicality to his speech as well, the way he dragged out syllables, used his lower register and then spoke softly when he asked questions with the slightest drawl. I'd wanted to keep listening to him.

If only he hadn't asked questions. I couldn't get any words out. I'd gone a long time without talking to anyone...well, other than Mr. Ame, but that didn't count. I knew he could hear me whether I spoke out loud or not. I'd just wanted this Ryan to keep talking. I'd wanted to keep looking at him.

Then I panicked and hurried away. I was here to find my purpose, whatever that may be. And what would I say anyway?

There were so many instruments lying about, sitting in... trailers? Yeah, that sounded right. I moved from trailer to trailer and found what looked like guitars, some with four strings, some with six—but they had solid bodies and strings like I'd never seen—and even some with twelve strings or more than one neck. There was such a variety! I spied shiny and sparkly drum sets, microphones and stands of all shapes and sizes, and other equipment I had no idea how to use. But the organ had called to me. It wasn't powerful like my calliaphone, and it sounded different, but I wanted to play more.

I wandered up and down the aisles as more and more people emerged from the long metal tubes. I tried not to stare, but they all looked so...different than anything I'd ever seen before. Many of them had brightly colored hair, ripped and torn pants and shirts that showed off limbs that were colored and marked like Ryan's. Some wore makeup, both men and women, and some folks looked like a wonderful blend of both genders. This place must be one massive theater.

Strange music assaulted me every few feet as I walked along the path next to a metal fence lined with brightly-colored fabric. While I had gotten used to the constant stimulation of the carnival, this gathering was louder, more crowded, and the heat was rising from the ground in waves though it was still morning.

"Watch where you're going, dude."

A young man who was smaller than I was bounced off of me. He glared at me, and then frowned. "Wait, that's cool," he said as he reached for my shirt. "That's an original Ben Davis shirt. Did you get that thrifting?"

I knew he was speaking English to me but I didn't understand what he meant. I shook my head and smiled, hoping not to come across rude.

"Oh! Hey," said his friend, and then he began to make hand gestures at me.

When I didn't respond, a girl with them put a hand on my back and spoke in a different language, maybe Spanish? I knew Spanish, but I couldn't get the connection between my brain and mouth to work.

I touched my throat and shook my head, and the three of them gave me the look I dreaded. Pity.

They waved at me and walked away, glancing back at me over their shoulders. The whole interaction stunned me. Why had they noticed me? As far back as I could remember, whenever I'd accidentally bumped into people, they'd kept on going as if I didn't exist. What had changed?

Screams and cheers rang out from the other side of the metal fence. I found a place where there was a gap in the fabric that lined the chain-link and saw a flood of bodies spilling in like a break in a dam. Hundreds of young people from all parts of the world, a rainbow of skin colors—with colors upon colors. So much color. And black clothing.

A shrill siren sounded and I covered my ears. I ducked down, fearing for my life. The crowd started running toward the left, so I followed them. The cacophony of sounds continued to swell into some sort of evil symphony, and then a man stepped forward dressed in black pants and a red and green striped shirt.

"Welcome to Warped Tour, motherfuckers! We're Ice Nine Kills!"

And then, all at once, thundering drums and squealing metallic sounds filled the air as if someone had turned on a massive band organ and turned the crank too fast. I pressed my hands to my ears again as I was caught up in the stream of colorful people until they carried me along with them to the foot of the stage. Bodies were lifted and carried over the crowd, everyone was screaming and jumping up and down as they packed in tighter and tighter. The man with the microphone growled and jumped around, taunting the crowd.

The ruckus ended and everyone around me cheered and clapped for a few beats until the music—Was this even music?—ramped up again. This time the singer, if that's what you could call what he was doing, carried a giant knife around the stage. He hacked at a person and blood splattered all over him...but then the person walked away.

I opened my mouth to shout but no sound came out. I was frozen in my spot, my limbs shaking, and yet I was fascinated with all that was going on around me. It was like descriptions I'd read of the famous gladiator battles in Roman history. The crowds would cheer as men fought to the death, urging on the violence and gore. These young people around me loved every movement on the stage, and there was something ultimately pleasing about the beat of the music, the skill it took to play such intricate fills on the drums or the ascending and descending sounds of madness coming from the guitar-type instruments.

The sounds of an organ emanated from the stage, but it was like nothing I'd ever heard and I didn't see any sort of keys anywhere. How did they accomplish such layered compositions without an orchestra?

Before too long, the group onstage was finished and the crowd around me began to move toward the next stage. A crew of workers rushed forward and began taking apart the equipment. I watched in awe, my mind completely overwhelmed with what I'd experienced—

"Hey, I've been looking for you. Kal, right? Here." A Black woman dressed in a rainbow top that showed her shoulders and stomach, and a pair of men's pants and boots, draped some sort of material over my neck with a card hanging from the end.

*Kallos Alexandrou – Stagehand*

I looked up at her. How did she know me? Was that my name? I know it had been on the ID card in my billfold, but it felt new, but I had no idea whether it had always been mine.

"Come on, I'll show you who you'll be working with." She grabbed me by my arm and pulled me behind the fence barricade. "Sorry to rush you, but I wasn't sure where I'd find you. Howie is the stage manager here at the Red Dawn stage, and he hurt his back so he's going to need help getting instruments set up. You can set up drums, right? And tune guitars?"

Somehow I knew that I could, even though these instruments looked foreign to me. And the wires! Everything was electric.

Suddenly I began seeing circuits and connections in my mind running so quickly, I nearly missed her giving the rest of the directions.

"Here's the schedule for today. I'm going to send Krish to find you a little later so he can show you to the bus where you'll be living the rest of the summer. We're really glad you could join us. The tour's been plagued with injuries, unfortunately. You are coming to us at a time when we can really use your help."

I smiled at her and nodded.

"Oh, right." She leaned in closer. "Your former employer let us know that speaking is sometimes difficult for you. Don't worry about it. A thumbs up is a good way to say yes." She held up her thumb. "The horns are a way to tell people you're good or you're happy." She made a fist and held up her index finger and pinky finger. "And if you need help, make the thumbs up, then lift your fist with your other hand and pull it toward yourself. Push it out if you're offering help. Got it? We've had a few deaf employees over the years. I picked up the important signs. Okay! I've gotta go deal with a few things, specifically the fact that catering hasn't shown up yet to make lunch for y'all." She rolled her eyes.

I made the sign for "help you" and her face brightened.

"You're a quick learner! Awesome. Come on. Let's find Howie."

I followed her around the back of the stage, noticing as we went that it was definitely a temporary platform. My gaze was drawn to the joints and structure of it, picturing how it would all come down and go back up at the next stop. I understood how these worked.

"Come on, man. How many times have I got to tell you motherfuckers to keep your goddamned frappacini expressive crap juice off my board! Fuck!"

"Ah, Howie?"

The big white fellow with a red face turned around and frowned until he saw who was interrupting his temper tantrum. Then he smiled and opened his arms wide.

"Chantal. Love of my life." He scooped her up and started to lift her but then he grunted.

"And *you're* not supposed to be lifting anything, my love."

Howie was nearly as tall as the Tall Man at the carnival. He was barrel-chested, bald, wore a backwards cap, and had a long mustache that came down on the sides of his lips to his chin.

"You must be my savior," he said, holding out his hand. "Howard Jones. Not either of the singers. I'm the man *behind* the magic." His handshake was firm and his gaze was curious. "You know a little something about magic, don't you?"

Did he know where I'd come from? But how?

"This is Kal," Chantal said. She pronounced it "call," which made me happy. Made me feel seen. Whatever this place was, it was good. "He's the strong, silent type. Knows instruments and builds, but may need a little coaching on boards and pedals. He's a quick study." She winked at me and patted my shoulder.

"How about dealing with idiots who put their damn *poop stew on my fucking equipment*!"

A few men muttered apologies and cleaned their coffee droplets off of Howard's intricate control board. I moved a bit closer and peered at the knobs, switches, and lights as my mind followed the pathways and junctions, all lit up and feeding into each other.

"I think you guys got this under control. I'll make sure Krish finds you, Kal, okay?"

I gave her a thumbs up as I looked around at all of the equipment and the men hurrying around with it.

She made the sign with the horns. "Right on. Okay. You need anything before I go?"

I shrugged. I had no idea what was happening and therefore had no idea what to ask for.

"Cool. See you later Kal."

Howie's arm came down heavy on my shoulder. "You ready to work?"

I gave a hesitant thumbs up and he laughed heartily. "That's the spirit. Okay, we got Backdrop Silhouette up next. Let's give them a hand."

He patted my shoulder hard—and I stumbled into Ryan.

# CHAPTER 4

**Ryan**

I was doing a few last-minute stretches when a big body rammed into me from behind.

"It's you! Hey, wait—"

"Sorry about that, Ryan. This is Kal. He's gonna help me out while my back is tweaked. You need anything?"

*Call?* He had an all-access pass around his neck that hadn't been there before. His name was spelled Kallos.

"Beauty." I'd spent a couple of weeks trying to teach myself Greek during my time in prison but I'd given up. It was a damn hard language to follow, but that word stood out to me. And this man definitely embodied its meaning.

He smiled at me, his golden cheeks reddening as he gave me a thumbs up.

Odd. But it was fitting. *He* was odd. He stood out. He was unique. Something made him seem like he'd been added in on a green screen, a special effect. Was he a CGI person? A hologram? It was almost like he glowed. I couldn't take my eyes off of him.

"He don't talk much. Anything you need, though, we got you."

I slapped hands with Howie, but I couldn't stop staring at this strange man.

"Here, Kal, how about you help Backdrop's drum tech?"

Kal nodded and took the stairs onto the stage two at a time with his long legs.

"Where'd he come from?" I asked. He seemed like a man out of time before, but now, watching him set up the drums with Mo, maybe I'd just been having a moment.

"Chantal brought him over to help. Doc says I'm not supposed to be lifting anything, can you believe that? We still got twenty-four dates to go. At least now I've got an extra set of hands. Hey, wait, don't touch that." Howie moved to Kal's side and pointed out something to do with the mic cords.

I let him get back to managing the stagehands. In addition to our techs, the tour had hands at each of the stages. I never paid much attention to their work before, but now? I couldn't stop staring at Kal's forearms as he tightened the cymbals on the stand.

"Wells, man. You warmed up? Don't need you blowing out your voice."

I turned to find Oscar stretching, pulling his fingertips backward with a sneer, his stupid bangs in his face.

"How 'bout I worry about my body and you worry about yours?"

"Because your body is required for the show to go on, you dumbfuck."

My lips pulled back from my teeth in something that might have resembled a smile to anyone not privy to the amount of animosity Oscar and I had for each other.

"That's right, motherfucker," I seethed. "And doesn't that piss you off?"

My limbic system kicked into high gear, and I balanced my weight on my feet, ready for a fight. I didn't do flight. It wasn't in my repertoire.

I felt a hand on my shoulder and was ready to throw a punch at whoever thought it was a good idea to touch me when I was in this state, but thankfully I caught a glimpse of plaid before shifting my weight.

Kal.

He made a thumbs up sign and pushed it up with his other hand, moving it towards me.

"Help? Oh, no. I don't need any help."

He looked at Oscar and a crease appeared between his eyebrows as tension built in his frame. For the first time, he didn't seem the innocent. No. Somehow I knew he was no stranger to physical violence.

I placed a hand on his forearm and moved into his line of sight, hoping to take the focus off Oscar. As much as I wanted to punch my bandmate in his smart mouth, I couldn't have him damaged either. I might have been indispensable for Backdrop's success, but Oscar was kind of important as well. *I guess.*

"Hey. I'm okay," I said in a low voice. "He's a dick, but I'm used to it. Thanks, though."

His body was completely still, stiff, as if at any moment he might pounce. I squeezed his arm and that got his attention on me instead of Oscar. His blue eyes widened and he stepped back. He shook his head and backed away from the confrontation, heading back to the stage.

I wanted to go after him. Nobody ever stood up for me. Well, maybe Silas from Hush, but that was because he was just as much of a hothead as me, only he came in a pint-sized package. Not even Gavin had stepped up for me.

Fuck, that's exactly who I did *not* need to think of at this moment.

I'd been about to climb the steps and look out at the crowd, but I needed a minute. I couldn't go onstage thinking about my dead best friend. The man I'd been in love with, only I'd never told him. I began to pace, my heart speeding up at a pace that reminded me of the kick I used to get from cocaine, which had me thinking about Gavin again…

"Dude."

Parker stood at my side. He knew not to touch me.

"I'm all right."

He waited a beat for me to continue.

"What? I'm fine. Fucking Oscar mouthed off again."

"You can't let him get to you," Parker said. "Let's get through this fucking set and then I'll talk to him, okay?"

Parker would try. He might get Oscar to cool it for a few days, but unfortunately, this storm had been brewing for too long now. It needed to come to a head. What the fallout would be, though, I had no idea.

And I kind of felt okay with that. I was beyond feeling like my life would be over if I couldn't sing for this band anymore. Gavin had shown me that I had worth, that my music had value, especially what we created together. I loved my band. But did I love it enough to keep putting up with this shit? Especially when it was fucking with my mental state? I needed to be on, needed to bring it for the fans, needed to keep myself contained so I didn't go off the rails again. If that happened, I might not make it back next time.

"You put the setlist up there for me?" I asked him.

Parker started our songs off, making him in charge of the setlist. Sometimes I'd fuck with him and go off-script. Not today, though. I just wanted to be done.

And that was a shitty way to feel when I was about to take the stage.

"Yeah, man. You ready? We can't be late. It'll fuck up the schedule for the whole day."

Nice. Another reminder of my failings.

I let my head fall back and took a deep breath. My leather pants were stuck to every square inch of my lower half, and my sleeveless t-shirt was already wet down the back. I knew my makeup was likely sweating off. The fucking sun on my face was like a damn tractor beam, sucking the life out of me.

"Let's do it." *Before I have nothing left to give.*

I stepped aside as my band took the stage before me. I'm not sure why it was a big deal for the singer to be the last one onstage. I knew how to make an entrance, of course. I'd been doing it for most of my life.

As Parker started on the kickdrum, I felt someone standing behind me. I spun around to find Kal.

He smiled. And he gave me the horns.

I wanted to kiss him.

Whoever sent me this angel today to interrupt the negative talk in my head, blessed be.

*Another town, another place,*
*another line upon my face.*
*Here today, gone the next,*
*and nobody knows my name.*

*I play so you can sing and dance*
*And hope someday I have a chance*
*To find someone to hold my hand*
*and join my lonely one-man band*

. . .

*To share the magic of a touch*
*Hope that's not asking too much*
*Cause I'm here today, gone the next*
*And nobody knows my name.*

The words were cleansing as I belted them to the heavens. It was a religious experience for me, between me and the audience. Singing was the one thing in life that brought me a guilt-free high, joy, and peace. Hearing the kids sing my lyrics back to me was all the affection I needed. Or it was enough to sustain me, anyway. And when the rain began to pour down on the overheated crowd, I counted it as a sign of grace.

*Ryan Michael Wells, you are a favored child of the gods. You shall reap the gifts you give unto others with your voice.*

I'd heard that statement from a priest in my youth. It was the only thing he'd said to me that wasn't a lie. I did anything anyone asked in order to keep the praise coming.

I stepped out from under the protection of the stage roof and turned my face toward the rain. I probably should have been concerned about the electrical nature of my profession. I held the mic to my lips and felt the shock rattle my teeth.

"What the fuck are you doing?" Burke never talked to me onstage, but today he shouted at me. "We're not grounded good up here."

I gave him a wink as I stepped into the hands of security.

Oscar spit where I'd just been standing. "Fucking hell, Wells."

And that added fuel to the fire.

I grabbed my crotch and sneered at him as I fell backward into the waiting hands of the crowd. I let them carry me as I crossed my legs and lay as stiff as I could. I started to sing one of my favorite songs over and over again, keeping the band from breaking into the next chorus. *"Here comes the rain again,"* that phenomenal song by the Eurythmics. Annie Lennox was my absolute favorite female vocalist and I loved to sing her songs. The crowd began singing with me and the music quieted except for Parker's drumbeat, which took over the rhythm of my own heart.

Eventually, Parker got impatient and started doing some complicated fills, and TJ picked up the bass line. My fun was over. I pointed toward the stage, and the hands carried me back to the security guards. When I was upright, I reached out, and Kal was there to catch me.

I gazed into his eyes for a long moment before thanking him...and missing my cue to start singing the chorus. Oscar and TJ carried the song and the audience sang along.

He lifted me with ease over the barrier and made sure I was steady on my feet before backing away. I picked up the chorus as I stared for a few more beats, and then I climbed the steps back onto the stage, earning an ugly look from Parker.

*Yay.*

The rest of the set went without a hitch other than me being unable to take my eyes off Kal. He remained at the foot of the stage with his arms crossed over his chest, watching my band play intensely. At one point, I sat on the edge of the stage next to where he stood and sang to him. It was during one of our not-slutty songs. It was one of the times I'd put a toe in the waters of self-expression and let the teeniest bit of myself show.

*Bury me with your disgust*
*Strike me down with your disdain*
*I'll come crawling back again*
*Whatever you think of me,*

*be sure it's been thought before*
*Behind every break is*
*Another closed door*
*However you try to knock me down*
*It's nothing I haven't endured*
*Greater men than you have tried*
*Push me, I will not fall*
*Kick me, I will not quit*
*Curse me, I will not give up*
*I will go on when you're long gone*

He watched me carefully, dropping his arms to his sides, and I thought maybe, just maybe, he might see through my shenanigans and slutty stage persona, although the latter I'd toned down today. Actually, for most of the tour I'd toned it down. I wasn't feeling it anymore. The new songs were a little mature, at least that's what the reviews of the new album had said. They didn't profess their love for it, but they did claim my lyrics had grown up a bit. I'd take their breadcrumbs.

It figured that on the last Warped Tour, I'd have an existential crisis. Whatever my problem was, the distraction of Kal kept me from being morose. Whoever he was, I wanted a healthy serving. However he'd gotten here, I hoped he'd stick around.

# CHAPTER 5

**Kal**

Ryan Wells had the voice of an angel and a body to tempt even the holiest of men, which I was not. Somehow I knew that from before, or maybe I figured it out by the way I responded to Ryan's performance on a primal, carnal level.

It felt like he was singing only for me, and I liked that. A lot.

When the rain started, I'd held my breath, worrying for his safety. I knew enough about electricity to know that water didn't mix well with all that was going on. But it seemed to bring out some sort of bliss in Ryan. He'd fallen into the crowd, and I'd been ready to push them all aside to get to him, only he'd risen above their heads like magic. He'd seemed enraptured by their caresses, and by the feel of the raindrops on his face. His smile had been serene, not like the one I'd seen when he'd argued with the fellow in his band.

That man had made me see red. I didn't like the way he'd talked to Ryan. At all. Ryan was special. I didn't have to know anything about him to see that. And to hear him? A gift.

As soon as his band left the stage, Howie directed me to start helping the techs tear down the equipment to make way for the next band. The pace was rushed. I had a hard time keeping my big self from being in the way of the men who'd been doing this longer than me. I'd wanted time to run my hands over the mind-boggling technology behind these instruments. I wanted to play them all, feel the sound travel through my bones.

When the next band was ready to take the stage, I moved to the area behind, sort of looking for Ryan. The next band was loud like the first one had been. Ryan's band had heavy guitars as well but their songs had melodies and harmonies that were pleasing to my ears once I got past the initial assault.

"Kallos? Are you Kal?"

A tall young man with brown skin and short black hair and a scar on his scalp approached me with the friendliest smile I'd seen since stepping foot into this festival.

I pressed my hand to my chest and nodded, giving him a little bow. He held his hand out to shake and I appreciated the gesture. He was taller than me, quite thin, and his eyes were vibrant and excited. I knew spending time with him would make his excitement contagious.

"I'm Krish. Chantal sent me to find you. But before we do anything, drink some water. It's ridiculously hot out here and your cheeks are bright red."

I touched my face and realized that, yes, I was quite overheated despite the rain we'd just had. I took the bottle he offered and drank a few gulps, the cool liquid immediately giving me relief from the heat.

"And I want to make sure you get some lunch. Now, I tend to talk pretty fast, though I do know some sign language, so stop me if you have questions, okay?"

I nodded at him and smiled. I really hoped that as my memories returned, my mind would kick the speech function into gear. If he started using sign language and I didn't understand him? It might cause these people to think I was unqualified for this position, and I didn't want that to happen. I had a hunch that this was where I was supposed to be, or at least it was a good place for me to land.

"You're working with Howie, huh? How's it going so far?"

Thumbs up.

"Great. I've met him a few times. He's pretty funny, especially at the after-parties. Lots of stories to tell about all of the tours he's worked on. Howie's been with Warped Tour for at least a decade. This is my first time being on the tour, but I've been going to shows for several years. I've seen a lot of these bands at other venues."

I gestured to him and then played a pretend guitar.

"Oh! Yes, I play. Some. But I'm a writer. I have a blog and I'm working on a book about the history of the tour. My boyfriend…" He smiled shyly. I wondered if it was because he'd said boyfriend. I wondered if that was acceptable in this place.

A hazy memory of two men and *wrong* tickled the back of my neck. That sensation was becoming annoying.

"His name is Silas," Krish continued. "His band, Hush, is on the tour too. I moved onto their bus, so Chantal said you can take my spot on the bus with her and some of the photographers. How about I take you over there and then we'll get you some food?"

I was in such a daze. Probably some of it had to do with the fact that I needed sustenance like he'd suggested. But everything about this day had taken on a dreamlike quality. I figured the best way to behave was to follow along. I had no alternative. I was sure the carnival would be gone soon. That door was closed.

"Hey, Krish. I was just going to tell Kal to go take lunch. You want to show him around?"

Krish grinned and put an arm around my shoulders. "Already on it, Howie. I'll take care of him."

Howie waved to us and I waved back, following Krish's lead. I had questions, wonderings, but I didn't know how to put them into words. Thankfully, Krish seemed to pick up on my mood.

"I'm sure you have lots of questions. I did when I first got here. Would it help if I point out things as we go?"

Thumbs-up.

"Awesome. Okay, how much history of the tour do you know?"

I shook my head.

"All right. Well, this is the twenty-fourth year of the tour, and it's the last time they'll go cross-country. We're all pretty bummed about it, but I think there will be something else to come along. Bands are trying new things for tours to get their music out there as much as they can. There are about sixty bands with us for most of the tour, a few special guests in certain cities, and we make thirty-eight stops. We're on date fourteen here in Nashville. You'll get to see a lot of the country as we travel, we won't make a lot of stops outside of the venues, but it's still a great way to see more of the country. Hey, where are you from, anyway?"

I had no idea what to say. I opened my mouth just as a slicing pain went through my head. I pressed my hand to the top right side, bending at the waist as it throbbed a few times before dissipating.

"I'm sorry, Kal. Are you okay? Maybe we need to sit

down." I shook my head and made a thumbs up. "Huh. Suffer-in-silence type, huh? Okay. But we really need to get more water in you." He gestured for me to drink more of my bottle. I finished and held it up with a shrug.

"Ah. Here." He tossed the bottle in a blue refuse can with the words RECYCLE PLEASE on it. "We try not to leave a mess behind us as we move from place to place."

I glanced around and saw more cans with TRASH on the sides overflowing with paper containers and food.

"Yeah, most of that stuff is compostable. We have a long way to go, but that's all of society. We'll get you a better water bottle you can keep with you, and see that station over there?" One of the tents had big tanks with faucets coming out of them and kids lined up to get their bottles filled. "You can refill it as much as you want. Sound good?"

Thumbs up.

"Awesome. You're going to have a great time with the tour, Kal. I can feel it. Do you prefer Kal or Kallos? My name is Krishnan, but most people call me Krish."

I shrugged.

"Okay then. Ready for more?"

Thumbs up.

"Over here are some of the nonprofits that travel with the tour. They help kids with information on birth control, mental health, and we even have a booth where you can sign up to donate bone marrow for cancer victims."

That word punched me in the chest, knocking the air out of me. I grabbed Krish's arm and opened my mouth to speak, but again, nothing would come out. I patted his chest.

"What? The booths?"

I nodded and kept patting him. What had he just said?

"Birth control? Mental Health? Uh, cancer?"

I grabbed him by the biceps as my eyes rolled back in my

head. For some reason that word—cancer—filled me with rage and sorrow.

"Kal? Hey, man, let's sit."

Krish guided me to a bench and we sat. He gave me another bottle of water and I downed half of it in seconds.

"Easy now," Krish said, patting my shoulder. "This heat is oppressive. Don't want you to pass out."

I held up my thumb, but my mind was reeling. *Cancer.* A devastating illness that attacked the body, usually resulting in death. What did cancer have to do with me? I didn't think I'd had it, and I couldn't recall any sort of thread to a person who might have had it. A family member? I must've had a family at one point. I knew what family was; I'd seen plenty of them at the carnival passing through.

I squeezed my eyes shut. There had to be a reason I didn't remember my past, and I had a feeling I was better off not remembering. I also knew people often ignored what was good for them when it came to curiosity.

I finished the bottle and watched people walking by. Affectionate couples, groups of screaming girls, packs of boisterous young men pushing each other and laughing. So much joy despite the miserable heat.

"Yeah, it's a lot. I'm used to this weather, though. I live in San Diego. But I don't love being out in it."

I stood and gestured for him to lead the way. We made it through the rows of tents to another fence and, beyond it, the metal tubes on wheels.

"Some of the bands share these buses and have their crew with them, and some have separate vehicles for their crew and gear. Then there are the younger or smaller bands who tour in a van with a small trailer. There's a lot of equipment that gets hauled from stop to stop, it's like a military assault." We passed about ten of the buses before he stopped in front of one with…a skeleton for a driver?

"That's Clarence. He's the bus mascot. Come on in!"

We climbed onto the bus and there were two men sitting at a table.

"Casey, Vinh, this is Kal. He's taking my bunk."

"Is he going to run off with a hot rock star too?" Casey asked, and they both started laughing.

Krish ducked his head. "Come on, guys. You know it had nothing to do with you."

"You never know. Maybe we're accidental matchmakers."

"Or we're so obnoxious we send our bus mates running for the first available guy or girl."

Ryan's smile flashed before my eyes.

No, that was preposterous. I couldn't even talk to him. But I wanted to.

"You guys have any shoots lined up today?"

The two looked at each other and then back at Krish.

"We might be hiding from the heat in here—"

"But don't tell."

Krish laughed and held up his hands. "Y'all are grown-ass men, you can decide what to do with your time. I just wanted to show Kal where his bunk and his things are."

"Oh yeah, Chantal dropped off his bag earlier. She replaced your labeled shelves with his name. It's like you never existed. Sniff."

I couldn't help but grin. Their camaraderie and sense of humor put me at ease. There had been few folks at the carnival who took the time to talk with me. Everyone was always so busy there wasn't a lot of time for conversation.

"Over here, Kal. See, this is your bunk, and you have your bag here and a shower caddy."

I peered into the bag, curious, and it appeared there were more clothes like the ones I wore. There was a plastic tray that held a toothbrush, toothpaste, and some bottles of what I assumed were for personal hygiene. Had Chantal put this together? Had Mr. Ame left this for me? How was it possible that everything I needed seemed to appear?

I touched the billfold in my back pocket and remembered what he'd said to me this morning.

*You shall have all you need.*

I knew there were unexplainable things about the carnival, but I wasn't on the grounds anymore. How was this magic accompanying me?

"Wow, this is great. Looks like you're all set. And here in the kitchen," he said, moving past me in the tiny hallway to the small kitchen. "We have the microwave and refrigerator. This shelf over here has your...oh, Corn Flakes, okay, and some cans of soup and crackers, some tuna... You sure this is all you want? We do make stops in between shows, I can always grab you something else. Like vegetables or fruit."

I peeked over his shoulder and saw familiar names but the labels looked different than I was used to.

"You won't need to eat on the bus much at all. Catering is awesome, and there's usually bagels or donuts or muffins around for breakfast. Plus, someone barbecues almost every night."

I nodded. The carnival fed us, but it was the bare minimum unless you wanted to pick through the leftover popcorn and hotdog wrappers. I'm not ashamed to say that sometimes I'd done just that.

But this festival was so welcoming. These people didn't know me and they were inviting me to share their home on wheels, and their food. I had a moment where my lungs refused to function properly. My eyes burned with shame. Who was I to deserve this level of charity? I was going to have to be sure I was a helpful part of the team here.

A feeling of regret passed through me, as if there was a time when I hadn't contributed, or perhaps what I'd contributed had been counterproductive or harmful.

"You need a minute?" Krish's smile was kind. His warm personality helped me remember how to breathe once more.

I shook my head and opened my mouth.

"Thank you."

His eyes flared as I pressed a hand to my throat, as surprised as he was to hear sound coming out.

"You're very welcome," Krish said, placing his hand on my arm and giving it a squeeze. "You need anything else here? Or do you want to go hit catering and grab some lunch?"

I placed a hand on my stomach, feeling a little grumble at the mention of lunch.

"Awesome. Let's go!"

We said goodbye to Casey and Vinh and left the cool bus for the heat outside. Krish kept up a steady stream of conversation as we walked, and I appreciated his explanations of things, such as how kids could use their little square devices as a payment method, and that it was also a telephone, and a way to listen to music and take pictures.

"You don't have a phone?" he asked me. "Well, if you want one, we can always grab one on a stop. They can be a nuisance, but most everything you do in life requires some sort of smart phone for communication."

That was something I'd have to consider. From what I understood, this music festival was only traveling for another few weeks and then I would need to find someplace else to go. Hopefully, I would find the answers I needed by then. And a purpose. My purpose as long as I could remember was to play music for people. I'd found myself surrounded by people who had a similar purpose, so I must be in the right spot.

Krish led us to an area covered by a big canopy with giant fans keeping the air circulating. "Today is burger day, and usually they don't mess up burgers, so you're in for a treat."

I followed as he picked up a plate and got into a line to be served. Krish continued to tell me about the food service as my mouth began to water. I hadn't realized how hungry I was.

Krish suddenly let out a squeal and jumped.

"Fancy meeting you here."

I turned to find Ryan smiling deviously.

# CHAPTER 6

**Ryan**

I watched Krish lead my new fixation into catering and I took several beats to simply admire him from afar. He wore his short-sleeved plaid Ben Davis tucked into his deep indigo Levi's with a handkerchief poking out of the back pocket, and a chain wallet in the other. I wanted to rest my hands on that thick waist and just hold on. If I slid my fingers into the back of his waistband, I could keep him in place, keep him with me, and bask in his light.

I had to check myself though. Was I fixated because I needed a distraction? Was I just trying to soothe my fragile ego because of the shit with TJ and Oscar? I knew I was in a vulnerable place. That's where I'd been the first time I'd hung out with Gavin after getting out of prison.

*"You know, so many people love you, Rye. They're going to forgive you."*

*Gavin and I sat on a bench on a humid night somewhere in the*

*South. It was the 2015 Warped Tour and I was fresh out of prison. Backdrop barely had time to practice before hitting the road with all sorts of requirements slapped on my being. Weekly therapy calls, AA meetings, total sobriety, abstaining from any sort of sexual contact with anyone employed by or professionally associated with the band, etc., etc.*

*Humiliating. And it all crashed down on me while watching our freakishly immature bandmates and friends shoot each other with water guns full of colored water and cans of Silly String. The yelling and screaming and the physical contact had me withdrawing to the sidelines. In the past, I would have been right in there with them. Gavin had been the only one to notice.*

*"I don't ever hear forgive," I said. "I hear 'we're good,' which to me means, 'I'm going to tolerate you for my benefit.'" I downed a can of cranberry juice, my new drink of choice. That and the free Monster energy drinks they plied us with during the tour.*

*Gavin brushed my hair back from my face and held onto my chin, forcing me to look right at him. "There's nothing to forgive, Rye. You fucked up. We all have. Loving is forgiving, and I love you."*

*If only he'd known I loved him too. I loved him more than he loved me. His was platonic, mine was idol-worship level. But he was with Mel, and talking marriage and babies with him, so there was no need to insert myself into the equation. He deserved to be happy. I didn't deserve shit.*

*"Hey, you want to go jam? I have some songs I've been working on, not really Hush material, but it's something, you know? I think you'd get it. Wanna come?"*

*"Yeah." I really did. I didn't want to be sitting on the outside looking in. I was a pariah. Gavin was offering me sanctuary and even if he fucking wanted help cleaning the toilet, I would have gone with him.*

*But what happened on that bus changed my whole belief system about music.*

*Alone, without the crutches of our usual musical partners, we reached out, we fucking soared through space and brought the stars back with us. We made magic.*

*It started that night and continued many nights after while we toured the country with our respective bands. Silas had gotten pouty about it, but when he heard our stuff, when we finally decided to tell our people, he'd understood. He'd loved it and been our cheerleader.*

*Then the labels had gotten involved and fucked everything up. Then Gavin was gone.*

I could use a cheerleader now.

"You better not be checking out my boyfriend, motherfucker."

Speaking of cheerleaders. My unexpected tiny Hobbit of a friend, Silas Franklin, cracked me up with his fists on his hips like he was going to do something.

"Your man is safe from me. His new charge, however…"

Silas cocked his head to the side and gave Kal a onceover.

"Where'd he come from? Or should I say *when* did he come from? Who tucks their shirt in anymore? And the cuffs on those pants? He looks like—"

"He stepped out of time. I know." That broad back was begging for me to free it from the confines of his clothes. "I want to draw him. Paint him."

"You want to paint *on* him," Silas cracked as he elbowed me.

I laughed but yeah, that was kind of the idea.

"Well, let's go get our mens." Silas hooked his arm through mine and made to sneak up on Krish. I grabbed us trays and stood right behind Kal. He'd done it to me, so I had no qualms about invading his space. Krish was chattering away to Kal about meat and it took all of my willpower not to lean closer and sniff the new guy.

Silas finally grabbed Krish's ass, causing him to jump, so I gave into temptation and leaned closer to Kal.

"Fancy meeting you here."

Kal turned quickly and, thankfully, looked as happy to see me as I was to see him.

Krish and Silas kissed like they hadn't seen each other in weeks rather than hours. Kal's eyes bugged out and he glanced around nervously, another move that made him seem out of time, or at least not from a place where public displays between men were common. But he didn't shrink back from the couple. No. He stepped forward as if to block them with his body, or to protect them.

Be still my black heart.

"Get a room." Los Morales, Hush's guitar player and Silas's stage-5 clinger, gave an exaggerated sigh. He was absolutely supportive of Silas and Krish, as long as they made room for him. He was straight as they came, but the dude was dealing with a lot of baggage I'd yet to discover, and he was attached to Silas, and now Krish, at the hip. It was kind of cute.

"Los, this is Kal. He's helping out on the Red Dawn stage while Howie's back is fucked up."

Los frowned at Kal. "Where'd you come from?" he asked with his arms crossed over his chest.

That crease was back on Kal's forehead. He looked between Krish and I to judge whether or not Los was a threat.

"Hey, cut out the tough-guy act, Morales," I said with an eye-roll. "Kal's good people. He got the glitch out of the mics finally. Whatever he did, I wasn't getting feedback."

"Sweet," Silas said. "We could use some of that magic over at the Left Foot stage. I keep hearing a buzz. Everyone says I'm hearing shit. Bowie told me my headset was haunted."

We all chuckled, even Kal, and then it was our turn to

grab lunch. Kal stepped back and let everyone go in front of him. I nudged him with my tray.

"You need to eat, man. Go ahead."

He blinked those blue eyes at me and opened his mouth as if he was going to say something. I lingered, wanting to hear his voice. I could wait all night. But then he shook his head and his cheeks reddened as he swallowed hard.

"Hey. It's all good. You don't have to say anything. I got you. Anything you don't want?"

Kal peered over the movable counters at the food and smiled at me, shaking his head.

"All right. Put your tray out and they'll put the food on there for you."

I talked him through the line and smiled at his choices. A plain burger, three scoops of fruit salad, some potato chips, a pudding cup, and a milk carton. I, on the other hand, went for the fruit salad, a veggie burger, and a Naked Juice. Had to eat healthy when I could. With these heathens, it might be another week before I saw a vegetable.

There was a ruckus at the entrance to the tent, and I groaned when I saw TJ, Oscar, and Parker coming in together. TJ and Oscar had beers with them, and with the heat so intense, they were already pretty trashed. It wasn't even one o'clock in the afternoon. I shook my head and turned away from them, hoping they'd grab food and leave the premises.

"You guys rocked, by the way," Silas said close to my ear. "I particularly loved the Annie Lennox bit."

"Thanks, man. I don't know. It was a vibe today."

I heard a snort behind me and turned to find the Terrible Two.

"A vibe, huh?" Oscar rolled his eyes. "That what you call it when you decided for the rest of us to change the whole fucking set?"

I sighed, really done with this shit.

"Sorry you couldn't keep up."

I knew before I'd even finished speaking that today was the day Oscar was going to make his move. I'd gotten comfortable, hanging out with people I knew had my back. I should have known better.

Oscar handed his beer to Parker, who swore under his breath, and then Oscar slammed his tray down with a loud crack.

"Come on, you guys. Knock it off," Parker said without hope.

I turned my torso sideways, but kept my fists down. If this was going to happen, I was going to let Oscar be the clear instigator. He approached me, bumping chests with me and breathing his nasty beer breath in my face.

"The fucking world does not revolve around you, asshole," he said, spitting in my face. "The sooner you figure that out, the better."

A big hand landed on Oscar's chest. It wasn't mine.

He looked up at Kal and his eyes flared. "What the fuck! Get your hand off me."

"Hey, no." I tried to get between them but Kal wasn't budging. "This isn't your fight, Kal."

His brow furrowed and he leaned in closer to Oscar, shaking his head slowly side to side.

"What the fuck is wrong with you?" Oscar looked from Kal's hand on his chest up to Kal's face. "Back the fuck up!"

When Kal didn't move, Oscar stepped back and Kal straightened. He reached out to pull me behind him. I must have been in shock, because I let him.

"This ain't over, Wells. I'll see you later."

TJ flipped me off and put an arm around Oscar. "Forget it, man. Come on. Not here."

Parker looked between us and sighed. He picked up a tray

and moved around us to get lunch. I didn't know what to say to him but I hated that this drama was getting in the way of Backdrop's business.

"Parker, man—"

"Save it. I'm sick of this shit. What is this, junior high?"

The words I'm sorry wouldn't come. I was, but I was hurt, too. He was done with me, and after all we'd accomplished together, after all we'd been through, I wanted him to be on my side.

"Fuck that guy," Silas said, putting an arm around me and guiding me to the table him and Krish had grabbed. "I'm sorry. I didn't even see him until Kal stepped up.

Kal was staring at me and breathing hard. As we locked eyes, his gaze softened.

"It's fine. I'm fine. Let's eat."

Krish and Silas sat on one side of the table and Kal waited for me to sit before taking the bench next to me. He left about six inches of space between us, as if he wasn't sure he was welcome.

He waited for me to start eating before taking his first bite.

"I didn't know things were so bad with you guys," Silas said. "That sucks."

"Yeah," Los agreed. "That's not like 'hey dick, quit leaving your funky towel in the bathroom' kind of shit."

I shrugged and took a few beats to chew my veggie burger, which was lukewarm despite it being hot as fuck in there. "It is what it is. I know I shouldn't take his bait, but I'm not wired that way."

Silas looked between me and Kal, and then he pressed his lips together to hold in a laugh.

"What?"

He snorted. "Sorry, I just never thought I'd see the day when Ryan Wells would need a bodyguard."

I put down my burger like *what the fuck,* but then I glanced at Kal. He was trying to look anywhere but at me and concentrate on his food.

"I don't need… Look. I'm trying to behave, all right? But that little prick gets in my face again… I'm not trying to start mess, I swear."

Kal turned to me, held up a thumb and pushed it toward me with his other hand.

"You want to help me?"

He did it again.

"Help me behave, or help me beat the shit out of him?"

Kal's lips turned up into a grin, and he shrugged as if to say whichever the situation calls for.

Oh, I *liked* having him around.

"Hey, did you guys know there's a carnival on the grounds?" Los asked. "It's like one of them old-timey kinds."

"Yeah?" Silas asked. "We should go! Tonight. We play at like four something. Why don't we go check it out after?"

Krish was all in, but Los was convinced he would be kidnapped by some carney meth freaks. I was down to get away from my band for a bit.

Kal was really interested in his food all of a sudden.

"You should come with us," I said to him, leaning close. "Might be fun."

Kal looked up at me, and I fell into his sorrowful gaze. He opened his mouth to speak, closed it, and then stood hurriedly, nearly upsetting the table.

"Kal?" Krish said, rising to his feet.

Kal gave me one last longing look, picked up his tray and left, setting it down with a bang on the bussing station.

"I wonder what's wrong?" Krish and Silas exchanged worried looks. I liked the effect Krish had on Silas the hothead.

"Probably worried about the freaks there," Los said,

dabbing at his mouth with a napkin. "Like, getting kidnapped, sold into slavery. You know, trafficking is a big problem. Pretty as he is, he best watch his back."

No. *I'd* be watching his back.

I picked up my shit and went after him.

"Wait. You want to meet up later or what?" Silas asked.

"I do. I'll catch you after your set." I waved and took off at a jog in the direction Kal went. After a few long minutes, I found him standing in the middle of the nonprofit section. He was staring at the Fuck Cancer sign next to the Hope, Love, Strength Bone Marrow Donor List booth.

"Hey, man." I placed a hand on his shoulder. "You all right?"

"I don't know."

He spoke, startling us both. His voice sounded raspy, like someone who had walked through the desert with no water for days.

"That's okay," I said. "You don't have to know. But you don't have to go it alone, okay? You stood up for me. *Nobody* does that. Lean on me if you need. If you want to. And Krish and Silas are cool. Whatever it is."

He nodded at me but didn't make eye contact. He just stared at the sign.

"You lose someone?" I asked him.

He grimaced as if he were remembering something painful.

"It's okay. Want to go talk to them? They're trying to get folks to sign up for the registry. They take a swab of your cheek, and if you're a match to someone who needs a bone marrow transplant, they call you."

He tilted his head sideways with a frown.

"For treatment. There's no cure for cancer, but there are some good treatments available. I talked to their rep a few weeks back. A lot more folks are surviving their battles with that fucking disease and living for a long time. All of Hush went and signed up after they found out their drummer Brains had cancer as a kid. Fucking horrible. I think I'd rather go back to prison than have that shit."

Kal put his hand on my arm, and I jumped, still not used to being touched so freely, but with him, it wasn't unpleasant. He tried to speak, and I could see the frustration as his mouth twisted.

"Hey, it's okay. It'll come."

He squeezed his eyes shut and blew out a breath. He pointed at my chest and then placed his hand over his heart. I wasn't sure what he was trying to say but I damn sure appreciated the gesture.

I placed my hand over his and gazed up at him. What a beautiful mystery. With all he'd left unspoken, it surprised me how much I could tell, what I could read from him. He didn't need to speak for me to know he was special. Someone was looking out for me when they put him in my path today.

My path. *Shit.* Being in my path might not be good for him. Between the assholes in my band and the overall aura of filth surrounding my name, that meant this special man would be tarnished just for being seen with me. I knew what people said, what the media would publish. Whatever his story was, Kal didn't need to get dragged down by my bullshit.

"Listen, man. Be careful here, all right? Watch out who you trust. There are people here who won't have your best interest at heart. Krish? Silas and his band? Howie and Chantal? They're good people. Stick close to them and you'll be okay."

Josh's face flashed before my eyes, and I knew what I had to do.

"Thanks again," I said. "Take care of yourself."

*Once when I was a kid, and my mom dumped me off with her*

*brothers for the third and final time, I found a puppy. I loved that little guy, and he looked at me with so much adoration, I brought him home. My uncles' place was rough. Lots of guys in and out, fights, drinking, and I had no one my age around, no one who cared about me unless I was cooking, singing, or cleaning up their mess. So I brought the little puppy home. He'd been a black and white pit bull and I called him Happy.*

*I knew it was a mistake the minute I stepped into the house with him.*

*Uncle Sean picked up Happy and looked him over.*

*"Right on. He'll be a big boy. Look at those paws! Once he's old enough, we'll teach him to fight."*

*And Happy knew no better. He wagged his tail and smiled his smile at me.*

*I was twelve years old, and I knew what his fate would be.*

*I went to my room, which was the master bedroom closet, and I curled up in the dark with Happy, holding him close to me as he slept.*

*That night, when my uncles left on their motorcycles, I put Happy in my backpack and I carried him ten blocks away to the fire station. I knew that the firemen took babies that no one wanted, knew about the depository because my uncles always told my mom she should have left me at one of them.*

*I unzipped the bag and kissed Happy one last time. I set the backpack carefully on the ground and pushed the bell.*

*I ran like hell, tears streaming down my face. I wiped them off before I got back.*

*The next school day when I didn't produce my backpack, my uncle beat my ass for losing it and made me carry a Victoria's Secret plastic bag some chick had left at the house with my stuff in it.*

Looking back at Kal's confused expression as I walked away, I prayed I'd done the right thing, just like I'd prayed that Happy had had a better life without me.

# CHAPTER 7

**Kal**

I walked back to the Red Dawn stage, the food churning in my gut, and Howie put me straight to work. The hours flew by as we set up and tore down for several more bands. On my afternoon break, I wandered until I found the Left Foot stage and was there in time to watch Hush. Krish spotted me and waved me over to the side stage to watch with him.

They were something else.

Silas was captivating to watch. You never knew what he would do next, whether it was throw his bass guitar to a tech, jump off the stage, climb on Los's back and scream into the mic with him. They were highly entertaining.

I kept thinking of Ryan.

That look he gave me as he'd walked away had me convinced he was a deeply troubled man. My heart broke for him. I didn't blame him for walking away. Who was I to think I could walk beside him in this unfamiliar world?

No. It was up to me to make a fresh start, not rely on someone else to help me.

I swatted at that creepy-crawly feeling on my neck once more—and then gasped as a realization hit me.

I'd been left behind before. More than once. By people who were supposed to care for me. People who I'd worked for, lived with. Family. I'd been a part of something...

A sharp pain stabbed the side of my head, and I sucked in a breath. These memories coming back in pieces were debilitating. I wished they'd all come back at once instead of this piecemeal process of torturing me.

Was I strong enough to handle them all? The ghosts from my past?

"They've really gotten into a groove with Bowie, their new drummer," Krish was saying. "He only started playing with them a few shows ago."

I shuddered when Krish looked away and took a deep breath. I tried to focus on what Krish was talking about and hoped it would keep the memories at bay.

Krish explained that Hush's drummer had broken his leg the first week of the tour when a meet-and-greet session got out of hand and some fans collapsed the table on him. He was back on the tour but couldn't play, so Bowie was filling in. Krish pointed to Brains watching from the other side of the stage.

The drummer looked miserable. His shoulders hunched over the crutches he leaned on to support his leg, which was protected by some sort of contraption wrapped around it. He bobbed his head to the music, but he seemed like he wished he were anyplace else. He must have, to see his band playing without him. He looked across the stage and our eyes met. I recognized the loneliness I'd felt as Ryan walked away.

Seemed like a lot of folks on this tour were struggling. How they continued to give their all while performing when they were unhappy astounded me.

"You should come hang out with us tonight," Krish said, pulling my attention from the sullen man he'd called Brains. Hush had finished their set, and Silas and his bandmates were throwing small plastic disks into the audience. The young people screamed and hunted around on the ground for them. "Ryan seems to really like you, and he could use a little lift right now. We all could." He glanced at me and gave me a sad smile. "I want you to know what you're getting into. Hush had a big blow-up fight last night. My best friend, Jake…he's Jordan's brother? Anyway, they're fighting, and Jake moved off of our bus and into the RV with the techs and Jessica. Ryan is fighting with his band. I think everyone needs a little space from each other, but they won't get it if they stay here and party. Add alcohol to this mix and it'll get worse."

"I don't know." My voice box decided to work. I cleared my throat and tried once more. I shook my head and pointed to myself as I spoke. "Make it worse."

"No way," Krish said. "It'll be fun. And maybe you can help me keep them in line." He winked at me, and I understood. Krish was worried about his friends and wanted to make them feel better.

I nodded and gave him a weak thumbs up. Then I gestured that I needed to get back to work and he told me to meet them after the show at their bus. "Ours is the one with the pink dingleberries. We just added them."

I loved how everyone personalized their spaces and had fun while they were on tour, but I was starting to see that a show like this could really wear on you. I was used to living on the move, but I was alone in my sleeping quarters. The carnival had been my life, and at this point it was all I could remember. Taking people out of their normal lives for a limited amount of time and forcing them to be together all day, every day, was a lot to handle.

Maybe I would go with them. I could be sure they saw the best the carnival had to offer. I could protect them. There were attractions that toured with the carnival that were… dark by nature. I didn't want any of them getting lost.

I hoped I wasn't breaking any rules. Mr. Ame had said my time was up. Surely I could attend the carnival as a guest? That wouldn't be breaking the rules, would it?

I worked alongside Howie, learning more about how the soundboard worked and learned how to use tiny tuning devices rather than tuning the instruments by ear. I loved learning all of these new skills. It gave me hope that I might find a permanent place after this tour was over.

"You're a quick study," Howie told me after we cleaned up the last act of the day.

The guests were filing out of the fairgrounds, exhausted, sunburned, and dehydrated. I heard one of the techs saying that there had been dozens of young people who required medical attention due to heatstroke. I hoped they were all okay. What a terrible way to end such a day of fun. I'd developed a film of sweat early in the day and it never went away, but the water Krish made me drink really helped. I thought about all of the folks here who didn't have someone to look after them, to care for them.

I thought about Ryan. Who was there for him?

I thanked Howie with a handshake and a nod.

"You're riding with Chantal, right? Be sure to check in with her and find out when their bus is leaving. We play in Virginia day after tomorrow, so you have a day off for travel. I'll see you bright and early on Thursday. Have a good time tonight." His knowing smile made me think of Ryan's parting words.

I wondered, who was watching out for Ryan?

I'd meet up with Krish and I'd be that person tonight. I owed it to them for being kind to me today. I'd help them navigate my world and be sure no one was left behind.

I made my way through the maze of buses until I found the one that belonged to Hush. There was some sort of booming music coming from inside, and I heard shouting. Alarmed, I debated rushing inside to see if anyone needed help, but then the door opened and Los dashed out, followed by another black-haired white fellow who was shooting him with…a water gun? But this was like no water gun I'd ever seen. It had several colorful tubes and a pump action that shot a stream of water six feet at least.

"And *that's* for giving me a wedgie. And *that's* for telling Roxanne I wet the bed. And *that's* for eating the last Uncrustables. And *that* is for swapping my toothpaste with the charcoal kind. Fucker. I thought I'd turned into a fucking zombie overnight!"

Los was bent over at the waist, laughing hysterically.

"You should have seen your face, dude. You were screaming 'what's happening' like the chick from *Poltergeist,* dude. It was epic!"

The man with the gun kept firing at Los until his gun ran dry, and then he lost momentum. He caught sight of me standing there and his eyes widened. "Whoa. You're the guy."

I held up a hand and tried to look non-threatening. I was not used to people paying any attention to me. I would need to watch how people greeted each other.

"Yeah, this is Kal. Kal, this is Jordan. He's our new guitar player. Kal is working with Howie while his back is messed up. Chantal brought him over today. Not sure where she found him, but he apparently works wonders. Maybe we should snag him when Theo goes back to school in the fall."

Jordan flicked his hair out of his eyes and stuck out his

hand. "Hell, if he survives this summer, I'd vouch for him. Everyone seems to be falling apart lately. First Brains and Mischa, then Howie. And did you hear one of the roadies on the Right Foot stage got electrocuted during the rain? Fuck, dude. I've gotten shocked before, but they had to take this dude to the hospital. Fuck that."

Krish came out of the doors with Silas on his heels.

"Oh great! You made it." He patted me on the back. "I see you've met Jordan?"

"Yeah, he came up as I was destroying Los."

"Fuck that. I got you way worse with the charcoal."

"*You* took my toothpaste?" Krish asked. He exhaled and looked up to the sky like a mother would when her children were being naughty. "I had to use Silas's bubble gum flavored toothpaste."

"It's the best!" Silas pushed up on tiptoes and kissed Krish's cheek. "And it makes you taste delicious. Er. You already taste great, despite that black shit."

The two of them seemed lost in each other, and Los and Jordan began making vomiting sounds. I had to laugh.

"Ugh," Los groaned. "Why don't you guys take that public display of tonsil jockeying and go somewhere else with it."

"You coming with us?" Silas asked him.

"Nope! Brains and I are going to play COD, and Jordan and Bowie have dates." Los frowned a little at that, but then he shook himself and shrugged. "Y'all can go to the creepy carnival without me."

Los and Jordan went back onto the bus and Krish smiled brightly at me.

"Are you ready? Did you need to go by your bus for anything?"

I shook my head. I didn't think so? However, They'd changed clothes and I was still in mine from earlier.

"Aren't you boiling in those jeans?" Silas asked. "We've

probably got some extra shorts around here. Maybe a tank top?"

And with that, I was ushered onto the bus, sent into the back room with a white t-shirt with writing on it and bright blue shorts to change into.

"We get samples from this designer. I love their stuff. It's like the softest cotton I've ever felt." Silas stepped back and gave me a onceover. "That blue really brings out your eyes."

"What the fuck do you know about fashion?" someone yelled from the front of the bus.

"I'll have you know..." Silas stormed away to continue arguing with his bandmates while Krish fussed over me and combed my hair. It felt odd, but I liked the attention. I felt safe with these men, though I wasn't sure why. Maybe because I knew some of them were like me. They also seemed to know how to get around, what was safe, and they seemed to genuinely care what happened to me despite the fact I'd just met them.

"Oy, the constant bickering. Not even my brother and I bickered this much." Krish rolled his eyes and smiled at me. "You get used to it, and it's all out of love between these guys, though some days I want to knock their heads together. Jessica tries to keep things settled, but there's a long history of dysfunctionalism she's working with. Do you know what I mean?"

I smiled and flipped my hand over and under, hoping he understood that meant I sort of understood? I thought perhaps I did, but then this overwhelming feeling of loss flooded me and another pain stabbed me in the side of the head.

"You okay? You need some Advil or anything? The heat got to me too today. I took some."

He pulled a bottle out of the cabinet and shook out two pills for me, and then he led me out of the bedroom and into the kitchen, where he handed me a cold bottle of water from the refrigerator. The tiny kitchens in these buses seemed quite modern compared to…

Yeah, things were coming back to me. I didn't know *when* it was, and I didn't know *when* I'd been before. But I had a feeling there was a lot more for me to discover. And that I wouldn't like a lot of it.

"You good?"

I gave him a thumbs up.

Brains, Bowie, and Los were all sitting on the couch with some sort of devices in their hands and they were staring at a large screen where little soldier men were shooting each other. I was mesmerized by the visual action, but Krish continued moving past them. They each reached out a hand to slap palms with him without tearing their gaze from the screen. I followed him out of the bus and Silas stepped in line behind me, repeating the palm slaps.

"Later dudes!"

The guys on the bus were too busy with their…game? This must be what a video game was. I'd heard my fellow stagehands discussing them earlier.

Once outside, Silas took Krish's hand and I followed the two of them. Silas was singing something unfamiliar, and I was surprised by the softness to his voice. Onstage he'd screamed and belted out melodies and lyrics about sorrow and hate and love. Now, his voice was that of a jazz singer. Soft, mellow, acrobatic. And Krish was all smiles beside him.

"You still on that swing kick?"

"I can't help it," Silas said. "That Squirrel Nut Zippers stuff is fun, and I totally want to see Bryan Setzer if he tours again."

We wove our way through the buses and again I wondered how they didn't get lost. Each one carried different music, shouts, laughter, and sounds like I'd heard from the video games on Hush's bus. Silas stopped at one with the door closed and he knocked a funny combination of times while slapping the door with his other hand, almost like he was making a drumbeat. He turned to me and winked.

"They hate it when I do that."

The doors opened before him and he nearly tumbled forward.

Ryan stood at the top of the steps. "What do you want, Franklin?"

# CHAPTER 8

**Ryan**

Despite Krish and Silas insisting I go with them to the carnival tonight, I'd convinced myself I would stay in, maybe write, maybe lay in my bunk and stare at the ceiling for many hours. I had this hollow feeling that, in the past, I would have filled with alcohol until I either passed out or found someone to fuck. Now that I'd made a promise, a commitment, that I wouldn't partake of mind-altering substances, music was the only thing that kept me from drowning.

I'd had it out with Parker before the rest of the guys left to go to a bar in Nashville and hear some local music.

"I know the guys are annoying, but Ryan, you gotta get your priorities straight, man. If you can't get along with them in the long run? Maybe we need to think about making some changes."

What he meant was, changes that involved *my* future.

Oscar and TJ had been embraced by the fans and were favorites at our signings, and they might accept me being out of the band by now. There had been a vocal minority who'd said I shouldn't be allowed back after my prison stint. But the majority had welcomed me. I'd received letters from other ex-cons and even folks still locked up that thanked me for showing them there was life after prison. That meant more to me than being worried about Parker's veiled threats.

"It's carnival time, dude." Silas hopped up the steps of the bus toward me and stuck out his hand. I grabbed it and pulled him into a bro hug, holding on a little longer than normal. He didn't know it, but he'd just saved me from yet another downward spiral. He'd done it once before, the night he'd sang "Angel's Son" with me. I'd been ready to say fuck it that night and go out looking for booze, but he'd agreed to my plan, agreed to help me finish the album I'd written with Gavin. Silas's friendship was one of the only positive things keeping me going right now. I should tell him, but he probably wouldn't believe me anyway.

"Shit. We're doing this. Okay. Let me grab my wallet."

I took a minute inside the bus to brush my too-long hair out of my face. It was scraggly at the ends. I barely looked presentable anymore. I grabbed a ball cap someone had given us from a canned water company called Liquid Death. "Murder Your Thirst" it said. So cheeky. I shoved it on backward and put on some lip balm, then turned back to Silas. He was bouncing his knees and looking up at the white board we had hung up on the wall for notes to each other. At this time, we had our schedule for the next five days, and then there were a couple of vulgar drawings.

"I can see you want to add something."

Silas grinned at me and picked up the marker. He hummed as he drew pictures of TJ and Oscar, and then drew a giant dick ejaculating on them. He popped the pen cap back on and turned to face me. His shit-eating smile made me laugh for probably the first time since…well, since I'd met Kal.

"I mean, it's not going to win me any awards, but you can tell it's those two, can't you?"

I sighed and gestured for him to exit the bus. "Yes, you can tell. I'll probably hear about it later."

He stopped and pushed past me. "Then let me leave my name. I don't want them thinking it's anyone other than me."

He signed the drawing *Love, Silas, July 2018.*

"There! Perfect. I always take credit for my shenanigans."

"Fucking Franklin. All right. Let's go. You get Los to agree to come? He seemed leery about hanging out with some colorful folks tonight."

"Nah, he's staying behind, but we brought someone else."

I followed him down the steps, watching as I went because I'd already stumbled twice getting off the damn bus. The steps were really funky. When I finally looked up, there was Kal.

He held up a hand and waved hesitantly.

I wanted to hug him even tighter than I'd hugged Silas. I couldn't believe how happy I was to see him. After I'd walked away from him earlier, I'd known it was the right thing to do, and yet it took all of my strength to keep putting one foot in front of the other. I wanted him near me. I wanted something *good* in my life.

Knowing full well I was an asshole for being happy, I grinned at him. "You survived your first day, huh?"

Silas put his arm around Kal and beamed. "He sure did, and if he survives the rest of the tour, I think we might poach him. Theo is going back to school and wants to be close to Merch Girl Mischa, so we've got an opening for a tech, and since we're headed to Europe, we could really use someone good."

Silas patted him once more and let go. Kal watched him with a shocked expression. I wondered what he thought about all that.

"I suppose it also matters whether Kal *wants* to remain with you heathens."

Silas looked at me like I'd just suggested someone might actually be immune to his charms. "What do you mean? What could be better than touring with us?" His confusion quickly morphed into laughter. "You're right. Kal, I won't be offended if you think me and my band of messy men are *too much* of a mess for you. So, do you have other plans? Headed home after Warped? What do you think?"

Kal opened his mouth and then shut it, his cheeks flushing. He shoved his hands into the pockets of his shorts—

Lord, whoever'd dressed him deserved my gratitude. His legs were paler than his arms, but they were sculpted like a statue I'd once admired in a museum, I forget which one. Long and lightly dusted with golden hairs that caught the fading light of the sunset.

My silence must have been noted by Krish. He cleared his throat. "We gave him some of the sample clothes from Roxanne's brand. It's so hot out—"

"Hot. Yes. Looks good."

It was clear I was ogling him, and though these guys were used to my quirks, it was an awkward moment. I'd drawn Silas once. He wasn't a good model, as he fidgeted and talked the whole time. I knew there were rumors about what happened at my drawing sessions. Nothing had happened with Silas. Couldn't say that for all of my models.

"Right, well. Shall we?" Silas gave me a look like *down, boy*. "I keep smelling that damned cotton candy and my sweet tooth is begging me for some."

I stood next to Kal and looked up at him. I liked the way he met my gaze, unafraid, unashamed, as if he were accepting my challenge, or challenging *me*. This back and forth had me fired up.

"We shall."

Kal and I fell into step behind the lovers and I wouldn't lie, their affection was infectious. Envy-inducing. I found myself wishing I could just as easily reach for someone's hand, have someone smiling at me like Silas always was at Krish.

"They are happy."

I nearly tripped over myself at the sound of his voice.

"Yeah—yes," I stammered. "They appear to be every time I see them. Kinda nice. Gives me hope the world isn't about to take a big crap, you know?"

Kal nodded and looked ahead. He had a stiffness to his walk, as if he weren't totally cool with what he was walking into. Like maybe he'd turn around and head the other direction if given the choice.

"I'm glad they are happy." His gaze dropped to the ground in front of him and his face scrunched up like he was concentrating really hard.

"Hey, you know you don't have to talk with me. You can say nothing and I'll still enjoy your company."

He glanced up with a quickness and gave me a shy smile. "Want to. Talk." He swallowed hard. "Difficult."

"I get it," I said, giving into my desire to touch him by brushing my hand down his biceps. His bulging biceps. Geez the guy was big, like, naturally big. "I remember one summer...I was a teenager, like fourteen maybe? I lived with my uncles and they were gone a lot. I stayed at the house, took care of things for them, cleaned up after their stupid parties. I didn't talk to anyone for days at a time. It was weird. I'd always been talkative, but I stopped. Wondered if they'd notice. They didn't. So I quit talking to them.

"When school started up that next year and I went to high

school, it was almost like I'd forgotten how to speak. I was uncomfortable, and the way I'd always dealt with that before was to goof around, act stupid. So I did. Made other kids laugh, made my teachers pissy, and I kind of felt at home. Running my mouth gets me in trouble. It fools me into thinking people are paying the good kind of attention, which is better than being ignored. Or at least that's what I used to think." I shook my head. "Damn, sorry. That's some of the weird shit that lives in my head."

We were almost to the entrance of the carnival when Kal stopped me with a hand to my shoulder, once more making me jump. He stepped back and pressed his hand to his chest and lowered his gaze.

"Don't be sorry," I said to him, stepping closer. "I'm not used to people touching me, but I could be. If it's you." I didn't know how else to make it clear to him that whatever my issues were, they had nothing to do with him. I looked down at the hand that had touched my shoulder and how big it was. I had a flash of his hands being all over my naked skin, and I shuddered. He started to turn, but I reached for it. "Don't stop on my account."

He nodded and removed his hand, but then he gave the sign for "help you."

"Yeah. It helps."

His smile faded and he looked up at the banner above the entrance.

*Welcome, Traveler.*

"Truer words, huh? We're all travelers," Silas said. He pulled Krish toward the ticket booth and yelled back, "I got you guys."

I waved and stepped closer to Kal, our fronts almost coming into contact.

"What is it? You okay with this?"

He kept staring at the sign. "I came from this."

I frowned. "You worked at a carnival? Really? That's cool."

He gave a half smile, but didn't say anything else as Krish and Silas joined us, gave us our tickets, and then took off at a jog for the ticket taker.

Kal and I followed. I had so much I wanted to ask him, but once we turned in our tickets, I was blindsided by the vibrant tents, the clear blue sky with white puffy clouds despite it being ten at night, almost like we were inside at Caesar's in Vegas. I didn't remember there being a dome over the carnival? But there was so much to see! It was like Baz Luhrmann designed the place and the cameras were all set on that fish-eye effect as I looked around. Like I was high without the drugs. I was ecstatic and terrified all at once, a manic panic forming in my gut.

I moved closer to Kal, a little overwhelmed by it all.

He slid his hand against mine and squeezed my fingers. "You're safe."

His words and the near-growl behind them shocked me enough to stop the maelstrom inside me. "Okay," I breathed.

We found Silas and Krish a few paces ahead with a massive puff of cotton candy. Silas had his whole face shoved inside while Krish giggled hysterically.

"Don't OD, man," I said with a chuckle as I pulled off a piece. It tickled my tongue as it melted and I immediately had a sugar rush. "This might be the best thing I've tasted in my life." I offered some to Kal but he shook his head. His gaze darted around us, as if he were making sure there were no threats to our safety.

"I've never seen a carnival like this in real life. It's wild!" Silas pulled off another hunk of cotton candy and shoved it in his mouth.

"Man, I went to one just like this as a kid," I said, feeling a wave of goose bumps pass over my skin. Something like déjà vu.

"What should we do first?" Silas asked.

"I wonder if they have a carousel," Krish asked. "I love those. My parents took my brother Viv and me to Seaport Village in San Diego after the Looff Carousel moved there in two thousand and four. It was so beautiful. Someday I want to go visit all of the historic carousels around the country."

Silas cupped Krish's cheek and rubbed his thumb along his cheekbone. It was such a sweet and tender gesture. One wouldn't think Silas capable of that level of tenderness.

"Let's do it, babe. After the European tour. I'm totally down. The one in Santa Cruz is incredible."

His words were like a gut punch. I turned around and had to bend over to keep from passing out.

"Ryan, man, you okay?"

Silas and Krish rushed to my side but Kal was the one who placed his hand on my back.

"I'm okay." I took a minute to breathe before I straightened up.

Kal pointed to a bench nearby and I went to sit down before I fell down.

"What happened, dude? Too much heat?"

I blew out a breath and planted my hands on my knees. "That carousel, in Santa Cruz at the Boardwalk, is where I was right before the accident."

# CHAPTER 9

**Kal**

I knew Ryan was carrying around a heavy load and he'd mentioned going to prison, but I wasn't prepared for the story he was about to tell. I led our little group over to a set of benches perpendicular to each other and sat next to Ryan. Krish and Silas took the other, both leaning forward to better hear Ryan speak.

"You mean the night Josh got hurt?"

Ryan nodded slowly at Silas. He took his cap off, slicked back his longish hair, and then placed the cap back on snugly, this time with the bill facing forward, perhaps to hide behind.

"We'd played a show at the San Jose Civic the night before and had a show the next night at The Catalyst. Having a night off in between was bad for me back then, probably still is. Idle hands and all that. You know how it is, Silas."

Silas nodded solemnly and took Krish's hand. Krish held it in his two.

"So you guys went to Santa Cruz, to the Boardwalk."

Ryan snorted. "We went to a few bars first. When I was good and hammered, going to the Boardwalk and riding the rides seemed like a great idea." I shook my head and looked down at the scars on the back of my hand I'd tried to cover up with tattoos. "Josh tried, poor guy. He tried to talk some sense into me. Kept suggesting we call an Uber, but you know how I am, or how I was, when I was loaded. There was no arguing with me."

He looked up at Krish for a minute. "Hey, I don't know that I'm ready to have my shit out there in your fucking book, all right?"

Krish held up his hands. "No way, Ryan. I only publish what I have explicit permission to write, and only if it takes place in the context of an official interview."

Ryan's lips curled up on the side. "Consent is sexy, friend."

Silas rolled his eyes and groaned. "Will you quit hitting on my boyfriend?"

"Sorry, sorry. Yeah, so I remember being obsessed with the calliope they had, and I wouldn't leave it alone." He rubbed at his lips and shook his head. "When I was finally done, I was ready to hit one more bar, and we took off in my rental car. Somehow I managed to make it back over the hill, but when we got to San Jose, well..."

Ryan shifted on the bench until his leg was touching mine, as if he were a live wire looking for grounding. I pressed my thigh to his and nudged his foot.

He gave me a sad smile, and I wished I could take him away from all this, somewhere he wouldn't have to carry this burden anymore. At least he was talking about it. I hoped that would lessen the pain somehow.

"Man, I haven't told this to anyone except my therapist,

and my AA group. I took the exit ramp too fast, we fucking went ass over elbow…I can't… Josh was crushed, man. And Tara and Tyler got seriously fucked up. At least those two left the hospital walking."

Ryan cradled his head in his hands, and Silas reached out for his knee.

"Dude, you've paid for what happened. More than most people who fuck up. Tyler and Tara got married, they have a kid. Josh went back to school and got super involved in the Paralympics. Yes, life was different for them than they'd imagined before that night, but you have paid for it. You have done everything asked of you, you've stayed clean." Ryan dropped his hands and Silas grabbed one. "I don't want this for you. Gavin wouldn't have wanted this for you."

Ryan's whole body tensed at that name, and he leaned away from me a bit. I moved closer. I didn't want him to float away.

"I feel like I'm in a fucking *Groundhog Day* situation with my band, man. I apologize, I do my part, they fucking find new ways to rub shit in my face, threaten me they're going to fire me. Fuck, Franklin, I don't know how much longer I can do this."

"Then don't."

I'd felt like I had to say something to stop his pain and that's what burst from my lips. I pressed them together, wishing I could take them back when they all looked at me in shock. I shook my head but Krish came and knelt at my side.

"No, you're right, Kal. Ryan, don't keep doing this. Find a way to disrupt things, take ownership of what you have control over, and the rest…"

"Appreciate that, Krish, but my band is my life. Kinda hard to amputate a whole life."

Silas and Krish continued to argue with him, but my attention was drawn by the whisper of a presence.

Mr. Ame.

*"Show him."*

I stood and held my hand out to Ryan, hoping he would trust me and take it. When he hesitated, I gestured for him to come and then gave him the help you sign.

Ryan gazed up at me, his eyes full of sadness. I wondered what was going through his mind. When I thought he'd turn away, he finally stood. He didn't take my hand, but he held his out as if to say, "you first."

I looked to Krish and Silas, and they smiled.

"You good, Wells?" Silas asked him

He nodded to Silas and they fist-bumped.

"Yeah. You guys go have some fun. We'll meet you back here…when do we have to be back?"

"We told Chantal we'd have Kal back by one. Buses leave tomorrow at seven."

Ryan nodded and raised his eyebrows at me as he walked to my side. He looked me up and down. I liked the way he looked at me.

"We're gonna, um, go find the arcade, yeah. Krish, want me to win you a big stuffed…thing? I am freakishly good at that water gun game."

Krish nodded and the two of them left to give Ryan and I some space. We waved to them, and I turned to take Ryan to what I hoped would make him happy. We walked past the purple tent that housed Madame Persephone and when Ryan's gaze lingered there, I sped up. Madame was kind, but she'd touched my hand once and shuddered, warning me never to have my fortune read.

Ryan asked about the dog sitting in the opening of the green tent, and I merely nodded, hoping he'd understand that Darius belonged there. His handler must have been close.

"This is a pretty wild place. Kinda reminds me of a place I went to as a kid."

Was it possible? Had he been here before? That seemed unlikely, given we were one of many carnivals, albeit a special one.

"Why'd you give up the carny life?" Ryan was still talking. "Seems like a decent gig."

I shrugged and then pointed to my left wrist.

"Ah. It was time. I get it."

He was quiet as we walked along. I sensed he was observing all that was going on around us. A woman on stilts passed us, and he smiled. A tattooed man with a forked tongue winked at Ryan. Ryan gave him a wide berth. I bumped him with my elbow and raised my eyebrows.

"Not a fan of snakes."

I laughed. Out loud. And it startled both of us.

"I like that sound," he said, moving closer to me, so close that our arms brushed as we walked. Each brush zinged along my skin as it had the first time we'd touched. Our walking pace was the same, we moved with a similar rhythm as if we'd always walked together, side-by-side, but I knew that was impossible. Ryan wasn't a man out of time like I was. He belonged to *his* time, though he did seem out of sorts. Perhaps that part in each of us was reaching out for the other.

I led him toward the back next to the carousel, and I knew the moment Ryan saw what I intended for him to see.

"Oh, Kal." Ryan gazed at the large Wurlitzer, which sat quietly in a covered pavilion. He admired the carvings of cherubs and the gold leafing, the automatons in the shapes of the muses playing different percussion instruments.

"I swear I've seen this one before," he whispered. "It's incredible!" He reached out a hand to touch the xylophone keys but then jerked back as if he were a little kid worrying about getting in trouble.

I gestured for him to go ahead. I knew he couldn't harm it. Everything under the protection of Mr. Ame was just that. Protected. As I'd been.

He ran his finger lightly over the metal keys and his smile was full of joy.

"I don't know what it is, but I love these things. How someone so lovingly created this, carving every section, figuring out how to make the gears operate every musical instrument. It's genius. Amazing."

I touched his arm lightly and gestured for him to come around and look at the back, but he hesitated.

"I don't know if I want to see it. It might remove the magic. That's silly, right?"

I shook my head and moved closer but I didn't touch him. My heart beat faster, thrilled by the idea that he loved these organs as much as I did. He thought it was magic, but I saw it as evidence of human potential. People were capable of creating such beautiful works of art, beyond our wildest dreams.

"I wish we could turn it on." he mused.

There was nothing I wouldn't do for him.

I went around behind it and flicked on the band organ.

"Wait, Kal! I don't want to get you in trouble."

The Wurlitzer began whirring and clanging and when the music started, it was thunderous inside the cavernous space.

Ryan clapped his hands together and bounced on his toes. He leaned his forehead against the machine with the youthful expression of a boy filled with wonder but who simultaneously tried to hide his excitement to avoid disappointment. He gasped as the music changed to a song he knew.

"'Daisy!'" He backed away from the Wurlitzer and began

to spin in circles, dancing to the rhythm as it rattled the wooden walls. He was doing a sort of one-man waltz that made me chuckle. Until he held out a hand for me. The next thing I knew, we were dancing together in circles, Ryan holding me close, neither of us really leading, not needing to. It was as if our bodies together functioned as one. Around and around and around we went until the song ended and the machine went still.

"This place is magic, Kal. Do you believe in magic?"

I didn't know how to answer him, or whether I *could* answer him. He was right. Many things about the Carnival of Mysteries were…without explanation. They existed in a time and space unlike any other. I'd gotten used to the unexplained.

I offered him a smile and a shrug. Somehow we were still alone in the pavilion despite the loud music, so when he closed the distance between us, I wasn't afraid to let him.

"You coming here, us meeting, this music…Kal, I needed this. I needed something to wake me from this perpetual nightmare where nothing changes, the bad shit stays the same." He swallowed, turned his ball cap backward, and pushed up on his toes, his hands resting on my belt. He whispered, "Tell me you need this too."

I couldn't *tell* him, but I could sure *show* him.

With one quick glance to be sure we were still alone, I lowered my head and brushed my lips over his. Merely a test, one brief moment of contact that left me awash with desire… and relief. Relief that I was safe, I was where I was supposed to be, doing what I was supposed to be doing. Kissing Ryan, even for such a brief moment, grounded me.

When I pulled away, Ryan gazed at me, stunned.

"I want to know who you are, but is it weird that I also don't *care* who you are, who you've been? I want the *now* you."

He snaked his fingers into my hair and tugged me closer so he could kiss me again. I let him take the initiative this time, allowing him to take the kiss deeper, letting him run his tongue over my lip. I'd let him have whatever he needed tonight. He held me tight to him with his grip on the waist of my pants. He was strong. I was stronger.

"This what you want?" he asked, tightening his hold on my waistband. "This okay?"

"Want." I thought perhaps I'd be forgiven for being a man of few words in this situation. I wrapped my arms around his back and pulled him completely flush with my body, and the contact made us both shudder and moan. I felt him hard against me and when his erection brushed against my hip bone, I was ready to explode and float away in a thousand pieces.

Ryan sighed and pulled away, pressing his forehead into my chest. "You make me want to run away and join the carnival."

I chuckled and he wrapped his arms around my torso.

"Want to make it better."

He sucked in a breath and pressed his ear to my chest. "You *are* making it better. Your voice is music to my ears. Your music makes me feel alive."

I wished I could give him more. I wanted to show him more, all of the treasures Mr. Ame had collected throughout the years. I wanted to show him the magic I'd built with my own hands. My calliaphone.

I took his hand and led him away from the pavilion, past the colorful tents, to the less glamorous section of the carnival.

There were trailers parked behind the attractions in various stages of disrepair, from various eras. Mine had been one of the older ones, modified to be pulled behind a truck if necessary, or loaded onto a train, depending on where—or when—we were headed next. I wondered what Ryan would think of how I had lived…how *long* I had lived this way. Even I didn't know that. I only knew by the sheer amount of technological advances that many decades must have passed since I'd joined the carnival, but I didn't know how I'd come to be there any more than I had this morning.

"Where are we going? Wait, how did you know this was back here?"

I stopped in front of my trailer. It was wooden with a faded advertisement painted on the side. My calliaphone was on the front half of the platform, covered by a decorative tarp, and the back half was the small space where I slept. I pulled the tarp off and my breath caught at the sight of the brass pipes and the fresh red paint.

"What is this?" Ryan walked around the front of the machine. "This should be in a museum somewhere! What a beauty."

I glanced over my shoulder at him and then climbed onto the platform. I took my place on the bench, stretched my hands out, turned on the machine, and wiggled my fingers, ready to play. First, I gestured for him to cover his ears, but he waved my concern away.

I played a few bars of "Meet Me Tonight in Dreamland" for him, and when I stopped he gestured for me to continue.

"Please, Kal."

He stood with his palms pressed together in front of his chest. It was a youthful pose I hadn't seen him make before.

I played more songs, and after each one, he pleaded "play another. Play another."

Finally, I stood from the bench and gestured for him to take my spot. His eyes flared and he scrambled up onto the platform and squeezed his fingers into fists and straightened them as if he wasn't sure he should touch the work of art before him. Little did he know that this machine had been around for a very long time and had taken the brunt of my frustration on countless occasions.

His boyish countenance had me worried. Who had made this strong and powerful man ever doubt himself? Who had hurt him? Such a wave of protectiveness washed over me that my muscles clenched and vibrated, ready to stand up for him, regardless of the foe.

I pointed at the bench again, and he carefully lowered his body, making himself small in the process.

"What should I play?" he asked me.

I pointed to the list of songs on the mechanical roll, in case he wanted to let the calliaphone play on its own. Then I pointed to his chest, right where I knew his heart ached for more of this magical music.

# CHAPTER 10

**Ryan**

I wasn't sure I liked the vulnerable place I'd gone with this total stranger. The whole experience hadn't been like sex with a random person. This was playing *music,* music that took me back to a time that Kal couldn't possibly know about as I hadn't told a soul, not my bandmates or friends, not in interviews. No one. A time when I'd felt electrified and terrified at the same time.

*All week, Uncle Rex had promised we'd go to the carnival set up at the fairgrounds. Part of me had been thrilled, the other certain that he would forget or something else would come up. Sure enough, early that afternoon, I'd put on my best shirt and pants, done the dishes, vacuumed, and even cleaned up some disgusting mess in the bathroom. I waited at the kitchen table for him to wake up and planned to make him breakfast, but when he got up he went straight for the fridge and grabbed a beer. Never a good sign.*

*"What the hell are you doing, Rye? It's not Sunday. Why are you wearing your church clothes?"*

*I had the newspaper open on the table and was reading the article about the carnival for about the fifth time. Uncle Rex walked over and looked at it, then he cursed.*

*"Shit. That's right, I said we'd go to the carnival. Dammit, Rye. Shirley's coming over and we were gonna... Fine. When she gets here, we'll take you to the carnival."*

*Uncle Rex was the uncle who paid the most attention to me, didn't treat me like a total pain in the ass. I remember being relieved and grateful that he'd been willing to change his plans with his date to take me to the carnival.*

*Shirley showed up two hours later. She was pretty, had artificially tanned skin and hair so light blond it didn't seem real. She wore black leggings and an oversized t-shirt with sandals, and every time she moved I noticed a bump in her belly. She'd pull her shirt out like maybe she was pregnant and didn't want anyone to know. I wonder if Uncle Rex knew?*

*My legs were cramped from sitting there waiting, staying out of the way, and making sure I didn't mess up my clothes. We climbed in her Corolla and drove across town. We passed under a banner and gave our tickets and I thought I was dreaming.*

*The carnival was like an old movie, with fabric tents rather than the regular fair rides with swinging metal arms and hundreds of colored light bulbs. Shirley and my uncle walked in front of me with their arms around each other, pointing out a group of acrobats tumbling and climbing on each other. I remember wondering if my mom and dad ever walked like that together, if I would ever walk with someone like that. I'd already had crushes on boys and girls in my fifth-grade class, but I knew that I should only let on about the girls.*

*"All right, Rye. Here's twenty bucks," Uncle Rex said. "You can spend it however you want. We'll be over here at the tables having a drink, okay? Go have fun, kiddo."*

*Twenty whole dollars. I added that to the five I'd saved up from doing the laundry and I was ready.*

*I walked the entire arcade first, which had different games than I was used to. I scoped out which games I had the most chance of winning a prize, and then I bought my tickets. I put enough tickets for the carousel in my pockets. I didn't like the rides at the usual carnivals. They screeched and groaned when they were working, and I'd seen a kid come off of the spinning cars with blood on her mouth where she'd smacked her face against the front of the car. No way was I going to end up like her. I'd been told enough times at eleven years old that I had a pretty face, and I wasn't about to lose what little advantage I had. But this place seemed more solid, even if it was a little surreal, and they didn't have dangerous rides like that.*

*I managed to win a big stuffed cheetah at the balloon dart contest by playing and winning enough times that I could trade in smaller prizes until I won the whole thing. But that meant I had to spend my carousel tickets. I thought maybe I could bargain with Uncle Rex for a little more money to ride the carousel. The wonderful music I'd heard all evening was coming from the ride. I'd seen the machine moving in the middle of all the brightly painted horses and I wanted to get closer.*

*I stood and listened to it as I watched the horses go round and round. The colors hypnotized me, the percussive music made my teeth rattle and the hairs stand up on my arms. I couldn't see anyone playing the huge machine. I wanted to get a closer look to see how it worked, but that would require more tickets.*

*I made my way back to the tables by the food trailers, but Uncle Rex and Shirley weren't there. I walked around the entire perimeter of the carnival and they were nowhere to be found. I figured maybe they'd gone in the creepy fun house. I raced over there, not wanting to miss them, but I wasn't allowed in without a ticket.*

*The only place left to check was the parking lot, but once I stepped out of the carnival entrance, my memory became a little hazy.*

*Next thing I recalled, I walked back inside the entrance and over to the tables where I was supposed to meet my uncle. I sat there with my giant cheetah...waiting. My clothes were torn and dirty.*

*A man played music in a pavilion away from the other tents. His back was to us and shiny pipes rose up in front of him as he played the keys. The songs sounded whimsical and happy. I wished I could have music like this always, make music like this. It made me feel like I didn't have a care in the world. Like magic.*

*A couple of women asked me if I was okay, and I told them I was just waiting for my uncle. By the time the music stopped and the lights were flicked on and off a couple of times to let folks know they were closing, I knew Uncle Rex had forgotten about me.*

*I knew better than to tell a grown up. The last time I'd been left somewhere, and I'd told an adult, a cop brought me home and Uncle Mack smacked me around for telling our family business. My mom came and got me then, and she tried to make it work, but I never made it easy. She always brought me back to her brothers. She couldn't handle me and working two jobs, and I got it. I never could manage to stay out of trouble for long either with her.*

*I started walking in the dark, trying to remember how many turns off of the main street it was to get back to their house, or whether Mom's was closer. If I went to the church, at least I'd be there in the morning when they all showed up and I could blend in. No one would even know.*

*I must have taken a wrong turn because it took a lot longer than I thought it would. It wasn't until I ended up outside the Circle K that I knew where I was, and by then it was three in the morning. I used the bathroom and was going to stay there, but some guys came in, and, well, that was the end of my cheetah. They had a grand old time ripping him apart in front of me, laughing every time I tried to fight them to get him back. It would have been a lot worse if the kid working the register hadn't come in to check the bathroom. He told the men to leave, sat me behind the counter, and gave me a beer when I said I couldn't go home 'til morning. He said he understood. He worked nights so he didn't have to be home either.*

*I passed out at some point, and when the sun came up, I managed to make it to church at the same time as my mother. She took one look at my fucked-up clothes and shook her head in disgust.*

*Uncle Rex merely gave me a pat on the shoulder. "Sorry, kid. Glad you made it."*

I shook myself as I fell out of that not-so-welcome memory. Kal placed a hand on my shoulder and squeezed with enough pressure to remind me that he was there, and that was all the encouragement I needed.

I spread my hands out on the keys and began to play "To The Shock of Miss Louise," which had been on *The Lost Boys* soundtrack. The first time Backdrop Silhouette had gone into the studio and I'd discovered they had an old Wurlitzer organ, I played around with it until I found a similar sound setting. I'd taught myself how to play the damned song during the downtime when the others were rehearsing and I was waiting for my turn to do vocals. It drove Parker and Burke nuts. I'd wanted us to incorporate some circus/carnival sounds on our first album. There was a song called "Bring The Magic" that would have been perfect, but they were absolutely against it. Our producer wasn't thrilled with the idea, said it had been done before, but I knew we could've done something special.

I should have known after that experience that we weren't totally musically compatible. The guys were phenomenal musicians, but they didn't want to stretch. They wanted commercial success. Parker wanted to follow the metalcore formula, and Burke wanted to show off his considerable lead guitar chops. Our original bass player, Sam, kept his opinions to himself and did whatever Parker wanted, so I was the odd man out. Back then I played guitar, too, but after our first tour, the label thought the performances would be much hotter if I did my thing rather than play. Then they pushed us to add a rhythm guitar player, as if my playing hadn't been good enough.

I thought back to that song and I played the part I'd written—that they'd rejected—and it made my fucking chest tight. I'd felt too much today, and the damned feelings had beaten the shit out of me, beaten me to a bloody pulp.

"Ry-an."

I gazed up at Kal, and he cupped my cheek in his big hand. It was the sweetest gesture, not at all like the scorching kiss he'd given me earlier. *Fuck.* I was still half-hard thinking about that kiss, but this touch shattered me.

"I've had enough." I closed my eyes. I couldn't take any more. I wanted to get shitfaced, totally smashed, and just… forget.

"Hey, guys," Krish called out as he and Silas trotted up.

"I thought I recognized that music," Silas said. "That was so freaking cool! Can you play it again?"

Silas's smile faded when I pulled my face from the comfort of Kal's hold and turned to look at him.

"Ryan, man." He stood next to the trailer and held his hand out for me.

I took it and gave it a squeeze. "I'm okay. It's been a day, though, man. I don't want to go back to my bus tonight. I don't…yeah, I don't trust myself. You guys have room?"

"Absolutely," Silas said. "Anytime. We should head back, though. They started flicking the lights. Probably this place is closing down."

I turned back to Kal, and his eyes were glassy. He ran his

finger over an engraved metal plaque on the side of the contraption and blew out a breath.

"Hey," I said, standing from the bench. "You okay? Why don't we walk back? We can, I don't know, hang out for a bit. Unless you need sleep. I can walk you to your bus..."

Kal sniffled, and his sorrowful gaze traveled over the trailer. Seemed like I wasn't the only one full of feels tonight.

"Do you need more time?"

He turned that intensity on me once more and shook his head. He held out a hand for me to go first off the trailer. I hopped down and Silas gave me a hug. When I turned back for Kal, I held a hand out for him, in case he needed help, but he hopped down gracefully. He pulled the tarp back over the organ and gave it one last loving pat before joining us.

"Is this what you did at the carnival?" I asked him. "Work with these machines? Wait—you worked at *this* carnival?"

He nodded. "Calliaphone. Organ. I played. I worked on them too, kept them tuned." He blew out another breath, as if speaking those words was the hardest work he'd done all day.

"Wow. This place is...I can't believe you worked here!"

He shrugged and looked over the trailer. He seemed to be saying goodbye.

"I bet you're going to miss them, huh? They're beautiful. Someday, man, I'm going to buy a whole bunch of cool musical contraptions and fill my whole house with them. Shit, I'll have one in the kitchen, one in the bathroom..."

That got him smiling, but he seemed far away. I couldn't help but worry that once we got back to the tour, he'd pull away. Or my dumb ass would. I wanted more time with him, but how was that going to work? Me talking, him listening, not saying anything about himself. His life. No. That wouldn't do. We'd have to find a way to communicate because I wanted to repay him for what he'd done for me tonight.

My step was a little lighter as we left the dark area around the trailers.

The carnival was deserted when we reached the entrance and there were no lights in this section of the fairgrounds. It was creepy, to be honest, and once we stepped out of the carnival boundary, I was about to say something to Silas when four men stepped into our path.

"You boys lost?"

They were like a stereotypical gang of villains out of a horror film. If they thought we were easy targets, they were mistaken.

I shifted my weight and made myself ready for anything.

# CHAPTER 11

**Kal**

"You boys seemed to have strayed a bit far from that freakshow they call a music festival."

These men were not like any of the people I'd seen at the music festival, nor were they roustabouts. Their intentions were evil, you could smell it on them. I wasn't going to let them hurt my friends.

"We're leaving," Krish said, his voice possessing the slightest tremor.

"You sure you don't want to stay?" The leader of this band of ruffians hooked his thumbs in his belt and sidled up closer to Krish. "Pretty lad like you could entertain the lot of us for hours."

I moved to Krish's side and the leader caught sight of me. His sneer faded.

"You don't belong here."

"And you do, Farm Boy? We're all here now. How about a dance?" He flicked his hand and a shiny blade extended.

*Blade.* That annoying twinge on my skin was back, but with it came a throbbing in my lower back.

My skin felt as if it had already been sliced open. Flashes of memories pierced the darkness around me. A crowd. Angry. Some had knives, others had big sticks. They'd come for us, for my uncle, and they were ready to shed blood.

"You want entertainment, you piece of shit, how 'bout I show you some stars." Silas stepped in front of me and faced off with the men.

*No.*

I couldn't get the word out. I reached for Silas's shoulder to pull him back at the moment one of the brutes took a swing. I was too late.

Silas's head snapped back with the impact of the hit. Krish shouted his name, but the diminutive singer shook his head, wiped the blood off his face, and his lips split to show bloody teeth as he grinned.

"All right, then. Let's go, motherfucker."

Ryan moved to step in, but Silas was already swinging at the one who'd hit him. A guy dressed in baggy pants and a tank top grabbed for Ryan, but he expertly pushed him away and took a swing. Krish was trying to avoid the melee when I saw a bald man dressed in black move around to intercept him.

Krish gasped as the guy hooked an arm around his throat. Out of the three, Krish seemed the least likely to hold his own, as Ryan and Silas were hanging in there. I went to Krish's aid, but a man in a green shirt stepped in front of me.

"Where are you going?"

An echo from the past sounded through my head. *"Where are you going, boy? This is your uncle's doing, but you'll do. It's time for you to pay for your sins, Callum Alexander."*

That name echoed through my consciousness, and I knew it had belonged to me once upon a time.

The green-shirted man shoved me against the fence and put a hand to my throat, attempting to cut off my air supply. I was flooded with memories. Flashes of a hospital clinic, sick patients screaming, family members crying, my limbs immobilized as I was pummeled with stones and bats.

*Oh Lord.* What did it all mean?

*Apologies, Kallos. I cannot intervene, but use these memories to give you strength. Fight for your survival. Walk your path.*

Mr. Ame's voice in my head jarred me from the flood of painful images.

"Kal! Watch out!"

Ryan's voice shook me from my stupor and I threw off the attacker's hold. I shoved at his chest and followed with a left hook that knocked him back into the shadows.

Ryan had fought off his attacker and was helping Silas deal with the leader, who was blocking them from getting to Krish.

I would not let any of my friends be harmed.

I rushed to Krish's side and delivered a blow to his captor's ear, causing him to let go of Krish, who fell to the ground. The man in black growled at me but I punched him in the face again and again, until he fell to a knee.

I was ready to deliver a final blow when Ryan grabbed my arm.

"Come on. Let's go."

Silas was trying to get Krish to his feet. I stepped in, scooped Krish up over my shoulders, and pushed Silas forward. Out of the corner of my eye, I watched as Ryan picked up a metal pipe and threatened the remaining brutes if they followed us. As I passed him, he backed away from the fight, keeping his pipe at the ready until we were far enough away. He tossed it into the bushes as we neared the corridor leading to the buses.

"Put me down, Kal, I'm okay," Krish grunted.

*Be well on your journey.*

I spun around and caught the silhouette of Mr. Ame at the entrance. He disappeared before my eyes.

I paused for the briefest moment to set Krish on his feet and puzzled over Mr. Ame's message. Silas pulled Krish forward, and Ryan followed.

I couldn't move.

That vision. I'd seen terrible things, done terrible things. Felt so much pain. This was how I'd ended up at the carnival?

"Kal, come on."

Ryan reached out for me, and I froze. Would he hate me when he discovered the truth? He was the first person to really see me in so long, and when I was with him, I felt like I might actually have a future, a reason for being here, in this time and place.

But there was a lot I didn't know, didn't understand. All of these men had been patient so far, but what if that didn't last? Could I really keep my past a secret from them?

"Let's go. It's okay, man, come with us. You're hurt."

I touched my face and sucked in a breath. Pain throbbed through my cheek and jaw and when I held my fingers in front of me, they were covered with blood.

"Please, Kal."

The *please* would now and always weaken my resolve when it came to Ryan. Even though I'd put him in harm's way, he still reached for me. Even though I'd hurt people, he'd tried to protect me.

We were linked, Ryan and me. My only hope was that I didn't bring more darkness into his life.

I took his hand and made my choice. I would walk my

path and survive. This time, I did not look back. I ran by Ryan's side until we reached Hush's bus. Once we reached the door, Silas pulled Krish to him and they held each other tight, murmuring to each other as they climbed onto their bus.

"We need to get you some ice," Ryan said. "And get someone to bandage your cheek. Damn. You might need stitches."

I stepped back from his gentle touch. I had so much to say to him, but once again the words would not come.

"Please, Kal. Come inside."

One of the young men who'd been playing video games earlier came trotting down the steps. "Who needs stitches... *whoa*. What happened to you guys?"

Silas started recounting the tale from inside the bus as if it were some action adventure while the young man stared at me. "Better not tell my dad," he finally said. "He already thinks you guys fight too much." He grabbed me by the arm. "Lucky for you, I paid attention all those times he tried teaching me first aid."

Ryan moved behind me and pushed me up the stairs. "Come on," he whispered. "Please."

# CHAPTER 12

**Ryan**

His poor face. He'd been really brave, taking on two guys, picking up Krish like he was a sack of potatoes, and getting us all out of that mess. But I'd known he was afraid. I'd seen the terror in his eyes when the guy in white grabbed him. He'd frozen in place for several beats. But when he knew Krish was in trouble, he'd snapped out of it and saved the day.

Now, as he sat on the couch being fussed over by Boy Wonder Bowie, his eyes darting around, uncertain, Kal seemed so far away. Something had triggered him, and if I were a betting man, I'd bet he was revisiting some kind of trauma. I was intimately acquainted with the trauma response.

"I can butterfly this, and we can see how it looks in the morning. Just don't rub it, pick at it, or get it wet, okay? It can come off in a couple days."

Kal nodded and gave Bowie a weak thumbs up.

"Hey thanks, Kal." Krish held out his hand and, after a brief moment, Kal accepted it. "For a second there...well, I'm glad we made it back."

Kal nodded and pointed to Krish's neck and then placed a hand over his own.

"Oh, I'm okay."

Bowie turned to frown at Krish. "Did you have pressure on your throat? That's no joke. It can swell."

Krish's eyes bugged out and he rubbed his neck absently. "Yeah, but I could still breathe."

"Fuck," Silas said. "I think we should go the hospital—"

"No more hospitals," Krish said with a groan. "I'm fine. You're the one bleeding."

Silas stood with his hands on his hips while the man on crutches tried to clean up his mouth.

"Your lip is split but your teeth are okay. I shouldn't have let you go," Los said quietly. His eyes were red and he wouldn't leave Silas's side. "I should have been there."

Silas rolled his eyes. "It was fine. We handled them, didn't we, Ryan?"

But I wasn't feeling as cocky as him. It was one thing for *me* to get physical. I hated seeing my friends in danger, and I considered these men my friends. The moment the ruffian's fist came in contact with Silas's jaw, my heart dropped. I couldn't have handled it if I got another person hurt.

I shook my head, and Kal reached out for my arm.

"Don't. Not your fault."

How did he know?

"What? No, Ryan," Silas scolded. "What the hell else were we supposed to do? Let some carney meth freaks drag us off and have their sicko way with us? No way. Nobody touches this ass but Krish, you hear me?"

Los cursed under his breath loud enough for Silas to hear him.

"Okay, and Los when he sleeps with us."

"Fuck off."

"I think everyone needs some sleep," Brains said. "Si, you and Krish go clean up and get some rest."

Silas lost his playfulness. "Ryan is gonna stay."

I'd been about to slip outside. I could always find a bench to crash on until it was time for the buses to take off in the morning. I'd done it before to avoid my bandmates.

Brains nodded. "Good idea. Kal should stay, too. We have room. Jordan is with Roxanne tonight."

"I'll text Chantal and tell her Kal is with us," Krish said, his phone already out.

I leaned back against the couch and pressed my thigh against Kal's. He pushed back.

"I'm almost done," Bowie said as he applied one more strip to finish closing up the half-inch-long cut on Kal's cheekbone. The area around it was really red and swollen. He turned Kal's head and frowned. "Damn. That's a helluva scar you have back here."

Kal reached up to the back of his skull, but he shook his head and shrugged.

I stood and moved around Bowie to take a look. Kal had a deep scar that was hidden by his hair from afar, but up close you could see the four-inch gash through the strands. It was still pink. "That might explain a few things about your speech. What happened to you?" I sat back down beside him and pressed a hand to his thigh. He shook his head once more.

"There, that should hold," Bowie said. "I'll get you guys some ice packs from the first-aid kit my dad sent. You should all take some ibuprofen, too. Krish? You okay?"

"Yeah, a little bit in shock. I've never been in a fight like that before. I kind of panicked, which sucks, because my brother taught me some stuff after boot camp. Guess it really is a use-it-or-lose-it scenario."

"Nah, babe, I don't ever want you to have to use it. I'm sorry."

"Not your fault, Silas. I was so scared when that guy hit you, but you just stood there." Krish chuckled, eliciting laughter from the rest of us. "No, really! You stared him down like 'did you hit me?' It was like a slow-mo action scene when the bad guy gets hit and, like, he doesn't move. It was actually sexy."

Silas stared at him for a minute, then glanced around at the rest of us before announcing, "Yeah, Krish and I are going to bed. Good night, everyone. Good night, Los. Thanks, Ryan and Kal. Thanks, Brains and Bowie. Goodnight, sweethearts."

Los groaned as Silas tugged Krish's hand and headed toward the back of the bus. Everyone else laughed, except Kal. He tapped my hand, pointed to his chest, then pointed outside.

"No," I said to him. "You're safe here. They're good people." I leaned close to his ear. "Neither of us should be alone tonight, man."

I said it as much for him as for myself. I'd always liked the Hush guys, and we shared a bond around Gavin, but I'd never bunked with them. They were so easy about including us, making us feel wanted. I hated it and appreciated it at the same time.

Bowie brought out some pillows and blankets. "These are extra. I guess one of you can take the couch and one of you can take the lower bunk."

"Thanks, man." I accepted the items from him. "Thanks for everything."

He nodded and gave us a little wave.

That left Kal and I sitting on the couch together. I turned to face him, and his eyes were already fluttering closed.

"Here," I said, placing a pillow on my lap. "Rest your head. I'll hold the ice pack for you."

Kal frowned but he did what I said. He lay down and pulled his knees up to keep his long legs from hanging off the sofa, and I spread the blanket over him. I held the ice pack to his right cheek and with my left hand, I brushed his hair back from his forehead. His deep blue eyes gazed up at me for several beats, and then I felt his body go slack as he relaxed. Soon his eyes jerked beneath his eyelids and his full pillowy lips fell open with a faint sigh.

How I wished I had my sketchbook. He was beautiful. I grew angry all over again that he'd been hurt, though he'd handled himself as if fighting was not foreign to him. He'd moved with purpose and agility. As I looked closer at the planes of his face, I saw the signs. A split in his right eyebrow, scars on his upper lip and the corner of his left eye, and a thin slice along his hairline.

Once the ice pack warmed, I continued to run my fingers through his hair. It was thicker than I'd thought, not coarse like mine, though. His was fine, but there was a lot of it. Guilt weighed heavily on my soul tonight and it dragged me into another memory…

*It was two weeks before I could visit Josh in the hospital. Well, I probably could have been there about a week sooner, but after getting bailed out of jail and detoxing, I'd thrown a pity party and didn't have the balls to face up to what I'd done. I wasn't too sure whether Josh would even want to see me.*

*"He's going to be excited you're here," the nurse said. "He's been asking for you. His parents have been by and his sister, but he's been hoping you'd come."*

*I had a lame-ass teddy bear I'd picked up, tucked under my arm, and I'd worn a plain hooded sweatshirt and sweatpants, tucking my hair under a ball cap and pulling my hood up over it. My tattooed neck was covered by a neck brace. I was hopeful no one would recognize me. The accident had mostly been kept out of the media, thanks to some quick action by the label's lawyers. My hands were still bandaged and my neck still hurt like hell. They were hopeful the fracture in my C-3 would heal on its own. I hated the dumb collar, but agreed to wear the soft one since I didn't want to become paralyzed or some shit.*

*Like Josh.*

*Even though we fooled around, I'd been upfront with Josh that ours was not an exclusive or even a forever thing, and he'd happily gone along with that. Didn't mean I didn't care about him. I did. But I'd never been in love, and I wasn't in love with him. The fact that I'd nearly made him a quadriplegic made me sick to my stomach, a feeling that would never go away.*

*The nurse led me into his room, where he was lying in the bed buried in cords and wires and tubes. Half of his long, curly brown hair had been shaved when they'd had to do surgery to relieve swelling on his brain. I knew this much from my lawyer.*

*"Joshua, your friend is here," the nurse said in that cheerful tone that nurses must learn how to achieve in nursing school. No one else could ever be that warm and kind and sterile all at the same time.*

*Josh's eyes opened after several flutters of his eyelids. I was grateful to see that he was breathing on his own. Apparently, he'd had a collapsed lung when they brought him in and he had to be intubated. Just the thought of something being shoved down my throat had me in a panic.*

*When he was able to focus and saw me, he beamed.*

*"Hey," he said. "Thank you for coming. Are you all right?"*

*Was I all right? Why the fuck was he asking me that?*

*"I'm okay," I said as I stood next to the bed. I took his hand in mine, because it seemed like that's what I should do, and he squeezed it.*

*We stared at each other, neither knowing quite what to say in this situation. Sorry I nearly killed you? Sorry you might never walk again?*

*"I'm sorry," I finally got out and tears flowed from my eyes.* I can't do this. *I wanted to run...for the first bar. This was too much, too intense.*

*Josh lifted his other arm, and I watched him struggle to bring it over and place his hand on top of mine, almost as if to say, "You're here now and you're going to stay."*

*"Hey, none of that. There's no blame here."*

*A sob escaped, and I tried to pull my hand back, but Josh held on surprisingly tight for someone with a spinal injury.*

*"Ryan. I got in that car of my own volition. Whatever you think, that's the truth. I knew how much you'd had to drink. I often feel like your invincibility will rub off on me when I'm with you. Maybe that was it, or maybe I felt like taking a step off the ledge and seeing what happens next." He brought his hand down hard on mine. "My condition is not your fault. It's the product of my poor decision-making, and I will live with it."*

*His smile faded only the slightest bit. "But you need to take a good look at your life. You're unhappy? Fix it. You're not well, take care of it. If I've learned anything from this, it's that tomorrow is no guarantee, and the world needs you and your music."*

*I tried to pull away again but the damn kid held on tighter. "I'm sorry, Josh," I said as tears streamed down my cheeks. "I don't know how to make this up to you. I'll let you be."*

*"You're not hearing me, Ryan." His smile was gone, but there was still that adoration in his eyes, and it made me feel about a millimeter tall. "If you really want to make amends? Yeah, that's what it's called. Go into treatment. Otherwise you're going to be right here like me, Ryan, or in a pine box. Don't let that be your legacy. You're too talented for that, and the world doesn't need to lose another rock star to excess."*

*He let go of my hand then and leaned his head back, letting his eyes fall closed.*

*The kid that I'd been scratching an itch with had just handed me my ass and given me an ultimatum I couldn't refuse. How dare I even consider not doing what he asked after what he'd sacrificed?*

*"I'll make sure everything's taken care of," I blurted out in a rush. "Doctors, specialists, rehab, whatever you need, Josh. I don't care if I never make another cent, I will take care of you."*

*He gave me a sad smile and sighed. "You'll do what you can. But what I really care about is that you get better, Ryan. I hate to see you in pain."*

*That hit me in the gut like a sledgehammer, bending me in half. My pain wasn't something I could ever get better from, but how did I tell him that? I could walk. I'd walked away from the accident. But I'd been a throwaway kid who found that the only way to keep people around was to keep them entertained, wowed, dazzled, and to keep the ride amazing at all times. It hadn't worked on my family, but it worked on everyone I'd come across since leaving home.*

As long as I lived, I'd never forget what Josh said to me that night, and in the years since, I'd done my best to walk the walk, slipping only briefly when Gavin died.

I instructed my attorney not to fight the charges, to enter a guilty plea, because from the moment I left that hospital room, I intended to take responsibility for my actions for the rest of my life.

The gentlest touch roused me from my thoughts.

Kal.

"So sad."

# CHAPTER 13

**Kal**

I woke from a deep sleep with my head in Ryan's lap, his tears dropping gently onto my face. I reached up and cupped his cheek, relieved he hadn't been injured in the brawl with the roustabouts. But his tears alluded to the worst type of wounds.

Ryan carried such sadness on his person, it weighed him down like the shackles he'd likely once worn. If my stupid voice would cooperate, I would ask him about his pain, offer to bear some of it for him. He belonged soaring in the heavens, not wallowing in sorrow. He'd been given such a gift, a voice to lift others up and ease their suffering. It wouldn't do for him to continue feeling this way. At that moment, I realized *that* could be my purpose here, to show Ryan how important he was, how his talent made others' lives better for a little while.

"Hey," he whispered. "How's your head? You okay?"

I nodded and pushed myself up to sitting, though I liked being close to him like that. He'd run his fingers through my hair as he'd held the ice pack to my cheek, a gesture that seemed foreign to him and which made it all the more meaningful.

I pointed to him and raised my eyebrows.

"Me? I'm okay. Tired. Wired."

I made the gesture for us to switch places, and he smiled. "Thanks, but I'm okay. I likely won't be able to sleep."

I pointed to myself and shook my head.

"You neither, huh? Man," he said, pressing his knee against mine. "Did you know those guys? That one guy in white seemed to know you."

I waved my hand back and forth.

"Sort of?"

Thumbs up.

He looked around the bus. "Hey, can you write?"

That was a good question. I knew I could at one point.

Ryan found a piece of paper and a pencil and he handed them to me, but my fingers didn't know what to do with the pencil. I tried wrapping them around, but I kept dropping it. As I bent over to retrieve the pencil from the floor, I spotted something familiar on a bottom shelf and reached for it.

"A Ouija board?" Ryan laughed, and I shrugged. I set the board up on the couch in between us and gestured for him to ask me a question. It was an older board, and the paper covering it was frayed at the edges. The planchette was made of lightweight wood stained black and it had designs burned into it.

"All right. Swore I'd never use one of these after seeing the freaky-ass *Paranormal Activity* movies, but I suppose this is safe." He tapped a finger against his chin. "How about, how old are you?"

I frowned at him. How did I explain that time had been

different for me since I'd joined the carnival? Instead, I moved the planchette around to the right digits.

He watched my hands move and mouthed the numbers to himself. "Twenty-one. Really? You seem much older. Okay, how about, I know speaking is hard for you and I know you had a head injury. Is it…do you have memory loss?"

I moved the planchette to *Yes*.

"I see. How bad is it?"

I hesitated because the truth would likely make him think I was mentally ill. *Not sure.*

"Okay. How about how long were you with the carnival?"

I moved the planchette to the number one.

"A month?" I shook my head. "A year?" I nodded. "Wow. That's a long time to be traveling around. Did you like it?"

I shrugged. I didn't know how to answer that. I thought for a minute and then started moving the planchette.

"Nothing…to…compare…it…to. Oh. Because you don't remember before?"

I moved the planchette to *Yes*.

"Wow, okay. So your…injury happened at least a year ago, yeah?"

Technically that was the truth. I didn't want to lie to him.

*Yes.*

"That is awful. I mean, there are things I'd like to forget, but not my whole life. But you remember how to play instruments. Did you learn at the carnival or have you always played?"

I moved the planchette to say *yes*, and he laughed. "Yes to the first or second part?" I moved the planchette to the number two. "Awesome. Different part of the brain, I guess. That calliope thing was pretty amazing."

I moved the planchette to say *I built*.

"No way! You built that thing?"

I moved it to *yes*.

"You're a craftsman, then, too."

I moved the planchette to *yes.*

"Cool, so you, like, rebuilt it?"

Hmm. That must have been what he thought possible. *Yes.*

"That must have been a big job."

I started moving the planchette rapidly.

"Had...a...lot...of...time. Right on. Do you remember where you're from?"

I frowned. A pain stabbed in the top of my head but not as bad as before. It was as if the man who attacked me unlocked a deluge of memories, and the more that came through, the less it hurt.

I had a flash of a radio, sitting in front of it. My uncle's voice. I moved the planchette before the memory faded.

"K...T...N...T What, like a radio station? K-TNT?"

*Yes.*

He grabbed a flat black rectangle-shaped device off of the table and touched it, bringing the screen to life. Ryan tapped on it several times and then frowned. "It says there are... Well, there's a few listed here. Oklahoma, Tacoma, Washington...wait...Muscatine, Iowa—"

I touched his arm and nodded.

"Huh. Iowa boy. Explains the clothes."

It was my turn to frown at him.

He grinned. "I don't know, when I first saw you, you seemed like you were from another time, but Iowa's kinda behind the times, right? It makes sense."

I rolled my eyes and he put my hand back on the planchette. "What else do you remember?"

Flashes of things, peoples' names...I started moving the planchette again.

"Herbert Hoover?" Ryan's expression was confused. "Oh, yeah, wasn't he born in Iowa? I don't know my presidents very well, and that was a long-ass time ago."

I didn't know how to respond. I knew time had passed, but I had no idea how much.

I moved the planchette to *Yes*. What else could I say?

"Wow. What about family—"

*No.*

My hands jerked the planchette, and Ryan flinched.

"Ah. I get it. Don't remember, or off limits?" His voice was soft. If the circumstances were different, I knew Ryan would absolutely understand my familial woes. I didn't want to go there. Not yet.

*Yes.*

He waved his hand. "Whatever you don't want to tell me, I'm fine with that too."

The thing was, I *wanted* to tell him. But how to do it without giving away the fact that whatever happened to me happened a long time ago?

"Left behind. Left me." Those words had been reverberating through my head since the attacker had grabbed me at the carnival. Pieces of my story had come together, and I felt like a huge bubble of pressure was under the surface of my skull, waiting to spill over. Like if I closed my eyes, it would all be there.

"Who left you? It's coming back, isn't it?" Ryan placed his hand on my knee. "Sometimes a traumatic incident can unlock memories you've hidden to protect yourself. Maybe that's what happened tonight? It's okay, it'll come back to you."

I shook my head. "Don't want it. Bad things, Ry-an." My vision blurred, and I sucked in a breath.

"Hey, shhh." Ryan put his arm around me and squeezed my shoulder. "Let's get some sleep, okay? It'll be easier in the morning."

I wasn't sure I agreed with him, but I nodded.

He stood from the couch and held out his hand to me.

"The bunks are pretty small, but if you don't mind, I really don't want to be alone."

I didn't either.

Ryan led us to the small hallway behind the booth where the men took their meals and, I could guess by the mess left behind, applied makeup for their stage shows. There was only one open bunk on the bottom level, and Ryan crawled in first.

I crouched down and peered into the darkness. Ryan made a "shhh" sound and then his hand reached out for me.

Having Ryan become my safe place was a scary proposition, but then I knew for a fact it was not in his nature to trust people, either. If he trusted me, that meant something.

I took his hand and slid onto the bunk next to him. It was surprisingly long enough for me to stretch out, despite my height. Once I settled down on my back, Ryan spoke close to my ear.

"Sometimes I dream, and it's not pretty. I'll try not to hurt you."

I turned my head to face him, and we were so close, I sucked in a breath in surprise. I couldn't make out his features in the dark, but I'd already memorized his face, I could see his gray eyes even with mine closed. The way his nose curved slightly from being broken a time or two, the deep scar on his neck that was visible above his tattoos. His dark brown hair with golden highlights from the sun…the way I wished I could wash it clean of whatever he put in it to create the messy style he wore. I knew it would feel good between my fingers.

I reached up and ran my fingers over the stubble on his cheeks, and he moaned quietly, the smallest sound of pleasure that let me know he was relaxing.

Ryan ran his fingers lightly over my chest and, hesitantly, rested his hand over my heart. "This okay?" His lips were close to my face. I felt the faintest brush of them against mine. I placed my hand over his and wished I had full use of my faculties. Since I couldn't get the right words out, I thought I'd tell him with my body.

I moved the fraction of an inch separating us and kissed him.

"*Kal*." He whispered against my lips, and with the *l*, he licked at them, sending shudders through me. I opened my mouth and our tongues met, greeting each other tentatively, curiously, our lips connecting soft as flower petals brushing together.

I'd never kissed another man before him, not like this. There'd been the hard smashing of faces together in a dark corner, fumbling with belt buckles and zippers, the furious thrusting against a stranger's hand until one or both of us found release.

This was different. We didn't rush, there wasn't desperation, just a pure and innocent need to connect with one another. Ryan seduced with his tongue, coaxing and flirting with mine. After a time, we rolled onto our sides to face each other and Ryan slid his knee between my thighs. I cradled his face in my hands, wishing to tell him with my kisses all that I couldn't say out loud. That I was amazed by him, inspired and aroused, and that I longed to shelter him in my arms as long as he needed a safe place.

"You are incredible, you know that?" he whispered.

We smiled together as we panted, our breath mingling in the closeness.

"You." It was one word, but I hoped it got my meaning across. As the noise of the day faded into the quiet of this moment, he was all I wanted to think of.

He ran his hands under my shirt. His nails were sharp, his fingertips hot. I wanted more contact, but I was thrilled with what he gave me. In the tight space, every movement we made caused desperate friction. The inability to get to more bare skin was frustrating and exciting at the same time. Made everything more intense.

"I want to keep doing this, but more than that," he said against my mouth, each touch sending thrills throughout my body, "I want to sleep with you, just like this. Close. Can I hold you like this, Kal?"

"Close." I kissed him again, though I felt myself being pulled under by sleep. Our kisses became lazy, small movements, enough to let the other know they were safe, cared for. Wanted. And I *wanted*. So much with him. I wanted the kisses, the touching, to go on, but darkness soon pulled me under.

THE MORNING CAME, and with it the worries. Would the fellows on the bus be distant or think I was too strange? Would I be able to do my job well enough? Would the others resent what had happened the night before and send me away? More than that, could I even navigate this modern time, and was it even worth it? To carry on?

What would Ryan think of me after last night?

"Whose turn is it to make breakfast?"

"Who needs to shower first?"

"Who busted out the Ouija board, dude? I didn't even know we still had that thing."

Ryan stirred from sleep and as his eyes opened, his body stiffening when he saw me. He had been sprawled across me, vulnerable in sleep. I lifted my hands so he could move—

"It's you." And with that, his face relaxed and he snuggled against me, closing his eyes and nuzzling my neck. "Did you sleep?"

I nodded and let my hands fall back onto Ryan's shoulder and his thigh that was draped across my torso.

"Good. I slept better than I have since we started this damned tour. You can do magic, Kal." He started humming a song as he ran a hand up under my shirt again, letting his nails graze lightly over my nipples. "You ever heard that song? By America? Wait, do you listen to any other kind of music? Like had you heard any of us before yesterday?"

I shook my head. "Only carnival, ragtime, and classical. Before my uncle left me—"

Ryan's eyes flew open and he placed his hand gently on my throat. "Keep going."

I gazed at him, my stomach churning. "My uncle, he did bad things. I didn't know. I worked for him. He...hurt people. Cancer."

Ryan shook his head. "Your uncle hurt people with cancer? What? Did he run a care home or something?"

I nodded. My body trembled out of control, the shivers, as if I were freezing, when moments ago I'd been warm and happy. Safe. Now I shook as if I was back on the frozen ground...in Iowa. My breath making clouds above me. I didn't know how to explain it all to Ryan. The memories assaulted me like the fists, stones, and sticks I was beaten with.

"He left me."

"Hey, hey, shhhh," Ryan said. He shifted so that he was the one cradling me. "You're safe now. You're okay. That's so fucked up though. Kal, I won't...I won't let anyone hurt you like that ever again."

I wanted to believe him, but I couldn't stop shaking.

"Hey, you guys okay down there?" I recognized Krish's voice.

The curtain pulled back, and I tucked my face toward Ryan and squeezed my eyes shut, not wanting these men to see me at my weakest.

"Yeah," Ryan said in a tone you'd take with a hurt animal,

being careful not to spook it. "We're doing just fine. Thanks for letting us crash last night."

"Absolutely." Silas's voice. "Can you guys even fit down there?"

"We're fine. But I think you're stuck with us until Virginia. I think I lost my phone in that nonsense last night, and I never let my band know I wasn't coming back to the bus."

"Shit. Uhhhh… Hey, Brains?"

"Yes. I'll text Parker."

Ryan chuckled and pulled me tighter to him. "Thanks, man."

I was sure they could all hear my heart pounding in my chest. I focused on Ryan's hold, his breaths, and I tried to calm down.

# CHAPTER 14

**Ryan**

I vowed right then and there that I'd hold on to Kal as long as he needed me.

Even though, holy shit. He'd been through hell, the poor guy. All that, and he'd saved our fucking asses last night. Then he'd taken me in his arms and brought out a protective streak I didn't know I was capable of.

I smoothed down his hair as he tried to catch his breath. His voice had come flooding back along with a fuck-ton of horrible, awful memories. I intended to see him through this. Like I wished someone had done for me.

"We're gonna figure out breakfast," Krish continued, making eye contact with me. "Take as long as you need."

"Yeah," Silas said. "We'll be leaving in a few minutes, driving through to Virginia Beach but hey, check this out. Bowie told us about this place he used to camp with his dad at the ocean, so we're going to have a motherfucking *campfire* tonight! At the *beach*!"

When none of us responded, Silas grew exasperated.

"With *S'MORES*!"

"Right on," I said, grinning at Krish. "Not really a fan, but the beach sounds cool."

Los's head appeared from the bunk above us. "You don't like s'mores? Man, Wells, what's wrong with you?"

"The list is long, my friend. Thanks, guys. Really. I…*we* appreciate you letting us tag along."

"We're glad you're here. Oh, Chantal texted me," Krish said with a grin. "She said 'tell Kal not to worry, see him at the venue for the show, and if you find a hot lesbian who needs a ride, send her over to my bus since y'all are into matchmaking. I could use a match.'"

"That's awesome." Not only had Silas and Krish connected on this tour, but so had Brains and his Navy man—who was strangely absent from these festivities—and Brains's replacement, the Navy guy's son, Bowie, had a little something going on with the guy handing out condoms at the festival. And then Jordan, their new guitar player, was hooking up with Roxanne, the singer from Just Like Love… Maybe there *was* some magic on this bus other than the magic man in my arms, who'd finally stopped shaking.

I glanced down at him and he was staring wide-eyed into the darkness, in some sort of daze. Probably overwhelmed with the memories he'd been hit with last night. I needed to help him compose himself before we crawled out of this bunk, which needed to happen soon or my bladder would explode.

I raised my eyebrows at Krish and he got the message.

"We'll give you guys a bit. I'll leave towels out for you and some clothes if you want to change? And breakfast will be… something."

"Fine," Silas said and gave an exaggerated sigh. "I'll make French toast."

The other guys whooped and hollered at Silas's pronouncement, which made Kal jump. I ran a hand down his back to soothe him. My new favorite activity.

"It's okay. Silas's French toast is legendary. The cheers are merited."

Kal tried to slow his breathing as Krish pulled the curtain partially closed for us.

"Thank you," Kal whispered. "For…all."

"You're so welcome." I scooted down a bit to lie face to face with him and I smoothed back his hair. "*So* welcome. So *very* welcome."

And I was gifted with his smile, like the one he'd given me when we'd first met and played the keyboard together, and in that moment, I wished we had days before we had to rejoin the tour, before I had to deal with my band. Weeks. Decades. I wanted endless time to explore this magic between us. I wanted to *make* magic with Kal.

But I really needed to make for the bathroom.

"Hey." I cradled his face and his eyelids fluttered.

"Hello."

"God, you're something else. Listen. We're gonna have a great day with our friends, okay? A long bus ride followed by some camping, and then we'll rejoin the tour."

He placed his hands over mine. "I don't like your band hurting you." That frown was back, and after watching him wail on those guys last night, a more noble guy might have worried for his bandmates.

"There's a lot of history there, but yeah, things aren't good. That's a worry for another day. Let's…relax today, okay? You can talk or not, tell them or not. I trust them because I trusted Gavin, and *he* trusted them."

"Ga-vin?"

*Oh...* "I need to tell you about him, but if I don't make it to the toilet in the next thirty seconds, I'm going to embarrass myself."

Kal's cheeks reddened and he smiled. He started to move out of the bunk but I held on.

"Hey. You're safe with them, you know? But if you don't want me touching you—"

"I understand. It's…surprising. That you can, that *we* can. In front of others. I…like it."

"Good. Me too. But you don't have to stay with me, you know. You can…" Ugh, I was making it weird, but I was trying to make it right. "If there's someone else you want, or you want to part ways when we get back to tour, I understand."

Kal shrank back, confusion on his face. He nodded and then climbed out of the bunk.

Not only did I make it weird, but if I kept up my weird shit, I was gonna make him leave.

I had to admit, as I stood up and stretched, that as much as I loved being close to Kal, sleeping in a bunk with a bigger man than myself wasn't exactly sustainable. I missed my bed in my house in LA. It wasn't a real rockstar place to live, but that's what made it good for me. I had a fleeting image of bringing Kal home with me. After the tour.

Like what? Like a roommate? A boyfriend? A pet? I was really getting ahead of myself here, but I couldn't help it. There was truly something extraordinary about him, about how I felt when I was with him, that went far beyond the fact that he wasn't part of my world. Beyond a distraction and beyond displaced infatuation. I was attracted to him, but it was more than that. He was the closest person I'd ever found, besides Gavin, who saw me for the fully flawed man I was and who didn't want to change me, save me, or flaunt me.

He seemed to just want *me*.

We'd see if that continued to be the case.

"I'll be right back."

He nodded and glanced around as if he were unsure he was ready to join the now singing group of men, who were belting out Simon and Garfunkel's "Fifty Ways to Leave Your Lover."

I dashed into the bathroom and couldn't help but groan as I unloaded far more than the recommended amount of waste from my bladder, and when I looked up, I snorted.

Someone had stuck a mirror on the wall at eye level that put the viewer's face in a mirrored "Employee of the Month" certificate frame. That was a preposterous proposition. For me. But then I took a look at myself.

I'd really stopped giving a shit. At least with my appearance. I still took care of my body, but I hadn't had a haircut in months, meaning whatever hairstyle I'd had at one point had turned into some sort of amorphous blob like a hedge that'd lost its shape. I'd foregone sunscreen so often my face was a combination of tanned, burned, and freckled. Yesterday's eyeliner was mostly gone but there was some black shit that had bled into the dark circles under my eyes and the establishment of significant crows' feet. And I forgot when I'd last shaved. I couldn't grow a beard, but I was successful at patches of sparkly stubble that put me somewhere between mug shot after a bender and a cast member on *The Walking Dead.*

*Wow.* And the press used to call me pretty.

I finished up, washed my hands, and figured I'd let Kal have a turn then take the guys up on their offer of a shower. Then maybe I'd attempt to polish this old heap.

The bus engine cranked on and as I opened the door, the beast lurched forward, making Kal brace himself on the bunks.

"Yeah, it's a little nausea-inducing until we get on the highway. Then it'll be better. Here," I said, gesturing to the bathroom. "Take your time. You want to shower?"

Kal nodded. "It's okay?"

I stepped closer to him. "With these guys, they wouldn't offer if it wasn't. Just be quick. I'll hop in after you. Krish left stuff in there for both of us. Take what you want."

He nodded, and I stepped aside to let him pass me in the narrow hallway. He paused in front of me, placed his hands on my jaw, and planted a kiss on my forehead. He stepped back as if it were the most natural thing in the world and as he closed the door behind him, I leaned back against the bunk, my hand over my heart to keep it from running away from me.

The care this man showed me…

I had to be careful. I needed, actually, to call my sponsor. I somehow needed to not let my feelings spin out of control, while on a bus, with semi-friends and a man who had tilted my world on its axis, and who I wanted to keep in my orbit.

Could I manage it all? Or would this turn out to be yet another epic Wells failure?

"Don't overthink it."

I spun around at Brains's voice. He occupied the middle bunk across from where we'd slept last night. He'd pulled back the curtain and was giving me the raised-eyebrow look.

"Oh, hey man. I thought you were up—"

"Nope," he said, popping his lips. "Just lying here, wallowing in self-pity, and I happened to catch the end of that conversation."

I sighed. "When I made it weird."

"Mm-hm. Look. I get it. But seeing as I recently had some experience with this whole feelings stuff, all I'm saying is, don't fucking wreck something that could be good because you let your bullshit get in the way."

"And what does the smartest guy on this bus think he knows about my bullshit?" I leaned against the bunk across from him and crossed my arms as the door to the bathroom opened and Kal popped his head out.

Not wearing a shirt.

"Okay?" He held up a couple of bottles that I couldn't make out. I held up a finger to Brains and walked over. Kal pulled the door a little more closed, his eyes wide.

"Relax," I whispered. "I won't look until you're ready to show me."

His lips opened and his pink tongue ran over his bottom lip.

"If you keep that up—"

He held up three little bottles in one of his big hands and grinned.

I pointed to each, shaking my head with a laugh. "Wash your hair with that, condition with that, use that on the rest of you. Got it?"

He smiled at me once more before pulling the door closed. And locking it.

"Probably smart he locked the door."

I turned back to Brains, knowing my little soldier was standing very much at attention after getting a load of all that golden skin of Kal's. From the waist up. He still had his shorts on. God, he was beautiful.

"And why's that?"

"Besides the fact you look like you'd eat him alive if given the chance, you do know whose bus you're on?"

"Good point. I recall the stories Gavin told me. What did he used to say, 'Beware: The Hush will be the last thing you hear.' Something like that?"

"There was the time Los picked the lock and put a pair of doves in the shower with Gavin. Los says, 'now we know what doves really sound like.' I can't even listen to Prince anymore without laughing."

I ran a hand down my face and shook my head. "Guess I should be thankful my band isn't that creative."

Brains shrugged. "I never minded it, not really. I missed them while I was gone." He looked up at the ceiling of his bunk and sighed.

"Hey, I'm sorry you and the Navy man are on the outs. I saw him in the bar in Nashville. Dude's pretty sprung on you. Surprised to see you here."

"The kid was pissed. What can you do?"

*Damn.* Brains had fallen for his Navy guy, and Navy guy's kid, Bowie, was now drumming for Hush. I could see that being all kinds of awkward.

"No way he stands in the way once he gets to know you better. Hell, even I'd want you for my stepdad."

Brains rolled his eyes but at least I got him to grin.

"Nice change of subject. Seriously. Why you trying to chase this one off? Seems like a good one."

"That's why."

"Hey. *You're* a good one."

I had no cute comeback, and Brains wasn't one for bullshit.

"I'm toxic and you know it. Tell me I'm lying."

"Tell *me* one of us who hasn't royally fucked up." He looked me dead in the eye. "You aren't toxic, Ryan. Haven't been for a long time. Gavin wouldn't have given you his time and his affection if you were. He may have been a mess, but he didn't waste his time with toxic people."

I shrugged because anything I said at that moment would have been thick with tears.

"Gavin was so proud of the songs you two wrote. He gave Silas a smidge of a complex with how much he talked about your talent."

"That was Gavin, though. He brought out the best in everyone."

"And where do you think your best went when he died? It didn't leave, man. You're still carrying it, although sometimes I wonder where, with those tight-ass pants you always wear." Brains whistled through his teeth. He winced as he tried to roll over onto his side to keep from craning his neck.

"Fuck off." But my grin said otherwise. I didn't take compliments well. Not serious ones. Sure, tell me I'm hot or a great fuck and I'm all over that.

"Look, you said you wanted to finish what you two started. Finish the album. I'll do it. I'll produce the album. But only if you stop it with that toxic bullshit, you hear me? Gavin didn't fuck with toxic people. Neither do I."

He held out his hand, and my arm felt like it was weighted down as I reached for his.

"You fucking guys, man. You make a grown man cry like you're the fucking Stones."

"'Start Me Up,'" Brains nodded. "Good one." The water shut off and I wiped at my face before Kal caught me blubbering out here.

"Last thing?" Brains pushed up on his elbows. "Don't fuck things up with this guy because you're all worried and shit. For fuck's sake, you act like you're Britney Spears with your *Toxic* bullshit."

"Fuck you," I said, but the laughter, once unleashed, it would not quit. When Kal came out of the bathroom the next time—dressed in a black knit shirt with an open collar, and lime-green shorts—the tears running down my face were the good kind. He gave me a concerned smile and I held up my hand.

"I'm fine, don't worry, but I think…" I turned to find Silas at the front end of the hallway. "Franklin, if you've got your clippers, maybe it's time I channel my inner Britney."

Silas clapped his hands together and rubbed them back and forth. "Oh, please say I can do it?"

# CHAPTER 15

**Kal**

Ryan went into the bathroom and Silas followed with his shears. Krish explained to me who Britney Spears was, and that Ryan was actually doing a good thing by letting Silas at him with clippers.

"He's really good with them. He cut mine off when I had to have part of my head shaved." Krish pointed to the angry scar on the side of his head. "Piece of metal cut me. Same incident where Brains broke his leg. Very beginning of the tour."

"Is it…always dangerous? Tour?"

Krish's eyes lit up when I spoke, and I tried not to be self-conscious about it.

"Things happen, sure, but this was a freak accident. Unfortunately, it took out a few of us. Could have been way worse."

I swallowed. "Don't like seeing you all hurt. I'm sorry."

Krish's smile was engaging, warm. He was the kindest person I ever remembered meeting.

"You got us out of there. It's all good. Now, let's go get you some breakfast."

I followed Krish into the lounge area of the bus. Los and Bowie sat across from each other in the booth, their heads bobbing to the beat of some music playing from somewhere. It didn't sound anything like the music I'd heard at the festival. This was full of horns, orchestral sounds, and an up-tempo beat.

"I can't do it. Why can't I do it?"

Los and Bowie stuck their tongues out at each other.

"My bio teacher in high school told us it's genetic," Bowie said. "Not everyone can."

"But that's not fair! Krish, can you roll your tongue?"

Krish produced a perfectly rolled appendage, and Los cursed.

"Am I the only one? What about the new guy? Can he do it?"

They all turned their eyes on me, and I shrugged. Yesterday, I couldn't talk. I wasn't sure I was ready to expose another flaw so soon.

"It's not genetic, that was disproven." Brains hobbled out of the hallway on his crutches and Los rushed to his side to help him to the couch. He lowered himself gingerly to a sitting position and handed his crutches to Los. "A guy called Sturtevant said it was genetic in 1940, but another guy named McDonald disproved it fifteen years later after studying pairs of identical twins. Some could and some couldn't. They still put that shit in textbooks and it's been debunked for half a century."

Bowie shrugged. "Doesn't surprise me. Being a Navy brat

meant going to some questionable schools." He glanced at Brains. "Don't tell my dad. He'd hate to hear me say that."

"Uh-huh. Anyway," Brains said, raising his eyebrow at Bowie. "You can train yourself to do it. Just takes practice."

"Hey is Silas going to feed us or what?" Los shouted.

"In a minute, sweetheart. I'm in makeover mode."

The clippers turned on, and his and Ryan's voices lowered to murmurs.

"Is he going to buzz him? I'm not sure Ryan has the skull for that," Los said.

Krish snorted. "Ryan has the skull for whatever he wants. Have you seen the way he controls a crowd?" Then he whispered, "He's so charismatic, he can do anything and they all love him."

Is that how people saw him? I wondered if he'd agree. Yeah, he'd seemed like someone who usually got what he wanted on the surface level, but I doubted anyone had ever given him all he truly desired. Or if they had, they'd hurt him. Terribly.

"I'll start the food," Brains said, preparing to hoist himself and his big leg brace off the couch.

I held a hand up. "I can."

I'd cooked before. For the patients. At my uncle's cancer clinic.

*Oh.* Sights and sounds came flooding through my mind as I prepared to take over where Silas left off. I picked up a piece of bread and dunked it one side at a time in the mixture, all while watching my hands do the same thing in another kitchen, in another time.

*"Make sure you get them evenly coated, Cal, that's it." The woman's voice in my head had a thick Southern drawl. "There's plenty of batter there, and everyone knows French toast day is special." She patted my shoulder and hummed as she passed me by to check on the ham she was baking for supper. "You get that batch*

*finished and then head on out and play your piano for the nice folks. Lots of families coming to visit today. Should be good weather for it."*

*I loathed family day because that was when the questions started, ones I had no answers to. "How do you know this treatment is really going to work? Why isn't our mama getting better? Is she ever gonna come home?" The kids broke my heart, but whenever I looked to my uncle for answers, Norman Baker would disappear. He could never be found when the families started asking questions.*

"Are you guys ready for the big reveal?" Silas called out, dragging me from this most unwelcome memory.

"Wait! Let me shower first!"

Ryan pushed Silas out the door and shut it while Silas cracked up.

"Okay but hurry! This is one of my favorites!"

"Oh God, is that good or bad?" Los flicked his own long dyed-black hair over his shoulders and continued practicing his tongue rolling.

"No it's great, you'll see. And maybe you'll let me cut yours off and finally grow yours out! I want to see your natural color—"

"No way," Los said, trying furiously to curl his tongue. "I'm not ready to go through life as a blond Mexican. No offense, Kal. Your blond hair is cool."

"Thank you." They all looked up, wide-eyed, so I turned back to my cooking and finished the first couple of pieces. Speaking was coming a little easier today but it felt rusty.

"I can take over," Silas said. "Those look great."

I nodded to him and sat awkwardly on the couch across from Brains, who was staring at me. He had one of those intense gazes that made you question whether you were having a friendly conversation, or a vital interrogation.

"Hey, Kal? Where'd you get your training as a gear tech?"

I clasped my hands on my lap. *Here goes nothing.* "School, and then with my uncle."

"You go to a technical school?" Brains had his left leg, the one with the brace, out to the side and his right was planted on the ground. He had one arm over the back of the couch and the other resting beside him. He didn't seem threatening.

"Music school." I had a faint stabbing feeling in my head as the thoughts became clear. The pain had been much less since the huge onslaught of memories hit at the carnival. But how did I explain my life without the time shift? "University professors came to audition students at my school, and they took me with them."

"A prodigy, huh? That makes two of us." He smiled faintly now, friendly, welcoming. "Where did they find you?"

"Iowa."

Brains nodded. "I remember reading about a movement during the Progressive Era when they sent music teachers out into the rural areas as a way to enrich the lives of the kids there. Before that, music was only taught in the city schools. Seems like a smart idea they had, but of course the Depression came along and wiped out most of the programs like that. It's too bad. My parents, like most upper middle-class white families, put me in piano and my sister in ballet. Luckily for them, I loved it."

I certainly couldn't tell him that the story he'd read was absolutely how I became a musician. Was obsessed with music, playing it, writing it, building machines to share it with the world. "My parents were farmers. They sent me to my uncle after I finished school. We worked on Wurlitzers together. He was in broadcasting." That was vague enough, hopefully I hadn't given too much away.

"You should see what he can do."

Ryan's voice startled me, and when I turned to look at

him, his appearance flooded me with...private feelings. Things I shouldn't have been thinking surrounded by others.

"Whoa!" came the chorus of reactions from Krish, Los, and Brains.

"I've never seen you with short hair," Brains said. "It suits you."

Ryan nodded. He was dressed in a white sleeveless shirt and loose black pants.

"Yeah, it always looked kinda scraggly, but like in a stylish way," Los said. "It worked for you, but *this*. Damn, dude."

"Isn't he pretty?" Silas asked, standing behind Ryan and peeking over his shoulder.

Before, Ryan's hair had touched his shoulders, and Los's description fit. Now, it was shorn up the back but Silas had left the front a little longer, letting it hang in his eyes. Then Ryan ran his fingers through it, and it made a pompadour of sorts.

It was appealing. So attractive. *Very* pretty, though Ryan was too rough around the edges to really think of him as pretty.

I couldn't hide my appreciation, and based on Ryan's grin, he was glad.

"Is someone going to take responsibility for the Ouija board being out this morning?" Los asked, breaking the spell momentarily. "Because we have a strict 'no fucking with the aether' rule on this bus."

Los stared at Ryan in a challenging sort of way, but I didn't get the sense Ryan would be bothered by it.

"Damn, you caught me Los," he said with an exaggerated sigh. "I was trying to summon a sex demon for you. Seems Hell is fresh out these days. Sorry. I'll try harder next time."

Los rolled his eyes. "Yeah, yeah, go ahead. Laugh all you want, but those boards are seriously creepy. Remember the night Gavin brought it on the bus? He got his great uncle Reinholt talking and I couldn't sleep for a week after that."

"Ah," Ryan said, rubbing at the back of his hair. "Makes sense now. It would be Gavin's."

The mood grew noticeably solemn on the bus as the men looked to each other. I didn't know how to inquire further, but I wanted to know who this man was that affected all of my new friends so much. Thankfully, Silas saved me from asking.

"Gavin's aunties who raised him are witches, and they practiced a lot of different ways of divination and communicating with those who'd passed on. He used to use the board sometimes when he was going through a difficult time. I packed it when we were getting ready for Warped. I thought it might be nice to have something of his with us."

Brains looked right at me and spoke. "Gavin West was a ray of sunshine and a cloudy day all wrapped up into one tiny human with golden-brown locks, a full beard, and stormy eyes that were often the only way for you to tell how he was really feeling. He was a brilliant guitar player, an empath, and a drama queen who wore his heart on his sleeve. Gavin and Silas were yin and yang, and it was my job to keep our band from going off the rails.

"We lived through his highs and lows with him, and after a particularly difficult tour, where his long-time lover broke things off with him, he went back to the apartment they'd rented together, and he left a dramatic scene for us to find." Brains's eyes filled with tears, though it was weariness I detected and not heartbreak when he spoke, as if he'd had time to accept the fate of his friend, and though he was heartbroken, he'd found a way to move on.

"Fucking Gavin," Ryan muttered, wiping at his own eyes. "I went to his aunts' place when I found out. I blew my sobriety getting wasted with them, trying to make sense of this gaping wound in our lives. They were so fucking sad, but they took me in and kept me safe while we went on a bender."

"I remember they used to come cook for us when we got back from tour," Los said, wiping at his nose. "They were awesome to us. They made the best pot brownies."

"They also used to get you drunk, Los, so they could take locks of your hair when you passed out," Brains said. "You were the only straight one. They wanted you for their love potions."

Los frowned and touched the back of his neck. "You're lying. Wait a minute—and you'd *let them*? I can't believe you! I was a good Catholic boy." He lost his indignance and cracked up. "No, I wasn't."

"No, you weren't," Silas said as he got back to making breakfast. "You were a good heathen though. They wanted you for your sex magic."

"Not gonna lie," Los said with a grin. "Cassandra's pretty hot."

"She hit on me the first time I met her," Ryan said, his cheeks turning a little red. He made his way to my side, and I scooted over so he could sit next to me. "If I hadn't thought Gavin would make me a victim of ritualistic murder for touching her, I probably would have taken her up on it. After he died, well, I assumed he'd come back from the grave and haunt my ass."

The guys all laughed but I was still confused. About Gavin, yes, but did Ryan like women, too? Ryan must have picked up on my bewilderment. He leaned in closer.

"Cassandra? Yeah, I'm bi." He winked, then his smile went from flirty to sad. "I told you I'd tell you about Gavin. This is the easiest way, I guess. Pieces to make a whole, unless any of you object?"

They all shook their heads.

"Cool. So, you went to school together, right, Silas?"

Silas nodded. "We did. At least, we were enrolled together. We didn't always *go*. Eventually we roped Los in, and then Brains found us. Voila." He gestured with the egg whisker and then cursed when he flung the mixture on the tiny counter. "Cassandra and Robin raised Gavin after his mom married his stepdad, who was a pastor of a church. He tried to pray Gavin's gay away."

There was some mumbling all around at that. So it *hadn't* been easy for all of them. That sounded more like the America I remembered.

"They let us practice in their garage and crash there as long as we cut the lawns and painted the house. Remember that summer?" Los asked. "It was so fucking hot out there, but we didn't care. You guys had already graduated, and I'd decided I wasn't going back if you guys were gone."

"You guys weren't together yet, right?" Krish asked Ryan. "Backdrop?"

"Yeah, Parker, Burke and I got together in two thousand ten in LA, like totally cliché, right? I'd been out there like four years already without much going on until I met him. Within a year we had a band and a deal, yada yada. I met Gavin at our first Warped, two thousand twelve. We were just acquaintances until the tour after I got out of prison."

Ryan paused long enough, it seemed, to see if anyone had anything to say about that.

"You were so brave," Silas said quietly, glancing at Ryan over his shoulder. When Ryan started to object, Silas put a hand on his shoulder. "For real, man. I barely handled a weekend in county jail. I don't think —"

"You do what you have to because there is no alternative. That's all."

"I hear you," Brains said. "But coming back and dealing

with all the shit the label's lawyers threw at you, *that* was fucking brave."

Ryan shrugged. "If I wanted to stay in my band and keep fucking around with the likes of you, that was my only choice. Most of the time it's fine. I miss booze sometimes, but not really."

"How did you and Gavin decide to write together? I've been curious." Krish's question served to animate Ryan.

"It happened while you clowns were all getting drunk after the shows. Gavin and I would talk, and he had all these ideas that he said you'd probably make fun of, Franklin. Sorry, but it's true."

Silas held up his free hand while he flipped pieces of French toast. "You're right. I did make fun of him. It was kind of hippie shit and I kept telling him there was no place in our angry chair for his hippie music."

"Which is where I came in." Ryan turned to me and likely caught on that I didn't understand the distinction. "Hey, mind if I borrow that guitar?"

Brains reached over and grabbed a lovely acoustic that someone had defaced by scratching "twat" into the finish.

Ryan looked it over and chuckled at the word. "I'm not going to ask," he said. He tuned it and played a few bars. "Okay, so you heard our set and you heard Hush, right?" He gazed at me as if I were the only one in the room as he spoke. "You get what we mean by angry music?"

I nodded.

"Hippie music is about peace and love and it's more—"

"Cheesy?"

"Corny?"

"Sappy?"

All the words used to describe it were negative until Ryan let out a little grunt. "How about optimistic, guys?"

They muttered their reluctant agreement.

"Gavin and I shared a need, a compulsion really, to find things to be hopeful about." He began to play a melody, one he seemingly picked out of thin air, and when he sang, that bravado was gone, and instead there was a smooth quality to his voice. He sounded like a completely different singer.

And I wanted nothing more than to close my eyes, spread my arms wide, and absorb his song like a much-needed balm for my soul.

# CHAPTER 16

**Ryan**

Playing the tunes I wrote with Gavin shifted something in my chest, making it easier to breathe, to think. Made everything hurt a little less. I played one of my favorites, one we called "More." When it was through, I strummed the guitar a few more times before looking up.

The fucking guys started clapping. They were cheering, whistling, and not in the sarcastic way Parker would when I'd try out something new. This was pure joy. I didn't know what to do with that.

"Fuck off," I said as I handed Brains back the guitar. "Way to make a guy feel all awkward and shit."

"Dude, Wells," Los said, and then he fucking sniffled. "I'm crying over here.

"Why didn't you guys release it?" Krish asked.

"Because Ryan's label said no." Silas said, handing a plate

of French toast to Brains. Then he handed one to Krish, then Kal and me. Los pulled some grapes out of the fridge and handed bunches to everyone. Silas served Bowie, Jordan, Los, then himself. I wondered if there was some sort of hierarchy between them. Silas always seemed like the leader of their little gang, like the others followed his lead, but the way he deferred to Brains and doted on everyone made me rethink my earlier impression.

"That blows," Los said. "I know Gavin was really disappointed."

"Why?" Kal asked. "Why no?"

He had that protective forehead crinkle going and I fucking melted. Right there. It was bizarre to have someone looking after me. I liked it too much.

Brains cut in. "Gavin was under contract with our label, Wreckage, and Ryan's band is under contract with Bloom Records. Our contract with Wreckage gives them a right of first refusal with any new material we come up with, whether it be as Hush or solo, but they're encouraging of us branching out. They can be flexible, plus after my first band split up, I studied contracts and made sure we had some autonomy. Wreckage was willing to work with Gavin to let him do the project, and correct me if I'm wrong, Ryan, but Bloom was unwilling to even consider a collaboration, even with a fifty-fifty split, right?"

"Right. They wouldn't let me take any time away from Backdrop. They said, and I quote, 'you've cost us enough time and money already.' We owed them three more albums then—now we have only one more left—and we were late delivering because my sentence had been extended three weeks because they couldn't get the parole board together..."

"Not your fault." Kal didn't look up when he spoke, if he would have, he'd have seen everyone gawking at him, and then at me. I shrugged and tried not to swoon. God, he was hot.

"I just want to finish the album. For Gavin. He loved those songs as much, if not more, than I did. *Do*. If nothing comes of it, so be it. At least we'll have his songs, right?"

"We need to get Jordan's brother Jake to take a look at your contract," Krish said. "He's getting his MBA, he's a whiz with all that stuff. Maybe there's some way?"

"I guess. I haven't exactly had the headspace to get anywhere with it. Not with rehearsing for this tour and trying not to get fired."

Silas took a bite of his toast and then held up a finger as he chewed thoughtfully.

"I wonder," he finally said. "If the *fans* knew this music was out there? Like if they *demanded* to hear it?" He nudged Krish, who, startled, juggled his plate and barely saved it from falling to the floor.

"What the heck?" He gave Silas an incredulous look. Silas stared back with eyebrows raised. "Oh… *Oh*, you mean like if news of the album's existence was leaked."

"I think we know a certain blogger who could bring the pressure." Los stroked his invisible goatee.

"I'm not above guerilla maneuvers," I said, holding a hand up. "But after Warped. Right now, I'm stuck with these guys and in a precarious spot. I don't want them to off me and fucking dump my body in butt-fuck Alabama or some shit."

A snapping sound drew everyone's attention to Kal. He'd snapped his plastic fork in his fist.

"Sorry." His worried expression had Silas fussing over him, grabbing him a new fork.

"No worries, man. Here you go. And here's some more French toast." He slid two more slices onto Kal's plate.

Kal's cheeks burned red, and he glanced up at me. I

winked at him, and his embarrassed expression turned to a bashful grin.

*That's it, baby.* I didn't want him to worry about me. If I could distract him, perhaps he'd loosen up a little more, and we might both enjoy that. I couldn't wait to get him alone.

"Grrr!" Los grunted loudly. He had a plastic fork in both of his hands and was trying unsuccessfully to snap it in half. "How'd he do that? These are hella thick."

Los's comic relief kept things from getting too heavy the rest of the day as we talked, laughed, snacked, and just hung out. We played more music and somehow it came out that I'd met Kal while he was playing Roxanne's keyboard.

"I'd love to hear you play," Brains said. "But our keyboard is busted."

"I can fix it," Kal said. He was trying hard to be helpful. He'd done the dishes after Silas cooked breakfast, and when we stopped for lunch, he'd insisted on cleaning up afterward. It was sweet, but I hoped he wasn't worried. It was obvious everyone already liked him. Otherwise they wouldn't have talked to him about going on tour with them this fall.

Silas and Los exchanged glances.

"I tried all I know how to do," Los said. "If you can get it working, that would be awesome. I shoved it under the love nest in back."

Krish groaned and Silas laughed. "It's okay, babe. I'll take Los's ribbing as long as I get to sleep next to you every night."

Los came back with the keyboard and put it on the table of the banquette and Kal went over to help them. I sat on the couch across from Bowie and Brains, who were back to battling each other on *Call of Duty*.

"Your guy seems to be relaxing. Talking more." Brains spoke without taking his eyes off the TV. "You find out any more of his story?"

I worried people might start asking questions Kal

couldn't answer. I didn't want to betray his trust, but I also wanted these guys to trust *him*. The truth was, I didn't know much about him.

"Only what he told us. I think he went through some shit. Don't want to speculate, don't want to add to his worries."

"Worries?" Brains asked. Bowie was listening carefully while pretending not to be paying attention. The two were on opposite teams and Bowie kept trying to sneak up on Brains, only for him to turn around and obliterate Bowie's character. No, there was no tension between these two.

Brains was good at getting people to confide in him. Gavin had told me on more than one occasion that I should talk to Brains about my issues with the band, that he was great at finding solutions to problems, but I'd always wanted to handle my shit on my own. Even now, though I was getting a little better at admitting I needed help, it was tough.

"I'll leave it up to him to share."

Brains raised an eyebrow at me. "You didn't ask. I'm just reminding you. Don't let a good thing go because you're caught up in your own shit."

He didn't look at Bowie, but I had a hunch his words were meant for more than me. Bowie cleared his throat and stood from the couch, mumbled something about the bathroom, glanced at Brains and then bumped into the banquette wall, bounced off the opposite wall, and slipped into the bathroom.

Brains shrugged and went back to his game. "Truth hurts," he muttered.

Before I could comment, cheers rang out from the banquette.

"You fucking did it, man! Right on. Dude, Brains, Kal fixed the old keyboard!"

I sauntered over while Los and Silas praised Kal's apparent heroics.

"This thing hasn't worked since the first day of the tour. We thought someone spilled on it or the electrical source fried it. But listen."

Kal played the scales expertly and the rest of the guys murmured their appreciation. Kal looked around, and at the urging of the other guys, he continued to play. The speaker on the unit was a little tinny but his playing held my attention. I was lost in the up-tempo composition when I felt a nudge against my foot.

I turned to find Brains giving me that intense stare once more. His eyebrows rose to his hairline before he turned back to his video games.

*Huh.*

I didn't normally settle in and get chummy with folks, and yet here I was, hanging out with these guys I'd only been acquainted with 'til now, spilling my guts about private shit.

Fucking Gavin. *This is your doing, isn't it?* For all I knew, his ass was haunting me. I glanced over at the Ouija board and frowned.

*Nah.*

The lack of sleep the past few...how many days had we been on tour? It all caught up to me and before I knew it, Kal was nudging me awake.

"We're here."

# CHAPTER 17

**Kal**

The fluttering in my chest made it hard to breathe. I wasn't sure if it was the excitement of knowing I'd be spending time with Ryan, maybe even alone, or the panic at yet another new experience. Would I do something wrong? Would my new friends think I was odd?

It was enlightening listening to their conversations on the bus. I learned a lot, especially about what each of them enjoyed and hated about life on the road. Personally, all of it sounded wonderful, especially if it meant spending time with people they cared about, and these men did.

We pulled into the First Landing National Park in Virginia as the sky began a fantastic color show signaling dusk was about to begin. I knew the plan was for us to park at a campground and watch the sunset on the beach. There was talk of making s'mores, which I knew involved marshmallows, chocolate candy pieces, and graham crackers. I remember them being all the rage when I was a teenager and apparently they still were.

The band's employees and their manager had left before us and stopped along the way to pick up sleeping bags, bug spray, and other essentials for sleeping outside, although Los and Jordan—who had ridden on the RV with the techs and Jessica—were having a hard time with the idea of being outside overnight, despite Bowie reassuring them there were no apex predators, snakes, or bugs that would cause them imminent death. With Bowie's father being a Navy corpsman, which I gathered was some sort of medical position, Bowie was appointed the supply master and charged with lighting the campfire. It was obvious this reliance upon his experience and extra attention had him feeling a little embarrassed, but he agreed.

Bowie was familiar with the campground, so he'd reserved two spots for them. The bus would have to be parked in the beach lot, but the RV and Bowie's boyfriend's van would be at the campsites. When the bus pulled into the beach lot, and I got my first view of the cypress trees and the wooden boardwalk, I'd sprung out of my seat at the banquette. I couldn't wait to see the ocean, but I wanted to be with Ryan when I did.

Ryan had fallen asleep on the couch opposite the gaming TV and everyone had tried to keep the noise down around him so he could get some obviously much-needed rest. I'd wanted to sit beside him, but I knew I'd have a hard time not touching him, especially his newly cut hair, plus I'd been asked to play cards by Los, who'd obviously thought I would be easily bested. He'd thought wrong.

"I still say you should come with a warning label," Los said, bumping me with his shoulder as he passed me to get out of the bus.

"I could teach you," I offered, and Silas burst out laughing.

"I could teach you," he sang, "but I'd have to charge."

Krish and Los joined in singing something about milk-shakes and boys in the yard as they filed past me.

"Lord, the musical choices on this bus," Brains said with a groan as he pushed himself to standing. Bowie hurried to his side and handed him his crutches. Brains nodded, and it was obvious things were still tense between them. I'd heard the other guys whispering that Bowie's dad and Brains were involved, and Bowie hadn't handled the news very well. That made me sad for them. I knew it had to be hard for them to be around each other, and I hoped it all worked out.

If there was a way for me to let them know how short and precarious life really was, I'd gladly do it, but I couldn't. Not without telling them the truth, that I wasn't from this time. I needed to figure out a way to answer their questions without exposing that fact.

"We'll wait for you two outside, but hurry," Bowie said from the top of the steps. "The guys want their s'mores."

I nodded and crouched down next to Ryan. I didn't want to startle him, so I gently nudged his shoulder. He looked peaceful even though he was in what had to be a terribly uncomfortable position with his knees pulled up and his neck bent at a funny angle. When he didn't move, I leaned closer to his ear and whispered to him.

His eyes flew open and he sat up so fast, we nearly knocked heads.

"Whoa, Kal." He reached out for my arm to keep me from jumping away from him. "Sorry, man. What's happening?"

"We're here," I said, unable to keep from grinning. "At the beach."

Ryan pushed his hair back, frowning as he likely felt a lot less of it than he was used to.

"Right. Virginia Beach. Camping. Awesome." He stretched his neck and back and stood up from the sofa, right in my space. "Hi."

All I could do was smile so wide my cheeks hurt.

I was beginning to wonder which was the actual surreal experience; the past year I'd spent working for a not-quite-what-it-seemed carnival, or the past twenty-four hours I'd been with my new friends and this enticing man before me.

"Are you ready for this?" he asked, adjusting my collar. "Sleeping in the outdoors? You ever done it before?"

A pit formed in my stomach at the vivid images of being left in a ditch outside my uncle's property. I shivered, trying to pull myself out of that nightmare.

"Kal?"

"Never camping." I tried to form a smile but from Ryan's expression, I wasn't fooling him.

"Glad I can be with you for your first time." His eyebrows shot up, and I laughed. So naughty.

"First time at the ocean."

Ryan's eyes widened and he took my hand. "Then let's go."

Outside the bus was pandemonium. The folks in the RV who I hadn't met yet were greeting the guys from Hush and there were hugs and some sort of square dancing going on? Ryan and I hung back while they chatted, until Los put his arm around the woman Ryan explained was their manager, Jessica, and called for order.

"Quiet, please. Quiet. Now, I was promised a campfire and s'mores. Bowie McNally? Hey, dude, what's your rank?"

"Your mom," said one of the guys, and everyone started laughing, which further irritated Los.

"I don't have a rate or rank, Los," Bowie said calmly. "Just because my father is in the Navy doesn't make it, like, hereditary."

"Wait," Los protested. "I thought titles *were* hereditary."

"That's in the nobility," Brains said, shaking his head.

"Really? So, could, like, one of us be nobility and not know?"

"Your mom's in the nobility."

"The nobility was *in* his mom."

"Gross!"

I turned to Ryan and spoke softly. "Are they always—?"

"A considerable amount of the time, yes."

Finally the large group walked from the bus down a long wooden boardwalk. "Down that way," one of the tech guys said, pointing to his right, "is where the campsites are, but we figured we'd take you guys to the beach first. This sunset is killer."

Ryan and I were near the back and it was frustrating to walk behind the guys who were strolling along at a snail's pace. I wanted to see the waves.

"There's no surfing here on the bay side," Jessica was explaining to one of the guys. "The water is pretty calm if y'all want to go swimming."

That was all it took to get the group moving faster. The guys, minus Brains, took off running, tearing their clothes off in the process.

"This isn't a nude beach, you exhibitionists. Keep your drawers on!" Brains shouted at them, but then shook his head as if he had little hope of being listened to.

"And please, God, don't break anything." Jessica turned and winced. "Sorry, Brains."

"You're right to worry," he said as he slowly swung himself forward on his crutches.

Ryan gestured for me to follow the others. "Feel free to run if the spirit moves you."

"I'd rather savor the moment."

Ryan linked our fingers together, making this my favorite

moment. As we reached the point high enough to see the water, I knew it was my *best* moment. Ever. My breath caught in my chest as I glimpsed the fiery orange horizon topped by deep blue skies sprinkled with dark clouds. The water danced and sparkled below the setting sun, stretching as far as I could see.

"The Atlantic Ocean is just around the bend, but this beach is part of Chesapeake Bay. Gorgeous territory out here."

I snuck a look at Ryan. I wanted to know if he was moved like I was by the beauty around us. He was…different here. His eyelids were heavy and his head sort of tilted back on his neck. It took me a moment to realize the difference was that his head was no longer on a swivel. His shoulders were relaxed, and there was a fluidity to his spine I hadn't seen other than when he was onstage.

He was at peace.

"You've been here before?"

"Not this particular beach but farther south than here, North Carolina, and up in New Jersey. On tour. Not for pleasure. Don't get much time for pleasure." He smiled at me. "You want to go in. I can tell. Go on. I'll be right behind you. Just remember, sand in your shorts doesn't feel too good." He winked and I laughed. Our fingers slid apart and, while I hated the absence of contact, I wanted to run like the others. I wanted that freedom, even for just a little while.

I made it to the water's edge and saw the piles of clothes the others had flung aside. I slipped my shoes and socks off and was thankful I'd been given shorts to wear again. I paused at the edge of where the water seemed to reach. The rest of the group was waist deep in the water splashing each other and screaming like kids. It was such a change from their performer personas. Instead of trying to look important and aloof, they could easily be mistaken for a group of boys much younger than they were.

I stepped forward and let the water run over my toes. It was warmer than I expected and as it pulled away, my feet sank into the sand. I stepped backward, worried I would lose my balance, when Ryan stepped behind me. He'd kicked off his shoes also and rolled up his pant legs. He placed a hand at my lower back when I stumbled.

"You're good. Some beaches you have to watch out for riptides, but it's not like that here. It's not as strong here like back home." His gaze seemed far away. He got like that sometimes, when I imagined the sadness came back to him.

"You live near the ocean?"

He smiled at me. "I've got a house near Laurel Canyon. Nothing big. You can see the ocean from my backyard. The beaches there are way more crowded than this."

"In California? With your family?"

Ryan sighed. "No family. Not anymore. And I haven't been home much. We started rehearsing in March in Las Vegas, recorded our new album, prepped for the tour, I went home for like a week? Long enough to do my laundry and pack to be gone for three months. When this is done, we have a break. They're still working out the details of our next tour."

"Do you like California?" Ryan's life seemed lonely. I knew that feeling all too well. There had been solitary times in my youth, in the music school, but my time with the carnival was the loneliest I'd ever been. I wouldn't want that for anyone. And it seemed that the fellows we were on this trip with had nothing but laughs with each other. At least most of the time. They argued like brothers, no mean-spirited harm upon each other.

But it wasn't like that for Ryan.

"I keep thinking I will," he said with a strong laugh that

seemed to surprise him. "I love Northern California, but after I got out of jail, I didn't want to go back. It felt…disrespectful to Josh."

"Disrespectful?"

"Yeah," he said, looking at his feet. He sucked in a deep breath. "You know, like it's wrong to be happy there after what I did."

I understood what he meant, but he was wrong. Like Silas said, he'd paid for what he did. No one expected him to suffer for the rest of his life. Not even the man who'd been hurt.

"The guys in my band mostly live in Southern California," he continued, "I picked a place in the middle of where they were but far enough away I didn't have to worry about them dropping by. I rented a place by the beach years ago, before I went to prison, and people thought it was their party pad. I had people in my house I didn't even know a lot of the time. My place now? I think it's haunted, but it's peaceful, and it's way the fuck up there so nobody bothers me. I have a studio, I can do my art—well, when I'm inspired, anyway." He turned to give me that up-and-down gaze that felt like electricity dancing on my skin. "*You* inspire me. Think you'd ever let me draw you?"

"Yes. How do you mean?"

He turned to face me and rubbed at his freshly cut hair once more. It sparkled in the glow from the sunset. He was absolutely arresting, *so* handsome, and he was asking to draw *me*?

"Depends on what you're comfortable with. I'd love to have you nude and spread out on the chaise in my studio. Or my bed. I've got skylights that let in the most surreal glow in the morning."

Ryan often went from plainspoken to seductive, but this was a request of a different tone. It was…sweet. And then he smirked. "What do you say, Kallos? Man of beauty. Want to come home with me and be my subject? I could draw you for hours and never tire of studying you."

I opened my mouth to speak and a larger wave splashed me above my knees, soaking the bottom of my shorts. Any good response to Ryan was gone, and instead I squealed.

Ryan laughed and reached for my arm to steady me. He was tuned into me and my needs, before I even knew what they were. How could such a selfless man think he had nothing to offer besides his music?

"Yes," I said. "Draw me. Whatever you want. You can have it."

His grip tightened on my arm. "I want it."

The sinking sunlight reflected in his gray eyes. I thought maybe he was wishing, like I was, that we were at his home. Alone.

"But first," he said with a sigh. "S'mores. And camping. I was thinking, though," he said, stroking his chin. "Maybe we bring our sleeping bags down here tonight. We can watch the sun come up in the morning before we have to leave."

In any other scenario, I'm not sure I would have willingly agreed to sleep outside. I'd done it out of necessity, and then once because I was unable to move. But with Ryan? I'd gladly sleep outside as long as I was next to him.

"Yes, Ry-an."

# CHAPTER 18

**Ryan**

You know you're with truly good people when there's not even talk of busting out booze, no sneaky looks like, "damn, we shouldn't in front of Wells." The Hush family did, however, bust out the marshmallows, chocolate, and graham crackers like they were going out of style. There were bags of chips passed around with canned salsa and bean dip, and various other savory snacks for those not into the camping staple.

"S'mores represent everything that's good about the world." Los spoke lovingly to his fourth treat. "You can't *not* feel like a kid while eating them, but, like, those few moments as a kid when everything seems like it's going to work out okay, the good guys are going to win, and everyone will get second helpings at dinner."

Silas hugged Los and kissed his cheek, at which, Los

wiped at his face. "Dude, you got me all sticky. Wait, don't even—"

"You walked right into that one."

It was down to myself, Kal, and the guys from Hush around the fire. The rest had gone back to the RV or, in Bowie's case, his boyfriend's van, and the chatter had slowed considerably. Everyone was beat. The beach had been a great idea, but tomorrow's show was imminent. The carefree attitudes had waned.

"Man, camping is fun," Jordan said. "We should do this again when the tour is over." Jordan happily licked melted marshmallow from his fingers as he spoke.

"We've only got two weeks after Warped is over before we head to Europe." Brains glanced in the direction of the van. "We'll have to make some personnel decisions."

If they were talking band stuff, I didn't want to interfere. I stood from the camp chair I'd borrowed. "This seems like a nice segue—"

"Wait," Brains raised his hand and looked at Kal. "The offer is there for you to consider, Kal. We're going to need a tech for our next tour. If Warped doesn't do you in, we'd like you to think about coming with us. To Europe."

Kal's wide-eyed gaze fell on Brains and then me. "Will you be there?" he asked quietly.

I shook my head. "I doubt it. I don't have details, but y'all already have an opener, right?"

"Just Like Love is a definite. Not sure if that's it. It would be cool to take like three bands with us, but we won't know for another few weeks."

Kal pondered the question while gazing up at me from his chair. What could I say? Our business was fluid, plans were often in motion and changed on the fly. It wouldn't be fair of me to, what, lay claim to Kal? As much as I didn't want there to be an expiration date on our adventure, what could I do?

Finally he stood, and handed his s'mores stick to Jordan.

"I'm honored you would consider me for this. May I give you my answer—"

"Yeah, dude. Sure. Take your time."

Kal nodded and then turned hesitantly toward me. I'd told him earlier I wanted him. He'd said yes. What was I waiting for?

"Thank you," Kal finally said. "And thank you for the s'mores. They've gotten better than when I was young. Good night." Kal grabbed our sleeping bags, gave me a look, and started marching into the darkness.

"Uh," Jordan said, sitting up. "Where—"

"We're gonna crash on the beach," I said. "Mind if I take the flashlight? I lost my phone."

Silas tossed me the flashlight. "Wait, you need anything else?" His eyebrows rose dramatically.

"I—"

He waved for me to follow him, and I called out to Kal to hold up. Silas trotted over to the RV and knocked on the door. Krish's head popped out.

"You guys done with your band meeting? I finished my blog, and I'm ready to— Oh, hi Ryan." Krish put a hand over his mouth and chuckled.

"Just need the go bag."

Krish's eyes flared. He reached behind him and grabbed a duffel bag and handed it to Silas. "Are you headed to the bus?"

"Yeah," Silas said, giving Krish a once-over. "Let's go." He reached into the bag, pulled something out all covert and shit, and he shoved a sandwich-sized bag into my hands. "Take this."

I looked at the bag, which had a label on it that said *Got You Covered.*

"This what I think it is?"

Krish giggled and Silas playfully punched me in the arm. "I'm assuming the old Ryan Wells treatment will work for you tonight. Better to be prepared, right?"

I didn't know what to say. I didn't want to assume anything with Kal. We hadn't even talked about... And why was I worried? It happened or it didn't.

If I wanted sex, it was usually there for the taking. I wasn't a dick about it, especially since I got sober. My interludes happened with less frequency these days, not for lack of opportunities, but more from my more discerning taste? Maybe? Sex wasn't usually something I spent a whole lot of mental energy on.

Which, of course, had been my problem. Now, it seemed like the right thing to do.

Perhaps the fact that I was having concerns was, like, mature. Maybe it was a good thing, leaving my unhealthy behaviors behind.

*He said you could have whatever you want.*

"Thanks. Night." I tucked the bag into my pocket and strolled toward Kal, Krish's and Silas's laughs following me.

I caught up to him on the path to the beach and we walked without speaking. I held out a hand to take one of the sleeping bags from him and he shook his head, pulling them closer to his chest. The walk to the beach seemed much longer than it had earlier, perhaps from the quiet or my uncertainty. When we crested the hill and the moonlight's reflection on the water came into view, I put a hand on Kal's shoulder.

"You sure you're okay with this? We can just sleep, right? Nothing else has to happen." *Such a fucking gentleman, Wells.*

Kal's lips quirked into a smile that was like nothing I'd

seen yet from the somewhat shy and reserved man. The vibe he was giving now made me think I was the one who should be on alert.

We found a stretch of sand that was protected on three sides by the bluff and Kal set down the sleeping bags.

"Are you tired, Ry-an?"

"A little," I said.

He looked down at the sleeping bags and nodded. "All right. I'll set these up so you can rest."

"Kal," I said, stepping close enough to take his hand, but not enough to spook him. "I'm sorry if I've been weird. It's been awesome meeting you, spending time with you… You've given me a reprieve in the middle of a storm, and I appreciate you for it." I didn't know how else to express what I was feeling. "I'm in recovery, and it's important for me to tell you how I feel and be honest."

Kal gave my hand a squeeze and let go. He turned to unroll the sleeping bags as I stood there like a gaping fish, trying to figure out what else to say, what I needed to say, what I *should* say.

He unrolled both of the bags, unzipped them, and lay one on top of the other. He kicked his shoes off, pulled off his sandy shorts, and crawled under the top layer. He stared at me patiently as if to let me figure out what my problem was.

"I'm telling you because I don't know what to do."

Kal blinked. "Aren't we sleeping? Watching the sun come up?"

"Yeah, but…I don't know."

He held a hand out to me and waited. When I didn't take it right away, he placed it on his chest. "I don't know what recovery is. Earlier, I told you that you could have whatever you want. I meant that. Even if you don't want anything."

I laughed, but it came out more like a sob. Damn. This man.

"Every time I think I need to offer you some involved explanation, you put me at ease. You're the new guy here. I figured I'd need to show you the proverbial ropes; instead, you've thrown *me* a rope one on several occasions."

He looked around, grabbed for the rope that held the sleeping bag rolled up and tossed it toward me. "Here. Come rest. Don't lose your way."

There he went, making everything okay. I shouldn't get used to this. Too much of a good thing usually meant *bad* things for me. Would Kal end up being good or bad for me?

I sat down on the sleeping bag and took my shoes off before pulling the top cover over me. I lay down flat on my back, my arm barely touching Kal's. We stayed like that for some time. The sky was black and blue above us with a scattering of stars of varying brightness. I followed the movement of what must have been a satellite for several moments and let my body relax into the sand beneath us.

"Ry-an? What is recovery?"

Surprisingly, I didn't tense up at his question. I wanted to talk about it. With him.

"Recovery is what we call the journey from being an active alcoholic or drug addict to living a sober life. Sober meaning, taking it day by day and abstaining from alcohol and drugs. It means making amends to the people you've hurt, setting boundaries to keep yourself from being or causing more hurt, and trying to live your best life. Being good to people, doing good."

I glanced at Kal, and he had that deep crease between his brows as he stared up at the sky.

"I don't want you hurt."

*My heart.* "I gathered that." I nudged his arm with mine. "And I appreciate it. But it's my responsibility to take care of me." His frown deepened. "Hey, thank you. For making this easier. *So* much. Come here."

I coaxed him closer and turned on my side so I could kiss him and once he had those big limbs wrapped around me, I was a goner. Our kisses sparked a fire that quickly had me gasping for air. He was so strong, I was consumed in a way I wasn't used to, wasn't sure I was comfortable with. It wasn't fear of being overtaken—I had no doubt that should I ask him to stop, Kal would adhere to my wishes.

It was a fear of losing control, or more, *giving over* control, in a sexual way, which I had fought tooth and nail to keep. Not saying there weren't times, especially as a kid, where I wasn't in control, but I refused to dwell on those unpleasantries.

I wanted to be there, in that moment with Kal, as our two souls sought comfort, pleasure, and wonder in the other.

Kal's strong hands pulled me flush against him, his thigh was tucked between both of mine. He slid his hands down to my hips, clutching, gripping, kneading and *needing*, and when that wasn't enough, he cupped my ass tightly and moaned against my lips.

A crinkling sound made him pause. He poked at my back pocket a few times. *The baggie.*

"Oh, that's…" I tried to reach for it, but he had my arms trapped. He pulled it out and held it up.

"Thanks, uh, Silas gave it to me. It's…condoms. And lube."

He quirked his head to the side and gestured for me to show him. I handed him the bag and he sat up to look through the contents. He held up each thing with a puzzled expression.

"Bowie's boyfriend hands these out. Silas helped himself to a whole duffel full," I said with a chuckle. "Seems him and Krish have been his biggest customers."

Kal stared at the packages, reading them, his lips moving ever so slightly.

"I brought them just in case. We don't have to use them. Unless, well...if we're gonna fuck, we need to use them."

His eyes darted to mine when I said *fuck,* and then back to the package.

"I've never used these before. Never done...that."

*Oh, my sweet Iowa boy*. The dirty son of a bitch in me pictured spreading his virgin ass out on the chaise in my bedroom and doing all the things—

"I will, to you. Ryan. If that's what you want me to do. I would like to."

My fantasy came to a screeching halt.

"Uh..." Shit. How did I explain without making shit weird? *Er*. Again. "I appreciate that, Kal, but I don't, uh... I don't... I'm usually the one who does that." Since when did I lose the Ryan Wells treatment, or whatever Silas called it? I sounded like a fumbling dork, not the prettiest guy in rock who made the girls swoon and the guys...well, scream my name over and over.

"Oh." He cleared his throat and put the items back in the bag. He handed it to me and lay back down, his eyes wide as he gazed up at the stars and chewed on his bottom lip.

"Kal? Listen. I told you, we don't have to do anything we haven't already done. It's enough, *you're* more than enough for me. And if you want more, there are plenty of other things we can do to and for each other that will feel real good."

"Want to. Feel good. With you."

He made eye contact, finally, his chest rapidly moving up and down.

"Well, all right, man of beauty. Let's discover what makes you feel good."

# CHAPTER 19

**Kal**

Ryan thought he was the one making things weird? Obviously, I'd misread the situation. Boys who sought me out liked that I was bigger than them, wanted me to…be in charge, I guess. I'd never wanted to take advantage or hurt anyone. I should have known that things with Ryan would be different than with anyone else.

"You said," he spoke against my shoulder, "that I could have whatever I wanted."

"I did." I could barely breathe, I was so excited. His breath on my cool skin, his body pressed against mine…I was hard and desperate, my belly doing flips in anticipation of what he would say next.

"What if I want…to kiss you?"

I turned and lifted his chin to kiss him, but he pulled back with a smile.

"Not like that." He grabbed my…

*Oh. Like that.*

I nodded. I couldn't have formed words even now that they had come back to me.

Ryan slid my boxers down and disappeared under the sleeping bag and...*oh...my*.

His mouth was hot, and wet, and the sensation was extraordinary. I wanted to watch what he was doing so I'd know how to do it to him, but when I tried to move, he stopped.

"You don't like?"

"I like. Want to watch."

Ryan looked around and saw that we were alone and he flung the sleeping bag back. "As long as you're not too cold. Doubt we'll get arrested, but if you see anyone—"

"Yes."

And *yes* was all I could think. Yes, *this*. Yes, *more*. Yes, Ryan, *please, Ryan*.

When the word erupted from my lips, he shushed me. "You're going to bring us company." But he was laughing now and couldn't get back to what he was doing. I took advantage of the situation. I sat up, reached for his hips, and tugged him up to sit on my lap, to give myself access. He grunted and put his hands on my shoulders.

"Are we going to wrestle now? Because that could be fun, too."

I reached for his pants, tried to unfasten them, but he put his hands on mine.

"I want to do you," he whispered.

I pulled his hands behind his back and held them with one of mine, bringing us chest to chest. We were both breathing hard, every movement brushing our chests together as he struggled against me.

"Why can't we both...kiss...like that?"

He grinned and kissed my mouth, his tongue hot and salty. I loved this closeness, but he gave finally in.

"Fine," he said, lying down with his hips near my head, his head next to my hips. "But if we get caught— *Ahgod,* Kal!"

I'd yanked his pants down, pulled him close to my face, and sucked his cock so hard, he groaned. I smiled in victory around him. I locked my arms around his hips and did what I thought he would like. I was rewarded with soft moans and then he rolled on his side, his mouth returning to its previous activity.

It was intense. Too intense. I hadn't felt the touch of another in a very long time, and certainly it had never been like this. I knew we had to be careful, but there was no rush, and if it meant hearing Ryan's soft sighs, I'd do this all night. Like before, on the bus, we were trapped by our clothes, tangled in the sleeping bags, and we were caught in the groove of the sand beneath us. I loved it.

Ryan's hand grabbed mine and he squeezed tightly. His cries grew more desperate. *Who's the loud one now?* I thought as he came, his spend coating my tongue, my throat, leaking from my lips as his whole body spasmed, shaking, shuddering, jerking in my arms. Every second of his pleasure satisfied me, made me feel whole in a way I hadn't ever dreamed. I savored the fact that I'd been the one to bring him such ecstasy, and I wanted to do it again, over and over, but he pushed my mouth away. He was firm but gentle, and I released my hold on him.

"Goddamn, you're good at that, Kal. Now let me have that dick. I want it. I want you."

This time I lay back and stared at the stars above us, paying attention to each lick, each graze of his teeth, each hot breath on my flesh. He took his time, and I delighted in the happy noises he made as he worked. Knowing he was enjoying himself let me relax under his hands.

When I knew I was close, I reached down to caress his jaw. He gazed up at me with a moan and placed one hand over mine, moving my fingers to the place where his lips met my cock, and the slickness of his tongue rolled over my fingers, sending shudders through me.

*"Ry-an!"* I moaned as the tension that had built in my sac, pulling my balls up close to my body, released in waves of what I can only describe as desperate bliss. Tears gathered in the corners of my eyes as I rocked into Ryan's mouth, my back curling up off the sand. He pulled off my cock and watched as the last few spurts of come landed on my belly, hot against my skin. I groaned as I fell back and before I could use my shirt to clean myself, Ryan bent to lick it up, kissing and sucking the skin on my belly. He ran his fingertips over my nipples and pinched at them, making me squirm.

"So fucking tasty, my beautiful man," he whispered as he covered my body with his. "You taste like fucking joy. I could suck you all night. Every night. And I don't usually get off that way, but you showed no mercy. You're so damn strong."

I smiled and ran my hands up his back, scratching gently, causing him to arch into my touch like a cat. "You feel good, Ry-an."

Ryan's smile turned pained.

"What's wrong? Did I…did I do something wrong?"

"Not at all. No. I'm just doing the thing where I make it weird, but right now it's only in my head. If I don't say it out loud, then it's not weird. Right?"

I ran my hands down to his hips, ready to hold on if he panicked and ran. I'd never hold him against his will. I would, however, challenge him if he started talking again about me leaving.

"Ryan, it's not weird. It's wonderful, what we do together. I want to do more."

"See, I'm not sure it's a good idea for you to hitch your trailer to me."

"Why do you say that?"

"I don't know! What if I'm bad for you, Kal? I don't mean to be, but I don't always treat people real good, and I don't want to do that to you."

"Then don't." What more was there to say. "Be you. I'm me. We forge our own path. Doesn't have to be like anyone else."

"But I could get addicted to you." He gasped as if he didn't mean to expose himself. "Not the sex, I mean, I could get used to you being here and make a bad decision…I could hurt you."

"I decide what hurts me." I didn't like Ryan talking like this. He thought he was a curse to people. Like his presence brought bad tidings. I refused to believe in that.

"I couldn't stand it," he whispered.

"You won't. Aren't you the one singing the optimistic songs? The one who talks about hope? Be that. Let me be here on your journey. I want to watch you stand tall."

"You don't have to say that. You can just be here tonight, and tomorrow—"

"Is that what you want?" I was confident it wasn't, but he obviously needed to say the bad thing.

"No."

"Do you want me to go? Find a companion in someone else?"

"No! Unless…"

"I don't want that." I reached between us and grabbed his cock, which made his eyes roll back in his head. He groaned as I squeezed. "I want this. I want to make you do that again."

His hips twitched wildly and then found a rhythm, but before long he put his hand over mine and froze.

"Wait. Here," he said, pulling a small package out of the bag. "If we're gonna continue this, I need…" He tore the package open with his teeth and reached between us to my hand. A cool liquid coated my fingers.

"Oh. I understand."

The lubricant obviously gave him more pleasure as he threw his head back and moaned. It was astonishing to see this man, who was always on alert, always looking for trouble to find him, shut out the world and allow himself to feel safe with me. To see him at his most vulnerable, to hold his trust as I gave him pleasure, was a gift I would never forget.

Ryan held himself up on his arms and threw his head back, his eyes closed as he thrust into my hand. I reached up with my other hand to caress his jaw, then ran my fingers down his throat. His strong arms and shoulders trembled as he moved, and when he dropped his head, I pulled him down to my chest and rolled with us, cradling him against me, supporting his weight.

"Let me take care of you," I whispered as I kissed his temple. He whimpered and turned his face into my neck as I resumed stroking him with one hand and hugging him so tightly against me with my other arm that he could barely move, allowing me to control the contact, control his pleasure.

"So fucking strong," he said, and then he bit down on the tendon of my neck. "So sweet and so strong." Another bite. More panting. "I think I just found my fucking kryptonite."

I squeezed him tighter. He struggled to move. He bit me again. I licked at his ear and he tilted his head back and gasped. When he started to shudder and arch his back, I knew he was close. I sucked on his earlobe and he cried out.

"Kal, fuck. Kal! *So…good.*" His moans carried on, accentuated by a sharp intake of breath every time I stroked his sensitive skin. "It's like you know what I need without me even telling you. I don't come like this. I always have to be in charge. But you make it better, more powerful. It's overwhelming and scary and thrilling and I fucking love it!"

I smiled in the darkness, thanking the forces that brought Ryan into my path, cleaned us up with my handkerchief and wrapped both arms around him. He pressed his face into my chest, reaching up under the fabric of my shirt to curl his hands together. Within moments his breathing grew heavier, his body slack against me, and I was grateful he slept. I didn't want to. I knew I should because in a few hours, I would be doing important work again.

I didn't want this night to be over.

I lay like that for a long time, kissing Ryan's hair, stroking his back, watching the twinkling lights of the stars above dance for me. One broke away and shot off into the atmosphere and I held on to the sight, wishing for Ryan to always feel this safe, for him to want me to hold him tight, for his soul to take flight like that star, breaking away from the things holding him back.

Maybe my purpose was to be his launching pad, a steady place for him to prepare, gather his wits before he broke away from his band. I would do it. Gladly. Even if it meant that our journeys could no longer follow the same path.

I inhaled the sweet, smoky scent of Ryan's hair. He smelled different after the campfire, delicious. Would it be wrong to wake him? Make his body shake and shudder for me once more?

As if I'd spoken my thoughts aloud, Ryan stirred in my arms and his lips worked against the tendon in my neck he'd bitten earlier.

"Did you sleep at all?"

I gazed down at him and I felt a surge, as if my heart leapt from my own chest and burrowed itself into his.

And as he smiled sleepily, hungrily, I figured my heart knew its own mind.

# CHAPTER 20

**Ryan**

Kal and I watched the sun come up, kissing, touching, and...*fuck,* when his giant hand wrapped around my dick for the third time, I wasn't about to deny myself another of the hottest orgasms I'd ever experienced. This time he held our dicks together, I held on to his shoulders for dear life, and we moved together until I thought I would die if I came one more time, or if I *didn't* come. I was a hot and sweaty mess when he was through with me, when he finally loosened his tight grip, and the cool morning ocean breeze touched my skin. I shivered, gutted that our time was up.

"I wish we had one more day," I mused with a sigh.

"What would you do with it? One more day?"

I snorted and gave his hip a playful squeeze. "You really have to ask?"

His cheeks reddened as he chuckled and looked away.

"I want to be on the beach, alone, none of the bullshit able to touch us. You and me."

He grinned. "You and me. Against the world?"

"Indeed," I said, kissing him again, wishing it wasn't the last one before we got out of our sleeping bags and prepared to meet up with the others. The sky was dim, the beach was empty, and I wished I could stop time. I didn't have that skill, but I did have an idea.

"Hey, we're kind of a mess. Want to join me?" I wiggled my eyebrows as I stripped off my shirt, then my pants. "Better than a shower, and it'll wake us up for the day."

I dropped my clothes on top of the sleeping bags and his eyes bugged out. Yeah, I wanted him to see all of me. I wanted him to remember this night forever, like I would. I felt like I knew his body even though I hadn't seen him naked. I *wanted* to see him. And we were running out of time.

I kicked off the blankets and made a run for it. We were about fifty yards from the water and thankfully there was no one on either side of our little burrow to see my white ass as I made my mad dash. I didn't wait to see if he'd follow me. I sprinted and splashed into the water up to my waist, ignoring the chill, and I dove in head first. Who cared if there were any finned friends waiting to bite my dick off? I felt more alive than I had in what seemed like centuries.

I popped out of the water and pushed my much shorter hair out of my face. I really liked what Silas had done with it. This whole excursion with Hush had done a lot to soothe my battered soul. I felt like freshly exfoliated skin: new, smooth...and a little raw. The haircut, the stories about Gavin, and my night with the unbelievably hot Kal, all of it would have left me flying high if I wasn't about to return to the den of despair otherwise known as the Backdrop Silhouette camp.

But then I looked back to find a nearly naked Kal—he'd

left on his boxers—running toward me down the beach, his long, thick thighs pulling his boxers tight with every step. His chest was so broad it was no wonder I'd felt trapped—and yet safe—in his arms overnight.

I didn't do cuddling. I didn't snuggle, but Kal was like my own personal weighted anti-anxiety blanket. Or a straight-jacket. Was I foolish to fall for this guy? I didn't get involved. I didn't *relationship.* I'd been in love with Gavin, though I knew it would never amount to anything. He was a safe target for all of my yearning. He'd never leave Mel.

Until he did. He left us all.

Kal wasn't a leaver. He was solid. Grounded. He was a mystery only beginning to unravel, but he was here, dammit, and he wanted me despite all of my efforts to push him away. That had to count for something.

He was a bit more hesitant than I was when he reached the water. He tiptoed cautiously into the surf up to his thighs, giving me a gorgeous view of a farmer's tan and freckled skin. And when he turned to look back at the shore…I saw his scars. Deep, angry scars, like the one on the back of his head.

"Kal," I whispered, moving closer. I turned him around to see his back and gasped. He tried to pull away. "What happened to you? It looks like you got stabbed! Cut with a helluva big knife."

When he turned back to face me, his beautiful blue eyes were red-rimmed. "They took out their anger on me. They had every reason to be angry. My uncle… He hurt people. I should have known, should have stopped him. They came for him and found me instead. They left me for dead. That's how I ended up at the carnival. Mr. Ame, he saved me."

I placed my hand over his heart, which was pounding less from the run than what he'd told me. "Kal, baby, it wasn't your fault. You're just a kid."

He shook his head and smiled sadly. "I'm not a kid, Ryan. I'm not that person anymore, either. I want to move forward, with the tour, with music. With…you. If you'll let me."

"Yes."

I didn't hesitate, even if I should have. He was throwing me a lifeline I desperately needed. In recovery, I'd learned the difference between leaning on people when you needed them and co-dependency. I had to trust that I was strong enough now. Being with Kal, and with the guys from Hush, it let me know that I truly did have people I could trust, people who cared about me, and it was time to let them be there for me.

"It's not going to be a picnic, being with me, Kal, but damn, I want it. Somehow. We'll get through the tour and… we'll figure it out. Somehow. Okay?"

He nodded, his lower lip trembling as he smiled. "I want it. Picnic or not. I'm no picnic, either."

"No, you're not a picnic," I said, wrapping my arms around his waist and pulling him into deeper waters. "You're a goddamned smorgasbord. I could fucking feast on you for days…weeks…months." I slid my hands in his boxers and felt him growing hard for me again.

"Years?" he said as I sucked on his collarbones. He held onto my waist for support and let his head fall back.

"Mmmm decades. Centuries. Fucking millennia, Kal. I'm serious. I know we just met, and I know I sound ridiculous, but I'm so serious. Be with me, Kal. Be beside me. For however long we have. Please. I know what I said—"

"I forgot it already," he chuckled. "Yes, Ry-an. I'm here. I'll be here for you, as long as you want me."

"Good."

We clung to each other and kissed without a care in the world, without concern we'd be taken out by a rogue wave, or that we'd be discovered, or—

A horn sounded in the distance.

"Shit. The bus. We gotta go."

We ran back for our stuff, laughing our asses off the whole way. I managed to pull on my pants over my wet body, and we tossed our shoes and shirts in the middle of the pile of sleeping bags, which Kal grabbed. Silas and Krish met us at the top of the rise on the wooden walkway.

"You kooky kids," he said. "We're gonna be late! Come on." But he wasn't mad. He knew exactly why were late. If he and Krish hadn't already been on the bus, they'd probably have been late too, judging by the hickey on the side of Krish's neck.

We got to the bus and brushed as much sand off of our feet as we could, promising to sweep the bus and clean the bathroom, though when that could happen depended on our schedule that day.

"Speaking of the schedule," Silas asked Jessica as we made it onto the bus. "Have they released it yet?"

Everyone was staring at me as we boarded, and that wasn't me being paranoid.

"What's wrong?"

"So," Jessica, their manager, said in a serious voice reminiscent of a death notification. "Chantal called me this morning looking for you."

I began to imagine the worst. Kal put his hand on my shoulder and stood at my back when I thought my legs would collapse.

"Everyone's okay," she said, placing her hand on my forearm. "Or, they're going to be. Um...I guess they went into Nashville after the show?"

"Yeah. I went with these guys to the carnival. What happened?"

Jordan snorted. Los elbowed him and whispered something. Bowie shook his head and whistled. Brains cleared his throat, which got my ire up.

"What the fuck, Brennan?"

Brains looked to Jessica and held up a hand as if to say, "I've got this."

"Are you familiar with the norovirus?"

I frowned. "You mean like the stomach flu?"

He nodded. "It's commonly mistaken for the stomach flu, yes. But noroviruses are spread through contact with feces or vomit from an infected person."

Los retched. "I can't. I can't hear this again." He put his fingers in his ears and started singing "la la la" as he speed-walked toward the back of the bus. He called out, "Let me know when you're done telling him," and slammed the door to the back lounge.

Jordan got the giggles and Jessica shushed him. Silas and Krish sat at the table with their hands over their mouths.

"So...what the fuck? What happened?"

"Apparently your brothers in Backdrop Silhouette found themselves at a strip club with an all-you-can-eat buffet. They proceeded to gorge themselves on hot wings and sausage while taking turns getting lap dances in a private room. At about the midpoint of their twelve-hour drive from Tennessee to Virginia, they all began to—"

"Oh, God," Jessica said, covering her ears. "I don't think I can hear this again, either." She went up front to talk to the driver and pulled the curtain behind her.

"What? Spit it out!"

"Your band is presently shitting and puking on themselves somewhere in a hotel near Roanoke, Virginia."

"Wait a minute," Los shouted, throwing open the back door. "Isn't Roanoke where all those settlers went missing? The Lost Colony?"

"No, Carlos," Brains said with a sigh. "That was an island off the coast of North Carolina."

"Thank God," Los said, holding his chest dramatically. "I

was worried they were done for. I mean, didn't those guys like eat themselves, or did someone eat them?"

"Go back to your corner," Brains said, waving him away. "That means, my friend, that you are without a band."

"Shit. Those poor fuckers. That's miserable."

"Are you done?" Jessica poked her head back in. "Because Chantal wants to know if y'all will be canceling, or…"

"I guess we have to. *Shit!*"

"Maybe stop saying 'shit,'" Bowie piped in. "Perhaps you have a different accent word?"

Jordan's giggles grew out of control. "Yeah, why do we say shit so much? Or like, 'I'm pooped' when we're tired? What's up with that?"

Brains stared at him blankly. "I'm surrounded by juveniles."

"Why don't you perform?" Silas asked from the table. "Ryan Wells and his guitar. A one-man band. I've heard you do it before, man. You're phenomenal. Corey Taylor does that shit and he sells out every time."

"That's not a bad idea," Brains said. "Si, you could join him for 'Angel's Son' like you did before."

"And Roxanne and I have the duet. I wonder… Hey, Jessica? Can I text Chantal from your phone?"

She handed it over. "She's on the line."

"Oh. Hello?"

"Hey, Ryan. I'm sorry about your band. Kevin needs to know what to do so we can finalize the schedule. You can cancel or—"

"Tell him I'm willing to perform acoustic Backdrop songs with a couple of guest performances. If he wants."

Kal squeezed my shoulder, and thank God he did. What the fuck was I doing, agreeing to go on without my band? "Wait—"

"It's a great idea, Ryan," he whispered. "You'll be great."

I turned to find him smiling down at me and, well, when he said it, it seemed true. I'd done it before, played guitar and sang, entertained rooms full of people many times. It had never been official, however. This would be in front of thousands of screaming Warped concertgoers.

Kal reached for my shoulders. "You can do this. I believe in you."

Goddamn it. If Kal believed it, I would too.

"Kevin is thrilled and says thank you. You're not on until late afternoon, the four forty-five spot. Gives you a few hours to prepare, I guess?"

"Yeah, thanks, Chantal. But wait, what about the guys? Are they being taken care of?"

"The driver was able to get them to the hospital before *he* got sick. They were all treated and released. Your label arranged for them to stay at a hotel while they recuperate."

"Good, that's good. Hey, can you or someone with the tour have some groceries delivered? Like Pedialyte, crackers, whatever they need? And bill me for it?"

"Sure, I can do that. Rick was the only one who didn't have severe symptoms. He's making sure they have what they need. He thinks they'll be able to travel in another couple of days. That may mean you filling in more than today."

"Whatever you need me to do." This was fucking serious. If we cancelled these appearances, that would put us out quite a bit of money. Hopefully my little show would be enough to keep the rabid Backdrop fans from being too disappointed.

"You're a lifesaver, Ryan. Thank you. And hey, how's Kal? I hear he's been hanging out with you guys?"

I smiled up at my beautiful man. "He's wonderful, Chantal. Thank you, I mean it. Thank you for hiring him."

She laughed in surprise. "Wow, okay. Maybe I could talk to him?"

I couldn't stop grinning at Kal, who really needed some dry clothes. He'd managed to wrap the sleeping bag partially around him, but it was becoming painfully obvious that we'd been up to some tomfoolery before running for the bus.

"Chantal wants to talk to you," I said, handing him the phone. He took it from me and looked at it funny before holding it next to his head. When her voice came through, he flinched before bringing it closer.

"Hey, Ryan," Brains said. "Why don't you guys plan on staying with us until your band recovers, okay? We'll find you something to wear."

"Great," I said, shaking my head. "Man, no clothes, no phone, no band. This is some shit."

"Stop saying that!" Los shouted again.

Jordan with the giggles.

Brains shook his head. "Surrounded."

I laughed, clearing more of the cobwebs off the old jovial Ryan. "Yeah. Surrounded by some pretty awesome people."

Brains looked around at his awesome people and nodded in agreement. "I am." But it didn't have that firmness I'd expect. Perhaps he was thinking of his awesome person who was missing. As if on cue, he gazed at Bowie, sighed, and then shook his head.

Bowie lost his smile and excused himself to go back to the bunks.

Kal ended his call with Chantal, handed the phone to Jessica and turned back around. He gestured toward the bathroom, and I nodded.

"Go ahead. You can go get cleaned up."

"Yeah," Jessica said. "We should be there early enough for you to head over to your bus before you need to get to the Red Dawn stage."

Kal nodded at her, gave me that sexy-as-hell smile of his, and then waded through the sea of activity in the kitchen. I would never not be affected by that man. My skin still tingled from our dip in the cool ocean water and his kisses.

"It's my day for breakfast and I've got banana bread and yogurt for all y'all," Jordan announced. "It's my mom's recipe so don't talk shit, all right?"

"Enough with the poop talk! Geez!"

I'd been dreading the return to the tour, but after the phone call, the dread began to dissipate. I'd been given a reprieve of sorts from the drama, but I had some major preparations to do. No biggie.

"Dude," Los said. "You can borrow our gear. Whatever you need."

I looked around. "Was thinking I should use the Twat guitar. Seems appropriate." For once I was being responsible, covering for my sick bandmates so we didn't lose money.

I knew somehow it would backfire.

# CHAPTER 21

**Kal**

We made it to the venue with enough time for me to make it over to the bus where my things were. Brains invited me to stay with Hush on their bus. He claimed it was for me to get to know them and decide if I wanted to go with the band to Europe. I appreciated my new friends. I also appreciated that I would have more time with Ryan, at least the next few days until he rejoined his band.

I brought my bag back to their bus with me and wore my own clothes. Ryan and I cleaned up our sandy mess and one of the techs volunteered to head into town and do everyone's laundry, since Hush wasn't playing until after Ryan.

"Guess I have to let you get back to work," Ryan said as we stood beside the bus, though the hold he had on my hand let me know he'd rather not. "I guess I won't see you until I play later." His palm was sweaty and his gaze darted around the parking lot.

"You're going to perform wonderfully," I said, lowering my head to speak near his ear. "They're going to love you."

That got me a small smile and a nod, but he finally looked into my eyes.

"You'll be there, yeah?"

"Yeah."

"That's all I care about. And we can watch Hush together?"

"If I am able. If I'm not needed."

"Sure," he said, staring intently at his feet. "Right. You have to work."

"I do. But after—"

"Yes. Please. I'll meet you at your stage."

He glanced around once more and then pushed up on his toes to brush a kiss across my lips. It was so quick, I didn't have time to do what I really wanted, which was to pull him to me and hold him tight until the uncertainty and tension was gone from his body. Instead, he turned to hurry away, forgetting I still had hold of his hand.

He was jerked back when I refused to let go.

"I will take care of you tonight."

He grinned and turned his body toward me. "Good. How about tomorrow night?"

I tugged him closer. "Yes. And the night after." This time I did pull him in for a kiss, and I don't think either of us cared if anyone saw.

Howie was grateful to see me as he seemed to be in more pain than before.

"You're a sight for sore eyes," he said with a wince. "That bus ride yesterday did me in."

"Maybe you should be resting," I said. "You need to take care of yourself."

He frowned and looked around at the other stagehands, all of them smoking cigarettes and drinking coffee. "Can't. Not with this lot. We've got a tour to finish. I'll rest when I'm dead."

I shook my head. "Put me to work."

"Listen to you, all verbose and shit. Found your voice, huh?" He patted me hard on my shoulder and gave a load of instructions, which I was determined to follow to the letter.

The day flew by. Thankfully it wasn't hot like Nashville, but it was humid for sure. My shirt was soaked by lunchtime. One of the other stagehands brought us all sandwiches and bottled water, which I ate in the shade while the band Just Like Love performed. Jordan from Hush stood with me, but all of his attention was on the singer, a woman named Roxanne. Her fire-engine-red hair was pulled up in curly pigtails and she wore white tights like a doll with a short black ruffled dress and heeled patent leather baby doll shoes. She had a deep, husky voice when she sang, and she growled like Silas and Ryan.

"She's quite good," I said to Jordan.

"I fucking love her, dude." He tore his gaze from her to grin at me.

"Does she know?"

His smile faded. "No. She's not ready to be serious. Too many issues with dudes in the past trying to mansplain how she should sing and perform. It's hard out here for women."

"I'm sure if you are patient and supportive, she will see that you're different."

He shoved his hands in his pockets and shrugged. "One can hope," he muttered, then he kicked up his chin. "What about him?"

I turned to see Ryan sitting under a tree with Hush's acoustic guitar, playing and humming to himself. He looked as though he'd shut out the world completely and was completely immersed in his task.

"I will take my own advice." I slapped hands with Jordan and went to prepare for the stage change, since Just Like Love was almost finished. I thought about what I'd said, be supportive and patient, and I wondered if that would be enough to keep Ryan's affections. I knew he was troubled, worried about his bandmates as well as when he would rejoin them. It seemed to me only a matter of time before things turned physically aggressive between them, and that was the last thing Ryan needed. I wouldn't allow them to hurt him, not if I could help it.

I didn't want to disturb him, so I got to work tearing down and I made sure to set up Ryan's stool and microphones myself. I knew his height well, and I recalled where he liked it set up, a little higher so he could sing with his chin up. I loved the way the muscles in his throat flexed, and how he caressed the microphone stand like a lover.

Loved that I got to *be* his lover, even if it was only for one night.

The crowd was about the same size as I'd seen in their previous performance and excitement buzzed in the air. I hoped this crowd loved him as much as he deserved. If this didn't go well for him...well, I wasn't sure how he would take it.

I tested the microphones, made sure the cords were out of the way, and I exited the stairs, shaking hands with Howie on the way by.

Ryan was waiting for me at the bottom of the stairs.

"All set?" he asked, and I nodded, stepping aside to let him by, but he stopped at my side. He placed a hand on my shoulder and pulled me down to speak into my ear.

"Stand where I can see you? For luck?"

I smiled at him. "You don't need luck. But yes. Whatever you want."

He cupped my ass slyly and pressed against me as he passed me to take the stage.

I watched him walk onto the stage with a little less cockiness than he had when he'd followed his band. Instead of the black leather and makeup he'd worn previously, he was wearing a worn pair of denim trousers, bright pink canvas shoes, and a tight white t-shirt with an illustration on it. He seemed lighter without his armor, but not quite as sure of himself.

"Wells, huh?"

I turned sharply toward Howie and his tone of voice. Was he implying something negative?

He blanched when he saw my expression.

"Hey, I didn't mean anything bad at all. Just surprised."

"Why?"

I figured he would say something along the lines of "didn't think you were homosexual" or "didn't think he'd notice someone like you."

"Nothing, just he usually picks partners who are bad news. Or all drama. It's nice to see him making good decisions that's all." He winked at me and chuckled to himself.

"Oh. Thanks." What else could I say?

I hurried down the steps in time to hear Ryan give an explanation of where the rest of his band was.

"The guys are really bummed to not be here and will be back just as soon as they're able. I talked to Parker earlier, and he said to tell you all that we'll be putting Virginia on the top of the list of venues for our next tour and folks who still have their Warped ticket will get special merch. We'll do everything we can to make this up to you. In the meantime, I borrowed this here guitar from the guys in Hush, and I thought I'd sing you a few songs. How about that?"

The applause was enthusiastic, not quite at the thunderous level I'd heard before, as though the crowd wasn't sure what to make of this turn of events but they were determined to be polite.

Ryan played a couple of songs I'd heard Backdrop Silhouette perform, a couple of songs I hadn't heard before, and then he paused for a moment, looking around the perimeter of the crowd until he saw me.

"This next song is…well, the parents out there will probably recognize it. It's an oldie, but it's a special one, and I'd like y'all to bear with me as I only learned it about an hour ago."

Laughter spread through the crowd, and then there was a hush as Ryan started strumming a song that sounded very different than any of those I'd heard him play before. This one was…optimistic. And when I listened closely to the lyrics, it sounded as if he were telling the story of us meeting, how it felt to see him for the first time, how unbelievable it was to feel such an instantaneous attraction.

"You can do magic," he sang, and the older folks in the crowd sang with him. They danced and clapped, and suddenly the kids were moved to clap and sway as well. When he started singing the *doo doo doos,* they chimed in.

It was beautiful. *He* was beautiful. The whole thing was… magic.

"Goddamn," Silas said, wiping his eyes. "That asshole. I gotta get up there and sing with him and I'm bawling like a baby."

Krish and Silas had joined me. I hadn't even noticed as I'd been fixated on Ryan's song.

"You better get up there," Krish said, giving Silas a push. "He needs you."

Sure enough, Ryan's smile was tight, and as he looked at me, his eyes were wide. I placed my hand on my chest and gave him a little bow, trying to let him know that I appreciated his song, and it seemed to brighten his smile.

"And joining me now is my good friend Silas Franklin from Hush!"

The crowd's screams grew to dangerous levels. Krish and I covered our ears and laughed.

"Thanks, friend," Silas said, placing his arm around Ryan's neck and kissing the top of his head. "Hey, what do you guys think of the haircut I gave him?"

More screams and laughter.

"Yeah, Franklin. If this singing gig don't work out for you, you can be barber to the stars."

Silas bowed exaggeratedly and the audience ate up their banter.

"Okay, seriously folks. You probably aren't aware of this, but besides being our guitarist and my best friend, our dear friend Gavin West was also a truly gifted songwriter."

The crowd clapped this time, and there were fewer screams but murmurs of appreciation instead.

"And when he wasn't with Hush, helping us craft the songs you all know and love, he liked to hang out with this guy right here and write hippie songs."

Ryan rolled his eyes, and Silas pinched his cheek.

"It's okay, sweetheart. It won't take away your street cred for them to know you've got a really big heart."

Affectionate laughter. Ryan blushed and when his gaze found me, I nodded. He did have a big heart. He was full of love despite what he thought of himself.

"Now, we can't play any of those songs for you...I know, I know," Silas said when the crowd protested. "You know how labels are. We can't play those songs for you, but we want to play a little song we know Gavin loved. What do you say?"

Cheers erupted from what had become a crowd twice the size it had been when he'd started. The photographers from my bus were there snapping pictures, many of the fans had their little handheld telephone machines out and were holding them up to face the stage.

"This is a beautiful song our friends in Sevendust wrote for a dear friend of theirs who they lost too soon. It's called 'Angel's Son.'"

The crowd gave their applause and many wiped tears away. Krish sucked in a big breath. "I'm so glad they're doing this one. They performed it a few weeks ago."

Krish and I stood shoulder to shoulder as we watched the two friends onstage harmonize together on lyrics that talked about the pain we go through when we lose someone we love, how hard it is to not be able to say goodbye. Ryan was a very gifted guitarist in his own right. The fact that he'd played such an emotional set while singing when he hadn't been doing both for a while was a testament to his talent and skill. I admired him even more.

When the song finished, Silas remained onstage and the two of them started in on an unfamiliar song.

"Oh wow," Krish said. "This is a Backdrop song. I didn't know Silas knew this one. They sound great together." He shook his head. "Man, Ryan sounds great today. Better than ever."

He did sound phenomenal. Maybe he'd realize that. Maybe he'd see he had other possibilities out there than the ones he thought he was stuck with.

Whatever came of this unexpected opportunity for him, I was certainly going to let him know how much I appreciated my song. And I would definitely take care of him tonight.

# CHAPTER 22

**Ryan**

My heart pounded as Silas put his arm around me and escorted me offstage.

"That was fucking brilliant," he said, kissing my cheek over and over like some little Italian grandma. "You are so fucking good, Ryan. Goddamn it, I could kiss you!"

"You *are* kissing me," I said with a laugh, but I didn't mind his affection one bit. The organ banging around in my chest had me worried I needed to find Kal...

He was waiting for me at the bottom of the steps with a giant smile. I flew down the steps and into his arms, nearly knocking him over, but my sturdy companion caught me and swung me around.

"How do you feel?" he asked, his voice tinged with worry.

"Great now. That was terrifying though. Don't tell anybody, but I almost puked. I haven't done that since the early *early* days!"

"I wouldn't tell a soul."

"Kal, I don't know if I could have done that without knowing you were here, would be here for me after."

"Yes, you could. You can do anything that you desire."

My eyes flared. "Be still my black little heart. Did you like your song?"

"How could I not? Did you write it?"

I wrinkled my nose. "No, silly. I'm not *that* good. No, I just gave a few updates to the old America song. You remember?"

His smile faded. "No. Now, let me finish here. Then I want to take care of you."

I knew exactly what kind of care he meant, and I was totally down with that, but I wanted more of the before time with him, too; when we talked, when he held me...and that had me worried as fuck.

"Fine, but I'm going to watch you. Now that I know what you can do with those hands."

Kal's nostrils flared and he shook his head. "You *do* know." He stepped back. "I'll be done soon."

Gone was any sort of hesitation from him, and I was left with the implications that my innocent Iowa boy was actually a bigger man than myself who could crush me in his grip but who took such tender care instead. I hadn't realized this was my type, but now that I'd had a taste, I was hungry for more.

"Hey, Ryan?"

Jessica approached me with a nervous smile.

"Hey, yourself. What do you need? And thank you, by the way. I appreciate all of your help."

She shrugged. "Not a problem, but I got a call from Parker and he wants to talk to you."

"Shit, yeah, I'm sorry. I need to get another phone."

"Let me get you one, okay? Rick said he can call your

carrier and report yours lost and that they'll transfer the number over. I'll get it for you after Hush's set. There's an Apple store not too far away."

"You're the best," I said, giving her a hug. "I hope these guys know how lucky they are to have you."

Her smile fell a bit. "Yeah, well, that may have been true at one point. Anyway. Not your problem. I'll see you at the bus later? Brains said you're staying with us?"

"Yeah, man. For some reason the Wells Curse hasn't spread to y'all yet. I'm happy to stay as long as I'm not infringing. More important, though, is that I appreciate you guys taking Kal in. He's had a rough go of it and it's good he made friends with Hush. I want to know he's taken care of, you know?"

She frowned at me. "A, you're not cursed, Ryan, and B, Kal is great. I hope he goes on tour with Hush. It's nice to have someone with manners around."

"Ha! I'll try not to take that personal."

She laughed. "You know what I mean. Anyway. You going to watch them?"

"Oh, yeah. I'll go with you."

I glanced back and paused to watch Kal lifting a cabinet, using his powerful legs and ass, flexing his back muscles beneath the gray heather t-shirt he wore today with some Dickies jeans. I sighed happily, thinking once more of getting him naked so I could draw every inch of his—

"You're drooling. Let's go."

"Do you blame me?"

Jessica dragged me by the arm, but I paused when I caught a glimpse of Kal brushing sweat from his forehead with his handkerchief before shoving into his back pocket, giving me a good look at his incredible ass. Suddenly my pants were too tight.

. . .

After dinner, some of the bands got together for limbo and a "guess that lyric" competition, but I was content to find a quiet spot with Kal and make out.

"Have you thought about it?" Kal asked in between smooches. We'd been doing that for a while, standing in between tour buses, out of sight of the partiers and out of earshot of others having amorous times on the buses around us. We talked, we kissed, it got hot, hands wandered, Kal would get me so fucking close to bliss, and then he'd stop, soothe me with his kisses, and then ask me a question. I praised the condom guy for the lube as this made for the best kind of torture.

"You getting me off? A thousand times a minute."

I loved his smile. If I were a spy and he smiled at me like he was right then, I'd cave under interrogation. Fuck, he could have anything he wanted if he continued smiling at me like that.

"Good. Keep thinking of it. But also tell me…have you thought about going on your own? You were incredible today. The crowd loved you. I loved you." He froze for a second, and it was my turn to smile. I knew what he meant, but damn. Now I had something else to think about. *Love.*

"I'm glad you loved…my performance. Oh, fuck, yeah… right there, that feels so fucking good!"

"I will if you answer me."

I laughed. "Yes. Yes, I have thought about it and always talked myself out of it. It's like any abusive relationship, you know? 'But we've been together so long. I know what to expect. It's easier if I stay. What happens if I leave and that's it?'"

"What if it's not? Ryan, your fans love you. They're always going to love you."

"You think so, huh?" I wanted to believe him and the guys

from Hush, but without my band? They were literally all I had in this world. Or had been.

"What if you could be surrounded by people who love you rather than fighting with those who are supposed to be loyal to you?"

It didn't help that he said this as he was sucking on my neck like the sexiest goddamned vampire on the planet. My knees were about to give out, and my dick was so hard every stroke of his hand was agony.

"Fuck, Kal, it's my fault things are this way—" I sucked in a breath as his grip tightened. He pulled back and let go, leaning on the bus behind him.

"I'm sorry—"

"No, no, no," I said, gripping his face and kissing him hard. "No, it's okay."

He put his hands over mine and pulled them down to his chest. "It's not okay. Ry-an, I don't want them to hurt you anymore."

My eyes and nose burned. "How are you real? Why do you even give a shit? Wait," I said when he looked away. "I'm sorry, Kal, I didn't mean it like that."

"I care because you deserve it. Because despite what you've done, what you think you've done, you matter."

Kal's hands trembled over mine, but his gaze was fierce. He gave me no quarter there, would not accept my "buts" or any of my protests.

I started to crack a joke, say something to ease the tension, but that would have been disrespectful. I heard what he said, and what he didn't say. I was blessed to have him in my corner and I owed it to him to acknowledge that.

"I want you to know that I hear you. I may not be ready to fully agree with you, but I heard what you said. And thank you."

He smirked. "I haven't given you a reason to thank me yet."

"Goddamn you, come here."

And we were kissing again, his hand was right back in my pants, making me want to scream within seconds.

"Please, Kal. Please, I need it."

"You can have anything—"

*"Yesss baby!"* I came so fucking hard, I slumped against him and he supported my weight with a chuckle.

"Baby?"

"Fuck, you're too fucking naughty for me to call you angel. You're too sweet to be a devil. I guess baby is the default."

"Call me whatever you want, just let me do that again."

I tried to ease my hips back and get my dick out of his reach because he was going to turn me into a useless pile of Ryan.

"Maybe devil is the right name for you." I pulled him close for a kiss, but when his hands gripped my ass, I grabbed his wrists. "Hey, Kal. I promise. I heard you, okay? And I'm thinking. And I'll try. Okay? I'm not good at this. My therapist gets on my case about shit like that, too."

He tilted his head. "Therapist?"

"Yeah. Actually, I have to call in tomorrow. Part of my parole. She's a pretty cool chick, rides me about my bullshit but can be gentle when I need it. I check in with my sponsor too once a week…I need to do that tonight. I should see if Jessica got me that phone."

Kal started to pull away and tucked his hands behind his back. "I'll give you some privacy."

"No, no. It's not like that. It's not a dismissal." I put a hand on his chest. "This is part of what I have to do to stay healthy. I have to exercise, in fact…shit. I've missed a couple of days. I exercise every day, have to avoid alcohol and drugs, talk to my therapist once a week, check in with my sponsor, and take my vitamins." I laughed. "It's a lot, but I look at it like medicine or physical therapy, you know? It's what I need to keep going. Not only that, but there are things I have to do in order to stay on the tour."

"I don't want to be in the way of any of that. I will go."

"Kal, that's not what I'm saying. I just want you to know everything, okay? So I'm not hiding anything. You okay with all that? My bullshit? I'd understand if it was too much."

He smiled and shifted his weight, clearing his throat. "I understand. It's not too much for me."

"Thank you. I'll see you on the bus later. Yeah?" I reached for his waist. "Can I tuck you in later? Tell you a bedtime story?"

I kissed him once more, licking at his lips until he let me in. I wanted to leave him wanting more, guess that was my M.O. Leave them all wanting more so they wouldn't find me lacking.

*Whoa*. Okay, Ryan, you mindfucked head case. Guess it was a good idea I was talking to Juanita tomorrow. It wouldn't do anyone any good for me to take a dive because my heart was all wrapped up in this magic man.

I mean, who could blame me? My life was going to shit and he shows up, turning me inside out and then putting me back together. Aftercare was another of Kal's gifts. One of the many, and I delighted in learning them all.

Later. After I did a little self-care.

Kal glanced back once as he walked out of our little tunnel between buses, the lights from the garbage can fires creating a stunning silhouette of his powerful frame.

Goddamn. And he could be mine if I could get out of my own way.

Jessica appeared beyond the bus so I figured it was time to get to caring.

"Hey, Jess," I said, trying not to scare her as I crept out of the darkness. She stood with a few women I didn't know.

"Ryan! Here..." She reached into her pocket. "I was coming to find you. One brand-new iPhone, and Rick was able to get your line hooked up. It's all charged and everything." She put a hand over it before she handed it to me. "It's kind of been dinging like crazy since I turned it on."

"I can imagine. Thank you for doing all this. You need anything, name it. I owe you big."

I kissed her on the cheek and took the phone. Sure enough, the notifications went on forever, but the top one was Parker, and given the situation, I walked back to my tunnel I'd shared with Kal and gave him a ring.

"Brother. You alive?"

"Ryan? Hey, man."

"You sound like death warmed over, man."

Parker coughed and moaned and then took a deep breath. "Finally quit with the intestinal pyrotechnics a couple hours ago. Tried to call you. Wanted to see how it went today."

"It certainly was weird," I said. How did I tell him it was the best I'd felt performing in ages? That my heart was still singing? "But I think it went all right."

"Good, good. Everyone's asleep, but I wanted to make sure everything was okay. Listen, man. I know y'all are driving tonight and playing New Jersey tomorrow. I honestly don't see us getting out of this shitbag hotel for a few more days. TJ and Oscar are still tag-teaming the bathroom. Burke and Ricker are better, but Burke said his hands are killing him, like some sort of joint inflammation thing. I'm afraid we are well and truly fucked."

"Don't worry about it, man. I'll figure something out. I'll talk to Kevin. If I gotta put on a fucking tutu and prance around in a G-string and combat boots for forty-five minutes, I'll do it for you, I don't even care."

Parker chuckled and then groaned. "Don't make me laugh, man. My abs are killing me from puking. What an awful fucking scenario. And I didn't even touch anyone in that place. The nurse thinks it was fucking shit particles in the food, for fuck's sake. Or like these fuckers in there jerking off and then grabbing some jerk chicken without washing their filthy fucking hands. Remind me never to go to a strip club ever ever again."

I pressed my lips together. "You mean like I reminded you last time, and you still went with your brother to that strip club in Tampa and got cr—"

"Jesus, Wells! Kick a dude while he's down. Listen, man, I need to get up and get some more Pedialyte but…I wanted to say thanks, all right? Other way around? We'd have had to cancel. There's no Backdrop without you, buddy."

I blew out a shaky breath. "Whatever. You guys get better, okay? I'll send some more supplies and I'll call you tomorrow, now that I've got another phone—"

"Yeah, what happened to you?"

"Went to a carnival. Maybe fell in love. Got jumped. Went camping. You know, a regular-ass Warped Tour adventure."

"Wait, wait. Go back to the middle."

"Got jumped? Yeah, I'm fine. We almost lost Krish, though. He almost became some carney's—"

"No, the other middle part. Love? What the fuck, dude?"

"Yeah, well…anyway…I'll check on you guys tomorrow. I'll find a place nearby that can bring y'all some chicken soup. Now that I've got a phone, I can hit up the fans in Virginia. Someone's gotta know someone."

"Thanks, man." Parker really sounded like he was hurting, so I ended the call by making him laugh again. He cursed me out. It was poetic.

Next call was to my sponsor, Rose. She understood the whole maybe-falling-in-love bit and she ran me through all the questions. Is he sober? "Probably?" Are you taking things slow? "Since I've known him all of three days now? Probably not?" Is it feeling co-dependent-y? "He's found me at a critical time, he's undergoing a huge life change, we're staying together on a bus? Remains to be seen." Are you being honest with him? With yourself? "Mostly. Both. Mostly both."

"Ryan, you have been sober this time for two years despite many trials and tribulations. I think you know yourself and know your limits pretty well by now. Make sure you're setting and respecting each other's boundaries and take care."

"I don't know, Rose. You sure you don't want to yell at me?"

She cackled. Rose was a tough old broad who drove trucks and rescued pit bulls. If there was cause to yell at me, she'd do it, no holds barred.

"Is he cute?"

"Really? Are we gonna have girl talk?"

And that's exactly what we did while I walked the perimeter of the parking lot. My cheeks hurt from smiling by the time I got back to Hush's bus. Rose promised to light a candle for me and we agreed to chat next week or sooner if needed.

"I love you, Mama Bear."

"I love you, too," she said. "Pain-in-my-ass rock star."

We signed off and I sucked in a deep breath.

What a weird fucking day. Good, but weird. And now, I planned to crawl into a bunk with my hunk and…yeah, I wasn't going to rhyme any more tonight.

# CHAPTER 23

**Kal**

I'd had a moment of uneasiness as I emerged from the space between the buses but then I heard Silas laughing. He had his band gathered around, as well as about ten other people I hadn't met yet. He was bent over backward attempting to get his body to pass under a stick being held by Los and Jordan.

I knew if I joined them they'd immediately welcome me into the fold, and that was a feeling I hadn't had in a very long time. If ever.

"The only reason you can get your scrawny ass under that pole is because you're already closer to the ground."

"You're just jealous, Matt. Being pint-sized has its perks."

A few more men and women tried to get under the pole at its current height and failed, mostly due to their level of intoxication. Prohibition had been in effect throughout most of my adult life before the carnival, so I'd never partaken of alcohol. My parents had been teetotalers, my father was an influential member of the community, meaning myself and my siblings were encouraged to always be on our best behavior.

It was strange, thinking about my family after all this time. My father, dark-haired, dark-eyed, and olive-skinned, was stern but kind. My mother, a blond goddess, statuesque and strong-boned like her Northern European ancestors, was reserved and protective, traits my father said I inherited from her. My sister Ellen, ten years my junior, pushed the limits our parents set, but Father adored her. Mother pretended to be annoyed with Ellen's antics while doting on her. And Zachariah, a toddler when I left, had us all wrapped around his finger.

I understood why they brought me to Uncle Norman. He needed workers for his various endeavors and had the means to feed me. I was sixteen and had a music education, which was not much help to anyone during the Depression. Being deprived of seeing my siblings grow up hurt then, and the more of my memories that resurfaced, a hollow space began to grow in my chest.

What had happened to them? Had they survived? The sensation of starvation echoed through that space, and I placed a protective hand over my stomach as the pain reverberated through me.

"Kal, hey man. We've got some hot dogs over here. You hungry?"

And there was Krish. Always there, checking on his friends, worrying about me. I let him walk me over to where a barbeque was set up and a man I didn't know yet handed me a plate with food on it and a bag of chips.

"Thank you," I murmured. These people had taken me in. Like family. I'd somehow stumbled upon this supportive group of men, and I intended to repay them for their care. It helped ease the hollowness in my chest, but I had this feeling that it would never dissipate completely unless I found out what had happened to my first family.

"You want a beer, man?"

Jordan stood at my side with a can in each hand. I looked down at them and Ryan's face flashed before me. I shook my head. "No, thanks." Never having a drink was the best way to ensure that alcohol didn't wreak havoc on my life like it had done to his. I didn't want to be another stressor for him, either.

"Cool, all right. I think there's some sodas and waters in the cooler over by Just Like Love's bus."

"Thank you." I walked over in the direction he pointed and dug around in the ice-filled box until I found a red can with a semi-familiar name. I cracked it open and drank deeply, causing me to pull it away coughing. I recalled the first time I'd had one. I'd choked on the bubbles that time, too.

A guy pounded on my back. "You all right? Oh, you're drinking the hard stuff," he said with a laugh. "Gotta watch out for that shit." He held out a hand. "Names Byron. I'm a tech for Just Like Love."

"Kal Alexandrou," I said, shaking his hand. It felt odd using this new name, now that I'd remembered my given name, although a niggling thought took hold. Why had Alexandrou felt right when Mr. Ame had given me the identification?

And then it dawned on me.

Because Alexandrou had been the family name.

With clarity, I now recalled Uncle Norman saying shocking things to me about my father, which I now believed were likely true. That my father had fled his home in Greece, adapted a more English surname, Alexander, and then he and my mother had run away from her home in

Muscatine because her father wouldn't allow her to marry him, despite all he'd done to fit in with small-town America.

They'd created a new life in Illinois, in Chicago…yes, I clearly remembered that place. And then a small town near the Mississippi River, which is where we'd been when the money ran out, the food supply dwindled, my siblings cried themselves to sleep…

"Hey, man, thank you for stepping in. I hear you're working wonders for Howie. And hanging out with Wells." He waggled his eyebrows and grinned. "How's *that* going?"

"Going?" I wasn't sure what he was implying but the conversation felt wrong.

"You know. I've just heard what happens with folks who hang out with Wells."

I stepped closer to this man with greasy hair and an unkempt beard. I smelled alcohol oozing from his pores as if he'd been drinking all afternoon.

"And what *have* you heard?" I said calmly, though the tension was collecting in my shoulders and neck. "I'm curious."

My calm exterior must not have been convincing, as he laughed nervously. "Well, you know. It's no secret he's *bi.*" He said that word like it was dirty or scandalous. "And everyone knows that he likes to like draw people in the *newd.*" Then his smile fell, and he tried to bolster his posture. "And some of his playmates have ended up paralyzed. You should watch your back."

He started to walk away, but I reached for his arm, which I held onto a little tighter than the situation called for.

"I'm not sure what you hoped to accomplish with that information, but you should keep your opinions about Ryan Wells to yourself."

He pulled his arm away and stumbled backwards,

running into Lysander, one of the guys I'd been working with on the Red Dawn stage.

"Kal, what's up?" He frowned at this Byron guy. "Everything all right?"

I nodded, but my expression probably said something entirely different.

"I was just leaving." Byron scurried away, and Lysander laughed.

"He was sure in a hurry. Everything cool?"

I took a sip of my Coca-Cola and put on a smile. Ryan had warned me people would talk. I was beginning to see what he meant. "It's fine."

"Good, because some people around here like to *run their mouths*." He said the last part loud enough for the retreating Byron to hear. Byron's shoulders flinched and he walked a little faster. "And I for one like the people *I* like to be happy, so *some people can go suck a bag of dicks*."

Byron broke out into a comical run then, and I couldn't hold in my laughter.

"I think he got the point."

"Awesome. Hey, I want to talk to you about the way you rigged Ryan's mics today. He sounded so crisp, you could hear each little crackle in his throat. Sounded sexy, man."

He was absolutely right, but that sexy sound had nothing to do with how I set up microphones. I'd wanted to pick up more of the rich tones I knew Ryan to be capable of. With him singing to only one guitar, there was more room to let his voice take over.

Lysander and I got to talking shop and a few other guys gathered around. I found myself talking freely and wondering how it was that I knew all of the specifics of today's technology.

*You shall have all you need.*

Mr. Ame had taken care of me in more ways than a bottomless billfold.

The next thing I knew, someone handed me an electric guitar and a toolkit. Under the parking lot lamp and a few flashlights, I was able to take it apart and work on the position of the pickups and the height of the strings. I'd taught myself to repair stringed instruments in music school, but given the fact that electric guitars such as these hadn't been invented yet, somehow Mr. Ame had made sure I had all of the knowledge amassed during the time I'd been with the carnival.

"Dude, you have the magic touch," Ross, the guitarist from Just Like Love said as he took it from me and played a few chords. "I destroy this thing every night and Byron can never get it to stay in tune. I always end up swapping it out."

Good to know I had an advantage over Byron the Instigator.

"Where did you learn how to do that?" Lysander asked. "Our program back at the technical school didn't teach us luthier stuff."

"Oh, I spent my time mostly working on pianos and mechanical orchestration apparatuses. I taught myself the stringed instruments. Back then, I needed to have as many skills as possible if I hoped to get a job."

"Back then? What are you, like twenty?" one of the guys asked with a laugh.

"What do you mean, mechanical orchestration?" Theo, Hush's drum tech, asked.

They had so many questions, I could barely keep up. "Mostly Wurlitzers, calliopes. Then I built calliaphones."

"What's a calliaphone?"

"It's a pipe organ similar to a calliope but smaller, portable, and not so loud it shatters eardrums." The guys laughed but they continued staring at me as if they wanted me to continue. "It, uh, uses compressed air for power, rather than coal like the original calliopes. It's more suitable for traveling carnivals like the one I worked at."

Where did my chattiness come from? I'd become comfortable with this group of men standing around the parking lot, and I was so wrapped up in this discussion of my true passion that I nearly forgot about the time differential.

"Pull up a picture," Lysander said. "I wonder if I've ever seen one."

I frowned at him. "Pull up a picture?"

"Yeah, on your phone."

"I don't have a phone."

"Oh," he said, and the other guys looked confused. "Oh, well, here, use mine." He handed me his personal device, and I stared at it blankly.

"I don't, um. I'm not—"

"You can fix the shit out of a Gibson but you can't work a smartphone?" The guys laughed but it didn't feel good-humored to me.

"I've never see—had one before."

Lysander burst out laughing. "Wow, a true relic. I've heard luddites still exist but I haven't met one in person. Where are you from, anyway?"

"He's from Iowa, boys."

Ryan's voice was a relief. He saved me from giving away my truth. I turned to find him smiling at me, and it was enough to erase any anxiety I'd had over the conversation.

The others laughed and the awkward moment was gone. He'd made it better, like he'd done from the start.

"Fuck off," Theo said. "I used to live in Iowa!"

"Explains a lot," Jordan said, and the two of them got into a playful shoving match.

"That makes sense, I guess," Lysander said. Were you, like, homeschooled?"

I opened my mouth to speak, but I feared I would dig myself in deeper.

Ryan wrapped his arms around my shoulders. "Enough questions, creeps. Kal, may I tear you away from your admirers?"

I turned and smiled. "Please?" I whispered.

"We'll see you guys in Jersey. Hey, Hush. Your driver says it's time to mount up."

The crowd dispersed and Ryan guided me away from the others.

"Thank you," I said. "I didn't know how to answer them."

"You don't owe anybody shit, you got that? Hey, look at me," he said, placing his hands on my jaw. "You don't have to tell anyone anything about yourself, about me, about the price of tea in China. You get to decide how much of yourself you share with people."

I placed my hands over his and took them in mine. I loved that he was here, that we'd met, that he'd run interference for me. But for how long? It wasn't fair of me to depend on him. I needed to stand on my own if I was going to make it, like I should have when my parents left me. I should have told my uncle I'd make it on my own before I got in too deep with his nefarious practice, starving or not.

Not that I thought Ryan would lead me into harm's way, not at all, but I also needed to make decisions based on the best way to take care of myself and be of service to others. I wouldn't be good for him or anyone else if I couldn't stand on my own.

We crawled into the bunk together again, but this time I lay in Ryan's arms and let the relative quiet lull me to a light sleep. He asked if I was okay, and I tried to reassure him, but I'd been jarred by the earlier conversations and I needed to shut down for a bit. I just hoped I didn't have too many more nights like this. I feared I would.

# CHAPTER 24

**Ryan**

The festival traveled to New Jersey for the next two shows, which were fairly close to one another. That gave us time for shopping and a nice dinner with a couple of other bands. Kal asked me to help him get a cellular phone and had me teach him how to use it. He didn't say why, but he spent a lot of time trying to figure out its features.

I showed him how to listen to music, how to search the internet, and with each new skill, he thanked me, but remained surprisingly tight-lipped when I asked him what information, in particular, he was trying to look up. I'd do anything for him, and I told him I'd help him if there was anything specific I could do. It was as if he'd never even heard of the internet, which was mind-boggling, though I figured there were still places where people didn't use it. I guess I never thought I'd ever meet one of them.

During the day, Kal worked the Red Dawn stage and would stand where I asked him to when I performed. He'd been quiet since Virginia, but we'd spent as much time as possible together and shared a bunk each night, despite razzing from the guys in Hush. Silas and Krish even offered to give up the lounge in the back for a few nights if we "needed more space" but since that was code for sex, and that made Kal seem uncomfortable, I politely declined.

I spoke to Parker every day and the guys seemed to be getting a little better, but they still couldn't keep down solid foods. The doctor told them they needed the rest of the week to recover. I ordered them soup and bread to be delivered each day. It was as if I was experiencing survivor's guilt or something. I had moments of remorse for having a good time when they were all sick.

Meanwhile, I kept up the band's commitments by performing each day, making sure I kept an eye on Kal when I sang "You Can Do Magic." I'd always loved those old 1970s soft rock tunes, but this one was becoming an all-time favorite.

The sets grew more involved as I hit up different acquaintances on tour to sing with me. Roxanne joined me on the second day in New Jersey, and we did our duet as well as a cover of Heart's "Magic Man," taking turns singing the verses and then harmonizing on the chorus. I changed the words up a little. I loved to do that.

I invited Spencer Charnas from Ice Nine Kills to sing Avenged Sevenfold's "A Little Piece of Heaven," which had the Hartford, Connecticut, crowd in stitches. It's such a naughty song, but that's what I loved about it. And then I invited Ahren Stringer and the guys from The Amity Affliction to perform with me in Pittsburgh on "Can't Feel My Face," which they'd covered on a Pop Goes Punk album we'd both appeared on. It was super fun.

Silas and I were planning to do a Beastie Boys tune in Toronto, but we needed a third.

"Come on, Los. You know all of those songs by heart. Like, you've memorized their entire catalog."

He rolled his eyes dramatically and sighed. "I guess. But if we're going to do this, I get to pick which song."

Which is how we ended up doing a rousing performance of "So Whatcha Want?" Roxanne found a backing track for us to use and we got very silly onstage.

Kal had been very confused by the song, which led to a whole lesson from Brains on the history of hip hop and the unique role the Brooklyn-based Jewish band played in what was an art form created by the Black community. He listened intently to everything Brains said, and Los made a playlist for him on his new phone. None of the guys treated him like this was a strange thing at all, but I was beginning to have questions.

My band was scheduled to rejoin the tour in Cincinnati, Ohio, so before I was back to being the lead singer of Backdrop Silhouette playing only our hits and the songs off of our mediocre last release, I put it out on my social media to the fans to pick the setlist for our Cuyahoga Falls stop.

"How does that work, exactly?" Kal asked me as we snuggled together in our bunk.

"Social media? Well, there are a couple of sites folks use a lot. I stick to this one because I can post mostly pics and talk about them or not. Sometimes I have a lot to say, some days it's like 'here's this cool mural I found.' People can comment. I don't always read them though. They can get pretty ugly."

"Ugly?"

"Yeah, you know. People say shit because it's not to your face. They hide behind their screens and criticize, bully, belittle. But then there are the folks who say things like 'I never would have gotten through losing my mom if it weren't for your music,' or the guys who are fresh out of prison who say 'if you can do it, so can I.' It's the best and the worst of humanity."

Kal was quiet for a long time after that, stroking his fingers up and down my spine and staring at the roof of our little hideaway. Above us, someone was playing games on their phone. I heard pages being turned in a book—probably Bowie or Brains—and someone else was snoring.

"You mean so much to so many people," Kal finally whispered. "You mean so much…to me."

"Come here." I was glad he'd said something. He'd seemed so far away, troubled, and I worried he was struggling with more than he'd said. "You mean a lot to me, too, Kal. You've made all of this better just by being beside me. I don't think I could have gotten through the past couple of weeks without you."

He frowned. "You could. You can do anything, Ryan." He cleared his throat. "I'm…struggling. My memories. What happened after…while I was with the carnival. I have a lot of questions. I want to find out what happened…to my family."

"We can find them, Kal. I can help—"

He placed a hand on my chest. "I don't want you to know." His eyes flared. "I'm sorry. Not yet, Ryan."

Now we were getting to the cause of his mood. "Kal, I told you. I don't care who you were before. I care about you. Now. You can tell me or not about your past, doesn't matter to me, but I can tell you're hurting and I want to help if I can. You've done so much for me. I want to be there for you."

"I don't know what I'm going to find. You can help me by…not helping. Until I'm ready."

"I understand. I do." I blew out a breath. *Honesty, Ryan. No matter what.* "I gotta tell you, man, that's really tugging on my 'you're not enough, Ryan' strings, but I'm gonna try not to take it that way."

Kal grabbed my arm and pulled me to face him. Rough. "You *are* enough." He kissed me, crushing me with his grip, pinning me down with his weight. "You could be *everything*. But I have to be something first." He pressed our foreheads together and exhaled a shaky breath before letting go and turning over. "Rest, Ryan. You have a big day tomorrow."

Tears pricked my eyes. He was good at this whole boundary thing, much better than I was. I curled against his back and tried to cool my shit. He was right. We were both in transitional times, and while it was nice to have him to distract me, he couldn't fix my band drama, and I couldn't fix his fractured memory. But together? We could be there to lend a hand when the other stumbled. That would have to be enough…for now.

By the next morning, the fans had responded to my call with ideas for a setlist that sounded like a blast. Word had gotten around and several of my fellow artists had texted to say they'd love to join me, so I sent out a group text and made a plan.

I took the stage with the "twat" guitar, which had become famous on the socials as several bloggers had written about my solo stint. The feedback was nice, not gonna lie. I made sure, when asked for comment by a couple of the journalists traveling with the tour, to say I was just doing my best to entertain the fans until my band was able to return. I knew better than to get on my high horse. I'd done it before and it had led to ugly fights with Parker.

One glance to my right and I saw Kal there, smiling at me like always. I adored his smile, his dated but perfect-for-him wardrobe, and his posture that said "approachable but no fuckery tolerated." I'd grown fond. He'd grown on *me*. My feelings had grown to…yeah, *that* territory.

"Hello Warped Tour, you wild motherfuckers!" I started playing "Bring the Magic," adding a little soul to it.

"Thank you, thank you. Now, the Backdrop fans have spoken, and I worked with my Warped family to create a little medley of songs we all know and love, and my pals in Hush have agreed to help me out."

Silas, Los, Jordan, and Bowie came out onstage to be my backup band, but we kept it acoustic. I wanted to make this as different from a Backdrop set as possible. We played a bit from Judas Priest, Metallica, Foo Fighters, and Queen, the last of which—"Somebody to Love"—had me searching for Kal again.

I scanned the crowd—the largest I'd had yet, maybe even larger than my earlier dates with Backdrop—and found him smiling yet pensive, as if he were thinking about our conversation from the night before. He caught me looking and even in the sun I could tell he was blushing. *Oh yes, Mr. Alexandrou. Just you wait until this tour is over.*

Yeah. After the tour. I'd take him home with me before he went to Europe. Okay, I'd *invite* him home with me and together we'd figure things out.

Hell yeah.

I tried to make eye contact with as many folks in the audience as I could. I waved at teenaged girls, winked at their moms, threw up the horns at the boys and felt pretty damned lucky to be alive.

And then I saw four faces I wasn't expecting.

Parker, Burke, Oscar, and TJ stood on the opposite side of the stage from Kal with arms crossed. They were dressed in their typical stage wear but they looked tired despite sunglasses and hats.

I saluted my friends in Hush and they said their goodbyes, leaving me to finish our set with a Backdrop classic, "Only Those You Love." I slowed it down a bit and when I got to the end of the song, I dragged out the last note, holding it as long as I possibly could. I wanted to hold on to this feeling, this positivity, this hope, to fuel me through the rest of this tour and then…

The rest was for Tomorrow Ryan to deal with.

One last strum of the Twat Guitar—I was really beginning to dig this thing—and I exhaled. That was it. The end of my freedom, the end of my leash, and the end of my peace.

Kal got right to work breaking down the set, but he came over to me under the guise of removing the battery pack from my waist that powered the monitors in my ears.

"They came back early. I'm sorry I didn't warn you, I heard after you'd already started."

I smiled up at him. "I love it when you manhandle me," I said with a laugh. "I'll let you take some more things off of me later."

He bit his lip and averted his eyes.

"I'll come find you when I'm done. Want to be there for you." He glared in the direction of my bandmates, who were waiting behind the stage.

I pushed up on my toes and kissed him, earning us a few catcalls from the other stagehands. Kal's cheeks reddened but he didn't step back.

My man.

"I'm good. I feel good. Only seventeen more dates," I said in a low voice, smoothing the crease on his forehead with my thumb. "Then…I'm going to end it."

Kal's eyes flared and he grabbed my waist. "Are you sure?"

I grinned. "These past few shows have reminded me why I'm a singer, why I joined a band in the first place. I want to find my love for performing again. It's there, I just need to make it happen, you know?"

"You can do anything you desire, Ry-an."

*Fuck whoever is watching.* I kissed him again, with a big hug and some tongue. He wasn't prepared for it but I heard that carnal little growl in his chest. He was feeling it too. I was out of control, and I couldn't even be bothered with propriety. Happiness was in front of me and I was going to hold on to it with both hands. And my tongue. And perhaps other parts of me.

Happiness was Kal, and I was going to have him and my cake and eat it all.

"Hey, Kal? Sorry, I need to get the rest of this stuff…"

Poor Lysander was trying to work around us, and even though we were out of sight of the crowd, we were making it difficult for the stagehands to finish.

I squeezed Kal's ass, which caused him to stumble.

"Yeah, get to work, beautiful. I'll see you later."

Howie let out a big laugh, and poor Kal's cheeks were the reddest I'd seen them yet.

"Thanks, man," I said, shaking hands with Howie.

He slapped me hard on the back. "Go get 'em, tiger."

"Meow," I purred back, making him laugh even harder until he strained his back. Then he cursed at me.

"Fuck you, Wells. Quit groping my stagehand."

I pranced down the stairs feeling every bit of my smug self, but mostly, I was just fucking happy.

They at least waited until I got offstage to confront me. With all eyes on us, TJ and Oscar shook hands loosely with me, and Parker accepted my hug, as did Burke. Rick gave me a side hug, as if he wasn't sure it was okay to touch me.

"Great job, Ryan," Rick said. "The tour is thrilled with your performances. You really saved the day. Oh, and I really like your haircut."

TJ scoffed but didn't make eye contact with me.

"Thanks, Rick. I was just doing my part to keep us on the tour. Losing that money and exposure would have hurt all of us."

TJ and Oscar looked at each other, and Oscar shook his head.

"Right," Oscar said. "Our lord and savior."

"Fuck off," Burke said to them. "I'm going to the bus."

Poor guy still looked a little green.

"We're going to go watch Waterparks," TJ said, and he and Oscar left, throwing me ugly looks as they walked away.

"That went well," I said, determined not to get riled up over those two knuckleheads.

"We gotta talk, Ryan." Parker had dark circles under his eyes and he'd noticeably lost weight.

"Sure, buddy, but we should get you to the bus—"

"Fuck, I'm sick of the bus. I'm sick of being inside. I'm sick of throwing up."

And I knew he was sick of me and sick of our band's drama.

"Okay, well, let's sit down then."

"Parker, want me to get you something to drink?" The Ricker, eager as ever, looked worried about him.

"Yeah, man. Some more Gatorade? We have any more?"

Rick put his hand on Parker's shoulder. "I'll find some. Be right back."

I walked with an arm behind Parker's back in case he fainted. He'd lost even more color in the time since we'd been standing there. There were some benches at the edge of the parking lot behind the stages, and I led him over to one away from groups of people.

"Thanks, man," Parker said with a laugh. "I haven't been that fucking sick since I was a kid. We had to get IVs and shit. The doctors we saw and the nurses they sent to the hotel took good care of us, but fuck. It sucked. I miss my bed, dude. Sucks being sick when you're not home."

"I hear you. I'm so sorry."

He held up a hand. "Nah, man. It's all good. Good you weren't there or you're right, we'd have been fucked." He grinned at me. "Your sets were awesome, by the way. I saw clips. It was nice to see you happy again. And Rick's right about the hair. It looks great."

I hadn't expected him to be kind.

"Thanks, man. Silas cut it, believe it or not. The first couple days solo was scary, dude. I was worried people would fucking walk away from the stage."

We laughed, but it was hollow, and Parker ended his in a coughing fit.

"You sure you guys are ready to play tomorrow?"

He shook his head. "No, but we gotta. I can bang on shit for forty minutes without dying. I think."

"Anything I can do? I feel bad."

Parker turned on me and his lighthearted expression was gone. "You've done enough, Ryan. You kept things going while we were gone, which we appreciate, but shit's gotta change. Burke is ready to cut. He's building this studio at his grandparents' place, and I overheard TJ and Oscar talking...I think they're looking to start their own gig." He folded his hands between his open knees and dropped his gaze to the ground. "Thinking this might not only be the last tour for Warped, but for Backdrop, too."

I exhaled and rubbed my hands on my thighs. This was not how I thought things would go down, but it actually made sense, and it might help take the focus off me as the problem if the others were looking elsewhere.

"Backdrop is our baby, Parker. I'm sorry if I let you down."

Parker leaned back against the bench and gazed off toward the stage where Wage War was now playing.

"We've had some good times. Made some good records, didn't we? Shit, we've got three gold records and a platinum single. We've done some shit to be proud of."

"Yeah, man. We have," I said, patting his shoulder. "And

you kept things going when I fucked up. I'm sorry to see it end."

Parker blew out a breath. "You'll be okay, though. Whatever happens."

"If you would have said that to me two weeks ago, I wouldn't have believed you. This isn't what I want, I don't want you to think that, but if it's over, I'll survive. I have to."

We talked a bit longer about the fact that we had one more album on our contract, not to mention the rest of Warped, but Parker was fading.

"Look, you need to rest, okay? Don't worry about it. I'll come find you guys in the morning when we get to Cincinnati and we can catch up, run through the set, see if you guys want to do any changes."

Parker pushed himself up to standing and his whole body sagged. Dude needed a nap or something.

"Do me one favor, Ryan?"

I stood next to him, ready to catch him if need be. "Anything."

"Don't fucking say anything about this. And if you talk to any press, cool it with the solo talk."

"What are you talking about?"

"Come on, Ryan. I saw what you said about these shows being a dry run for your solo project. I know you've got that album you and Gavin wrote. Just, be cool until we can unfuck this situation, all right?"

"What the fuck are you talking about? I never said *anything* like that. There is no solo project. What the hell?"

"It was on the rock sites, dude. Look, I don't even care anymore about your shit with Gavin, all right? Let us work this shit out before you start anything else, okay?"

"Parker, I swear to God, I have nothing planned and I've said nothing to the press." Who the fuck was talking? I trusted that it wasn't Krish. I knew he wouldn't fuck me like that, but had it been someone else in the Hush camp? Maybe Kal?

No way. He wouldn't have spoken to anyone. I hated that I even had to worry, but something in my gut told me that he'd never do me wrong like that. No matter who tried to get him to talk. All I had to remember was that protective forehead crinkle or any of the times he'd stood up for me.

I tried to speak again, reassure Parker, but the look he gave me was the same look he gave me at our last meeting before I went off to prison. Disgust. Disappointment.

"I wish I could believe you, Ryan. Too much has happened."

He walked away, leaving me sputtering. How did we go from a positive resolution to "this is all your fault?" *Again*?

# CHAPTER 25

**Kal**

Everything conspired to keep me from finding Ryan that afternoon. The second-to-last band blew out the sound board and Howie used very colorful language while trying to fix it. When he was unable, he and Chantal got to work trying to track one down for the next day. They moved the last band to one of the other stages, and sent me to help out over there. Of course, this band had more equipment than the power could handle at the smaller stage, they complained the whole time, and then the power blew, the backup generator failed, and there was a shouting match between the band's manager and Chantal, who did her best to smooth things over without having to involve Kevin.

"I'm sorry, Chantal. I did the best I could to fix the circuit breaker—

She put her hands on my arms and shook her head. "Uh-

uh, Kal. Don't apologize. These guys think they're so important they need twice the amount of equipment as everyone else, even though we send out specs way before the tour. I don't want you to worry, okay? This is not on you." She rolled her head around on her neck and sighed. "Now I've got to track down another backup generator as well as a new board. And shocker, we're not exactly in a hub of music equipment here in Ohio!"

"Let me work on the board some more. I think I can fix it."

She sighed. "I won't say no, but if you can't, don't worry. We're still making calls. We'll either find someone, or we'll have one of the stages go kumbaya and play acoustic sets or something. We'll figure it out."

I had no idea what kumbaya meant but I understood her sentiment.

I spent another two hours with Lysander on the board and we managed to fix it enough to be used carefully, but not perfect. It was late when we finished, and I had no idea where Ryan was. I was tired, thirsty, and I wanted a hug.

Something buzzed in my pants. My phone? I hadn't used it yet to communicate with anyone. I pulled it out and a picture of Ryan's face was on the screen, making a kiss at me. I pushed the green button and then it was him for real.

"Where you at, babe?"

"I'm sorry," I said, feeling like apologies were not enough today. "Lysander and I have been working on the board and we just finished."

"Hush's bus is ready to leave. Can you get here?"

Ryan's smile was strained. I hated that I'd been kept away from him, especially after I heard that his band was there. I feared the worst had happened after he'd left.

"I'll run. Tell them I'm on my way."

He sighed and his smile relaxed. “Thank you. Please hurry.”

I hung up the phone, said goodbye to Lysander, asked three people to point me in the direction of the parking lot as I was turned around, and finally made it to the lot to find all of the buses lining up to leave. I searched frantically for Hush’s bus and finally saw Ryan hanging out the door waving to me, so I took off running.

“Whew. That was close,” he said as he pulled me onboard.

I apologized to the driver, who waved and said not to worry. Ryan led me past the video game players, who all slapped our hands. This time they had TVs going on both sides of the lounge and all six of my current bus mates were fixated on the screens.

Ryan led me past the bunks and back to the lounge, shutting the door behind us. All of the bedding Silas and Krish usually used had been folded up neatly and put in a corner and, from what I’d seen when the door was open, it appeared that they’d cleaned up after themselves.

“The guys all wanted to play this new game tonight so I asked if we could have this space to talk.”

My hands grew clammy and I tucked them in my pockets. Was this it?

Ryan frowned. “Hey, what’s wrong? What happened? Are you okay?” He reached for my shoulder but I sidestepped him.

“I’m okay. You want me to go? Is that it?”

He opened his mouth, and then closed it and sighed. “No *fucking* way. Kal, why would you think that?”

I shrugged, the burning feeling in my chest threatened to take over.

Ryan took my arm and led me to the platform. “Sit. Please. What’s wrong?”

I sank down and put my head in my hands. “I feel like I’ve

been saying sorry all day. Everything blew up and I tried to fix it but—"

"Whoa, whoa, hey, I heard about that, and it wasn't your fault! Sometimes that shit happens. You can't repair something that's imploded. You're good, but that's like superhero level. Hey." He placed his hands gently on my cheeks and kissed me softly.

It was exactly what I needed, but I was afraid to trust that everything was okay.

"What happened? With your band?"

Ryan pressed his forehead to mine and sighed. "Seems I might not have to quit after all. Looks like we're done."

He explained to me that the two jerks wanted to start their own thing, that one of the members wanted to get into recording, and that Parker was ready to call it quits. "We've got a lot to discuss, and it's probably going to be an ugly divorce, but that's it. I feel weirdly relieved."

I tried to muster a smile, but I was honestly worrying about everything tonight, and I didn't know what this meant for Ryan.

"I'm glad, Ryan. You'll do great, whatever you decide to do."

He sat up straighter and spoke in a soft voice. "I was hoping that whatever I decide to do will involve you."

I wanted to believe him. I wanted to believe that I would not have to walk this earth without him, but I was *afraid* to want it.

I leaned forward and placed my forehead on his shoulder, too tired to fight my need for his touch any longer, but too vulnerable to ask for what I really wanted.

"Baby, what's wrong?" He brought his arms around me without hesitation and held me to him. "Did someone say something? Did someone hurt you? Kal—"

I put my arms around his waist and tucked my nose into

his neck and just breathed. This was the one place that everything made sense. I didn't want to think about anything else. "Lay with me?"

Ryan nodded and lay on his side with his arms open. He was wearing a pair of soft, loose pants, a black t-shirt with the sleeves cut off and deep grooves that opened down to his waist. I hadn't had the opportunity before to admire his body art in the light. His arms were covered with black and gray ink from his fingers to his shoulders, and even on his neck and throat. Symbols from the Ouija board, five-pointed stars, the all-seeing eye, a black cat, a crow…

"Are you a witch?"

Ryan smiled and waggled his eyebrows. "Maybe? Why?"

"Those symbols. Witches are known for using them, but also spiritualists. My grandparents believed in Spiritualism.

"I've always been fascinated, but after meeting Gavin's aunts, I was hooked. They taught me a lot. I'd love for you to meet them, they're really cool." He pressed his lips together. "I think they'd be really happy to see me right now. With you."

"You think so?"

"I do. They'd probably think I had to use a love potion on you. They always give me shit for being too much of a brat for anyone to really fall in love with me, but I know they find me entertaining."

"You wouldn't have to use a love potion." I ran my fingers over his arm and recognized a quote from Edgar Allan Poe. "'All that I love I love alone?' Why alone?"

He sighed. "You haven't learned by now that I have a flair for the dramatic?" He ran his fingers over his belly, lifting his shirt. He had dark golden hair in a thin patch between his navel and the top of his pants. There was more writing on his skin there, but my eyes were tired. I wanted forever to study him, every inch of his body. I feared forever wouldn't be enough.

"Do you still talk to them? Gavin's aunts?"

He put his chin in his hand. "I do. I see them whenever I can. They live in a beautiful place up in Northern California. You can walk to the beach from their property in the redwoods."

"I'm glad you have them in your life. You should never have to love alone."

I lay beside him and he pulled me close. "My beautiful man. My Kallos."

And there was no more talking, only loving. He said so many things, made so many promises, which he'd been careful not to do up to this point.

"Let me love you, Kal," he whispered as he unfastened my pants. "I want to hold you always. I want to be with you."

*Always.* I knew that was an unreasonable pledge, seeing as we just met, and his work might very well make us part. Mine, too, if I continued down this path. But if I had this night, these memories, I could always call upon them to ease me if I no longer had him beside me.

His kisses were different this time, eager, sweet, his touch soothing, caring. It was just as consuming as when we'd been on fire for each other, but it was more. Whatever had happened with his band earlier didn't seem to have him in a negative state. He was emboldened as he pulled me under him, used one of the lube packs from The Condom Guy, who I had yet to meet, and he used his hands to get us both off, together.

We moved as one, breathed as one, and when we came, we cried out as one. I'd never been this close to another person before, either physically or emotionally, and while it was everything I'd never allowed myself to hope for, I couldn't shake the feeling that it could easily be taken away.

No matter how tightly I held onto Ryan, he may not turn out to be mine to hold.

"Soon we'll be away from tour buses," Ryan said, accentuating his point with kisses along my shoulder. "And I'll make love to you in a real bed without clothes on and with no place to be for days."

I looked around the space and smiled, stroking his back under his t-shirt. "At least we made it out of a bunk."

Ryan laughed softly, but his breathing had evened out and he was deep asleep in moments.

I, on the other hand, was wide awake.

I eased myself off the platform and was as quiet as I could be as I left the lounge and used the toilet. When I came out, I realized everyone was in their bunks asleep. The bus was rocking gently as the driver took us to our next destination, Cincinnati, Ohio.

I sat on the couch for a bit and looked out the window, watching the occasional road signs and lights, but it was mostly darkness. The driver took an exit off the highway and as he rounded a corner toward a large gas station, an orb of light flashed in my eyes.

I turned and rubbed them, as they were sensitive since I'd been in the dark for hours, but when I opened them, the orb was still there. It traveled slowly through the bus's front lounge, eventually stopping on the shelves next to the couch.

It landed on the box for the Ouija board.

My mother's family were indeed spiritualists. It was one of the bones of contention between her and my father, who felt it went against the church. I knew my mother had owned a board that she kept hidden from my father. I recalled seeing her use it at night when I was supposed to be asleep, or using it when her aunts and uncles came over. When Uncle Norman came, before he made his money and was too busy to travel.

Why were all of these memories coming to me now? It was as if my subconscious had been trying to work out the mysteries of my life while the rest of my brain was trying to keep up with living in this modern time and do a job I was learning as I went along.

The orb bobbed and slid across the box as I watched. I suppose the explanation could have been the wind blowing a tree branch in front of a streetlight, but there was something animated about this particular light.

Curious, I went over and pulled the box from the stack. I set the board up on the couch next to me and sighed. The driver had his curtain closed, there was no movement from the bunks, so I thought I would see what something, or someone, wanted me to see.

"Is it right… Sorry. I mean, am I meant to be here?"

I touched a finger to the planchette, but it didn't move.

"Who is here with me?"

The planchette moved under my finger. It vibrated with warm energy and swirled around the board. It landed on the word *Good*.

I hoped that meant someone with good intentions. I took a deep breath and asked the question I'd most been struggling with.

"What is my purpose?" Since I was having anxiety about this very topic, I figured it couldn't hurt to ask.

The planchette began to tremble and then slid slowly to the letters M-U-S-I-C-R-Y-A-N.

Goose bumps rose on my arm and across my torso as I gasped. This was such a specific message. I knew a lot of what was broadcast through Ouija boards was either random pieces of words traveling through the aether, or the person controlling the planchette's intentions. There were no clear answers, no way to determine the distinction between what was desired and what was real.

"I'm supposed to be here for him?"

*Yes.* No hesitation. No moving around, just a direct slide to the word *yes.*

I thought about what was holding me back from taking Ryan's hand and following him into the sunset once the tour was done. Why was I so afraid?

"What happened to my family?" I knew there was nothing I could have done, nothing I could do now to put them at peace, but until I knew my whole story, I wouldn't feel whole.

The planchette moved and stopped. Moved and stopped. H-U-N-G-R-Y it finally spelled out. Tears filled my eyes, and I gasped again. I needed to know, but there was such a feeling of dread welling up in my chest.

H-E-L-P

P-E-A-C-E

S-A-D

S-U-R-V-I-V-E

What did it all mean?

"Why did they never come back for me? How can I find out what happened? How can I honor them for trying to do right by me? How did this happen?" I put my head in my hands and tried to steady my breathing. I didn't want someone to find me sobbing over a Ouija board.

Scratching noises startled me, and I looked up. The planchette was moving of its own volition in a large figure eight on the board, and then it stopped for several seconds before going back to the letters.

M-U-S-C-A-T-I-N-E

*Right.* Mr. Ame had said to go to the address on my identification card if I needed answers.

But the planchette hadn't stopped.

F-O-R-T-U-N-A

"Do you mean fortune? What does that mean?"

H-O-M-E

I jumped as the bus driver put the bus in gear again, and it lurched forward. Home? Did that mean my fortune was at home? But whose home? I touched the planchette but it had gone cold. The bit of supernatural energy coursing through it was gone.

I ran my hand over the board, shocked to find a lingering warmth.

"It was the friction of the planchette." But I knew as I said it, it wasn't true. Someone had paid me a visit and given me some pertinent advice. I folded up the board and placed it carefully in the box before placing it on the shelf with the board games. I rubbed my shaking hands on my pants and made my way back to the lounge. I didn't want to wake Ryan, but I needed…closeness, I needed to hold him as my insides were trembling.

He'd shifted to the far edge of the platform bed and was curled up as if he were trying to keep warm. I curled up against his back and wrapped my arms around him, feeling him instantly relax.

"Don't go, Kal. Stay with me."

He spoke in his sleep, but to hear him say this wish aloud…after the visit I'd had? I wanted to do just that.

WE SLEPT ENTANGLED LIKE THAT, my body surrounding his. It was nice to have a little more room to stretch out, but I wanted this closeness. I dreamed of making a home for the two of us, sleeping like this every night.

When the sunlight filled the back of the bus the next morning, I started to roll onto my back with a smile on my face and—

"Mmm, ten minutes longer."

I opened my eyes to find Ryan's sleeping form in front of

me and realized it wasn't his voice. Something was keeping me from rolling over. *If not Ryan, then who?*

I looked over my shoulder and got a face full of Los's hair.

"This bed is community property, pretty boy."

I spit his hair out of my mouth and pushed myself up a little. I found him lying next to Silas, who had Krish half on top of him on the other half of the platform.

"Sorry guys," Krish said, his eyes still closed. "We made sure you were decent before we came in. Los had a nightmare."

"We all sleep together at our house in Oakland," Silas said with his face smashed against Krish's forehead. "Hope you don't mind."

Los rolled over and curled around my arm. "You make a good addition." He squeezed my bicep. "You make a good pillow."

Ryan leaned over me and brushed Los's hair back from his face. "As long as you remember he's mine, Morales. You can sleep with him, but that's it, and only if he consents."

"Do you consent?" Los asked me, still without opening his eyes.

"Yes?"

"Good." He threw a leg over me, and Ryan burst out laughing.

I turned to face Ryan, whose smile was infectious.

"Yours?" I whispered.

"Mine, baby." He kissed me, being sure to add in slurps and moans, which made me laugh. I pulled him on top of me, trapping Los's leg.

"Man, I just want ten more minutes to *sleep*." He pulled his pillow over his head and curled up in a ball, which led Silas to crawl on top of him and start tickling him.

"It's my turn to make breakfast," Krish said, sitting up. He pulled on a t-shirt and squeezed Silas's foot before getting up and leaving the back lounge.

"Need some help?" Ryan asked him.

Krish grinned and stretched. "Nah, it's yogurt and fruit. Nothing fancy. I don't have what I need to cook Indian breakfast. I'll try to pick some stuff up when we get to Detroit."

"I'd *love* that," Ryan said. "I'm happy to contribute toward the cause. I'm also famous for my cinnamon rolls made from scratch if you'd like me to take a morning."

"Oh please, that sounds scrumdidlyumptious," Silas said. "Make a list of what you need. We're going shopping."

"I can cook," I offered, but Silas had already closed the door, leaving Ryan and I alone…with Los.

"You can do a lot of things," Ryan said, kissing my neck. "Cook stuff, fix stuff, tune stuff, in fact, you're *really* good with your hands."

"I'll show you—"

"Still here, guys. And no, I don't like to watch." Los rolled away and tucked the pillow over his head tighter.

Ryan looked at him and then laughed, shaking his head. He smoothed my hair back and sighed. "I should go find my band. We've got to work out what we're gonna do for our set today." But his hands weren't ceasing their exploration of my body. He divested me of my shirt and was working on my pants when Los groaned and threw the pillow off of himself.

"Fine! Bone away, you pervs. God, way to get my day off to an *erect* start."

Ryan burst out laughing. "Thought you didn't like to watch?"

Los covered his eyes and stood from the bed, ran into the wall, and then peeked between his fingers to get to the door. "I can hear though. Damn. Carry on, ya heathens. I'm going to eat my yogurt and scones or whatever the fuck Krish is making." He said the last with an English accent before shutting the door behind him.

Ryan gazed down at me and waggled his eyebrows. "Well, since we have his permission, how about we continue our heathenry?"

He yanked my pants down and with his mouth, he made me see stars.

# CHAPTER 26

**Ryan**

Sure, I might have been postponing dealing with things by staying in bed with Kal, but I wanted a little more time in our cocoon of safety and…love.

Oh, Cassandra and Robin were going to have a field day when I told them about Kal.

That weekend we'd gone on a bender, the two of them had a lot to say about my love life.

*"You know we love Gavin like he's our own son," Cassandra said. "But he was not the one for you."*

*"My darling, you were in love with* idea *of Gavin, not the real Gavin with all of his quirks. You are a survivor." Robin poured us all more of whatever concoction she'd put together. Lots of sweet and alcohol and mind-numbing goodness.*

*"But how am I ever going to know, you know, whether someone will love me for me or for what I can do for them, who I am?"*

*"You definitely have the dramatic side like Gavin did,"*

*Cassandra said, rolling her eyes. "Ryan you're, what, twenty-eight years old? Give the Fates a little time to place the right one in front of you."*

*"What if she's already in front of me," I asked Cassandra, feeling a bit full of myself, and we all know how that tended to turn out. I waggled my eyebrows at her and she laughed.*

*Robin groaned while Cassandra brushed my hair back from my face.*

*"If you weren't already meant for someone else, I'd take you up on that suggestion, but I do have a sense of self-preservation and I'm trusting my divination that there's someone waiting for me."*

*"Ugh, Cassandra, you need to quit pawing our guest. Here's the deal, Ryan, you need to quit looking. You need to keep working your steps—well, after you sober up. God, we're bad influences. Heal yourself, and be ready to offer something to someone, because this person the Fates will send you is going to need you. Specifically you. You're going to have to be strong enough for both of you. Help them find their path, and they will walk with you on yours."*

All of the conversations I'd had with Kal, everything that had happened up to this point…I couldn't help but wonder. Were those witches for real? Did they know what I'd been up to? I needed to call them. Soon.

I returned to the Backdrop bus and went inside to find the band in the middle of a meeting. Without me.

"Good morning." I walked in and felt their eyes boring into me. "How are you all feeling?"

TJ and Oscar grumbled, Burke and Patrick said, "Okay."

After a few more attempts at conversation, we eventually turned to the topic at hand.

"Anything we need to change for today's set?"

TJ snorted. "Well, we ain't doing that soft rock America shit."

I opened my mouth to say something but then I thought, *no. He's not going be my problem much longer.*

"I think we'll be fine, thank you, Ryan." Parker nodded at me as if he knew I'd held back. We discussed specifics, and then TJ and Oscar left the bus.

"I told Burke about our conversation," Parker said.

Burke nodded. "It's cool. I'm tired of performing anyway. I thought it was what I wanted, I did. But honestly, making music is the best part of the process for me, and if I can get my studio going…I think I'll be good."

"That's great. I'm happy for you, Burke. You're going to be great."

He nodded and looked down at his coffee cup.

"Yeah, so if we can keep it together for the next three-ish weeks? I'll put a call in to our lawyer and see what we need to do."

I swallowed hard. "Uh, yeah, okay. Whatever you need me to do."

Parker and Burke nodded but were avoiding eye contact. This was awkward. Worse than any breakup I'd ever experienced. There was nothing to say. None of us wanted to save what had brought us all a good deal of money and notoriety. We weren't the biggest band out there in our genre, but we'd had a few massive hits that defined an era. No one would forget us, at least no one who listened to any type of hard rock music, but we weren't immune from becoming one of those "whatever happened to" sob stories.

Well that wasn't going to be my fate. I wasn't done making music, and as soon as Backdrop Silhouette was in my rearview, Ryan Wells was going to reinvent himself, starting with the music I wrote with Gavin.

And I was going to make sure that my new muse, Kallos Alexandrou, and I were on a path together. Somehow.

Our set was mid-afternoon, which gave me plenty of time to get my exercise in, give my therapist a call, and leave a message for my sponsor. One foot in front of the other.

Following my path. My path to...well, my path out of the nightmare. The *Groundhog Day* of band drama was coming to an end, and I couldn't wait.

I started to put my makeup on, but I realized I hadn't worn it the past few performances. I'd felt okay without it, so I left it off. And I dressed in black dress pants, my patent leather loafers, and a black embroidered dress shirt that had a bit of a '50s vibe. I felt different, so why not reflect that? We didn't have a damned dress code, not since the early days.

Fuck it. I was comfortable.

I got to the stage early enough to spend a few minutes with Kal during the set before ours. His smile was bright when he greeted me.

"I like this," he said, fingering my collar I'd left open by a few buttons. Then his gaze dropped to my slacks and his lips twitched.

"I like you liking this."

Kal's cheeks got red but he still pulled me in for a quick kiss.

"I have to watch the board. I'm afraid my fix won't hold." Then his gaze seared me. "I'm going to see you later." It sounded like a threat, and I got a semi just thinking about what we might get up to. I didn't even care if we ended up sleeping with the whole fucking Hush brotherhood.

Then the band before us finished and Kal winked at me from behind the board. The rest of the stagehands began their flurry of work getting our stuff set up. I did some stretches, enjoying the way my slacks had more give to them than the leathers. And my loafers were much lighter than my heavy boots. Kind of like my soul right about now.

"Okay, Frank Sinatra," Oscar snorted. "Where's your fedora?"

TJ laughed at me, and for a split second the unstable Ryan

almost reared his ugly head, but I let it go. *Let them ridicule me.*

Then I got a load of the crowd through a gap in the fence. And the signs.

There were kids holding signs that said things like "Ryan is Magic" and "Wells For President," and my favorite, "Back-TWAT Silhouette." I was laughing my ass off when Parker walked up.

"What's so funny?"

I jerked around and lost a bit of my exuberance.

"Oh, just, some creative signage out there. You good, man? You have enough to drink today?"

"I'm fine," Parker said, shaking his head at the crowd. "You ready?"

"Yeah. Let's do this."

He gave me an incredulous look, shoved a set of sticks in his back pocket and went over to the stairs to stand with TJ and Oscar, who did not look enthusiastic about our impending set.

*Shit.*

They went out onstage and started the set with the usual intro, but when I walked onstage and started singing, the screams were deafening. I paused mid-stage and smiled, throwing off the song. I waved to the crowd—the biggest I'd ever seen at a Warped Tour. Man, the kids were sitting on top of the fences lining the performance area, they were smashed against the barrier even at the beginning of our set. There was more security than usual, and the stagehands, including Kal, were all helping to pull kids over who were getting crushed.

"Wells, what the fuck?" TJ bumped me with his shoulder. "Pick up the song!"

I glanced at him and made a mea culpa face before turning back to the crowd and picking up the lyrics. I went from one side of the stage to the next, waving at and pointing to the kids with signs, giving them the horns.

I'd never, ever felt such love from a crowd, and my heart was bursting. I wanted to sing my heart out for them, more than I'd ever wanted before. I couldn't believe I'd ever treated this like a job, like these people owed me anything.

I was in love. True love. It was better than sex, better than drugs, better than walking out of prison after a year and a half. It was the best thing that had ever happened to me, and I wanted to spend the rest of my life showing gratitude for this blessing.

I floated through the set, pushing myself to perform my best. I stepped down into the walkway in front of the stage and shook hands with as many people as I could while I sang, signed some shirts, took selfies with folks, and had a blast, all without missing a beat. Gone was my cocky, slutty, grabbing-my-cock onstage persona. I'd thought I'd needed that.

Word must have gotten around about my solo performances because in between songs, people chanted things like "Ma-gic Ma-gic Ma-gic" and "Bea-stie Boys" and "Si-las Si-las." I kind of forgot about the sections when Burke played his solos and continued schmoozing with the crowd. I was having too much fun, damn the consequences.

I decided to do a little damage control in between our last two songs, and I introduced the band. I hadn't done that in a long time, and they all looked a little surprised, but I wanted to make a point. We were a band. I was not a solo artist. Yet.

Then it was over, and the crowd kept screaming my name. The band came forward to wave, and we usually took a bow together, but they fucking walked offstage and left me alone.

I dreaded taking the steps down to the backstage area. Kal gave my hand a squeeze as I passed him, his expression serious, and he had the protective forehead crinkle going on.

I loved this man.

And I loved Ryan Wells, and that was what fueled me forward.

"Nice fucking Ryan Wells love fest out there. You have that planned with your fucking groupies?"

"Great set, TJ," I said, ignoring his comments. "Thank you."

"Fuck you," Oscar said, getting in my face.

I stepped back and held up my hands. "You need anything from me? Otherwise, I'll see you guys tomorrow."

Oscar's eyes flared—and he went for it. He shoved me hard in the chest. So hard, I stumbled over my feet and fell against a cabinet, landing on my ribs, taking my breath away. I'd been relaxed and floating on such a cloud, I hadn't been ready.

I sprang to my feet, in shock, but before I could get balanced, Oscar clocked me in the mouth so hard, I spit blood like a fucking movie special effect, and it sprayed on Burke's clothes.

"Shit, not here, dumbass!" TJ said, trying to pull Oscar back, but he was fuming like some sort of raging bull. He shoved TJ aside, and I barely had time to put a hand up to block another face shot before he landed a punch to the ribs that I'd just fallen on.

Then Oscar flew backwards and went sprawling over the back of a park bench.

The shouting started, and I looked up to find Kal standing over me, blocking anyone else from touching me. A crowd of people came forward and from my spot on the ground, I saw Brains and Parker shouting at each other, Jordan pushing Burke, Los and Silas going after TJ and Oscar—

I tried to shout but I couldn't get any air in.

A voice boomed over the area as I collapsed against the fence.

"Enough! Knock it the fuck off!"

Howie stood at the top of the steps with his hands on his hips.

Kal reached to pull me up, but my side hurt so bad, I held up a finger for him to wait. I was bleeding steadily from my mouth, and I had such a fucking headache. I'd forgotten what it felt like to get my bell rung. I'd been careful to avoid getting hit for so long.

A couple of security guys showed up and escorted my band back to their bus, while I sat there trying to figure out what the hell had happened.

"Ryan, are you okay?" Chantal was there. "Let this medic take a look at you."

I wanted to protest but I was spitting blood and bits of teeth. Thankfully I wasn't expected to speak because I was seriously shook.

Kal was explaining what happened to Chantal, and more security were talking to the guys from Hush. I tried to make my thoughts form a coherent pipeline.

Backdrop Silhouette was done.

I'd managed to not be the one to destroy it, at least not by doing something even stupider than my previous stupidity.

I had no idea what would happen next, but relief coursed through me, easing some of the pain.

"You need to get checked out, Ryan," Chantal was still saying. "The medic thinks you've got rib fractures and you're going to need to see an emergency dentist."

"In fucking Cincinnati? I think not." It hurt to talk, hurt worse to cough, and I was struggling to breathe normally.

She put a hand on my shoulder and leaned closer. "I'm telling you this, but it's not for public knowledge yet. Management is *furious*. TJ and Oscar have been making comments to the media about changes coming to your band and their frustration with the decision to have you perform when the band was out sick. You have done everything we've asked you to, Ryan, and Warped is indebted to you. I don't want you to worry about anything—"

"But we're off the tour, huh?"

She nodded with her lips pressed together.

"Good," I said, and I meant it. I hated that we'd be the laughingstock of our metalcore community, but I couldn't care anymore. "My mental health comes first." I hadn't meant to say the last aloud, but I had to remember that.

"Come on, let's get you to the hospital, okay? You need anything off Backdrop's bus? Because they're out of here. We won't have that shit on tour."

"I don't blame you. Yeah, if you don't mind, Parker or Burke will know where my shit is. Wait. Can I talk to Kal first?"

She smiled. "Yes. I figured he'd want to go with you to the hospital."

I nodded and smiled as she squeezed my arm gently. She stood and made room for Kal.

"Hey." I reached up to smooth his forehead crinkle away but my hands were covered with blood. His face was beet red and his jaw was twitching as if he was trying really hard not to tear some fucking guys limb from limb. "I'm okay."

"No you're not. I'm sorry." His eyes filled with tears, and he blinked them away and blew out a breath.

"This isn't on you, babe," I said, wishing I could touch him. "It was a matter of time. Listen, I'm going to go to the hospital, but you're needed here."

Kal's eyes flared, and he swallowed hard. "I want to go with you. Keep you safe."

"I know, and I want you there. But you're needed here. Let me go get checked out and I'll meet you back on Hush's bus tonight, okay?"

"Ry-an…"

"I know. I do." I wanted to tell him I loved him, that I was strong enough to do this, but that I desperately wanted him to never stop holding my hand. "I'm trying to be strong," I whispered. "But any second I might start crying like a baby and I don't want anyone else to see that, okay? I got a rep to protect." I winked at him, and then sucked in a breath when I smiled and my jaw protested. "I'll see you soon, babe."

He took my hand, even though I tried to keep it away from him, and pressed our foreheads together. "I'll wait for you."

"Please. I'm coming back to you, I promise."

"Mr. Wells, we need to take you in."

Paramedics had brought the fucking ambulance around and were waiting with their gurney.

"Ah, man. Can't I take a Lyft or something? Do you even have Lyft in Ohio?"

The female paramedic rolled her eyes at me. "Management insists. Guess they don't want to get sued by a pretty boy who got his ass kicked."

I barked out a laugh, which hurt and made me have to count to ten before I could get back to smart-assery. "Rawr. You think I'm pretty, huh?"

Kal helped me up and the paramedics took over, hoisting me onto the gurney.

My heart broke when I looked back at his face. But thankfully Krish stood with him, one hand on his back. I knew Hush would take care of him.

He would be okay.

Now it was time for me to get okay.

# CHAPTER 27

**Kal**

Ryan didn't come back that night.

In fact, he didn't return to the tour.

He called from the hospital to say he needed to get back to California to see his dentist or else he might lose some teeth. I was livid to discover he also had two broken ribs and a bruised lung. It was a good thing that Oscar person was no longer on the tour, or he wouldn't be breathing any longer.

"I'll miss you, baby," Ryan said. "I'll find a way to get back to you soon, okay?"

But once he returned to California, his troubles multiplied. In addition to dental appointments and being in a lot of pain from his broken ribs, there were meetings with his attorney, his parole officer, and a court appearance. He decided to sell his house to cover his expenses after losing out on the revenue from the tour and the band breaking their contract with the label, leaving him temporarily without a home. He didn't want to be anywhere near them, wanted to cut all ties.

We talked every night he was gone, but the longer he stayed away, the less it seemed likely he'd be back in my arms anytime soon.

The tour replaced Backdrop Silhouette with one of the bands from a smaller stage who'd consistently been bringing in big crowds and who'd had a hit song that summer. There was talk of having Ryan travel with Hush—the band didn't want him alone—but he said he wasn't allowed to leave California because of his parole, though he had a date set in the new year to be released from his parole obligations. The fact that he hadn't fought back when his bandmate attacked him led his parole officer to recommend he be excused. It was good news, but it seemed so far off.

Hush asked me to stay with them and offered me a contract of employment to start after Warped was over, as well as an apartment to rent in their building in Oakland, California. I needed to work, and I liked the guys in the band a lot. It made the most sense for me. I decided to mention it to Ryan and see what he thought.

"It's a good gig, and you'll get to visit Europe." His words were encouraging, but his expression on FaceTime was forlorn.

"They said we'll be back in time for the holidays."

"By then, I'll have my own place, maybe up here in Fortuna—"

"Fortuna?" My run-in with the Ouija board flashed before my eyes. Wasn't that part of my purpose? But I had to know…

"Yeah, with Gavin's aunts. They invited me to stay, rent a cottage on their property. But Kal, you need to do what's best for you. It's not fair of me to—"

"I miss you," I said.

He exhaled a harsh breath into the phone. "I miss you. So much. We were just getting started, you know? At least that's how *I* felt."

"We *are*," I reassured him. "And we will continue. I have two weeks in between Warped and when we leave for Europe." I paused, unsure what Ryan's reaction would be. I'd thought long and hard about what I should do, though there really was only one scenario that would make it possible for me to have some sort of normal life.

"You could come here. The cottage is small, but it's mine, and they can't wait to meet you."

I blew out a breath. "I'm going to Iowa."

Ryan was quiet. "To Muscatine? Oh, Kal, why? I didn't think there was anything left there for you."

"I still only remember parts of my life. I need to know what happened to my family after they left me, and what happened to my uncle after he left me for dead. I need to close that door."

He nodded and chewed on a nail. "I know it's important to you, but Kal, those people… Just know, *I* wouldn't leave you. I won't. I'd bring you here right now and keep you safe."

"I want that, too. But I have to know."

"I know you do, and I know you want to do it alone. Know that my heart is with you, wherever you go. And parole or not, Kal, if you need me I'll be on the next flight out of here."

I smiled at him and touched the screen, wishing I could touch his face.

"You have my heart. Wherever you are, Ry-an."

Los whipped open the curtain on my bunk and his eyes went wide.

"Oh, dude, sorry. I didn't know you were on the phone. Hey, Ryan!"

Ryan wiped at his eyes and gave a tired smile. "S'up, Morales."

"I'm gonna borrow your boyfriend later for a pillow."

"Fuck off, Morales," but there was no venom behind it. "Find your own pillow."

Los laughed. "I'm just kidding, but I am going to borrow him. I have some stuff I want to record and my pinche four-track isn't working."

"I'll help you," I said to Los, and then I pulled the curtain out of his hand and shut it. "In a few minutes."

"Are you guys gonna have phone sex? Because damn. I'll have to put in my earbuds—"

"Are you bothering Kal?" I heard Silas smack Los in the back of the head and Los's patented "ow." This was such a common occurrence on the bus. "Leave him alone, dude."

"My boyfriend, huh?" Ryan had a sly smile now. "You good with that?"

I smiled and nodded. "It's what I want."

"Good. Don't forget it."

THE TOUR ENDED in Florida on August 5th and the next day I climbed onto another bus bound for Iowa. Krish and Silas tried to convince me to fly on an airplane, but I wasn't ready for that much modern technology. At least not by myself. The bus had been tough enough to get used to, though I knew I'd have to fly with the band when they went to Europe. Silas and Krish had rented a car and planned to drive back to California together after soaking up the sun for a few days, so they drove me to the Greyhound bus station after loading me up with snacks.

"You sure you're going to be okay?" Krish asked. I was so lucky to have met him. I wasn't sure how to tell him how much his looking after me meant.

"I am. I'm worried about Ryan."

Silas patted my shoulder. "Me too, but don't worry. We'll call and check up on him. He's with Gavin's aunts. They'll look after him. You guys will be back together before you know it."

I wanted to believe Silas's prediction.

Krish told me to let him know when I was ready to come to Oakland, and they'd help me with transportation. It was good to have friends like Hush. *Family* like them.

It took me two days on the bus, with only a few stops to use the bathroom and grab food, to reach Muscatine. My body was stiff and sore in the worst way as I climbed down the steps for the last time. I had no desire to be on a bus again for a long time, but the minute I left the bus station, I knew I didn't want to stay in this town.

Krish had shown me how to use the maps application on my smartphone before we parted. I was grateful he hadn't ever asked me why I didn't know how to do what seemed to be so simple for everyone else. I plugged in the address on my identification card and I started walking.

I soon realized why most people preferred to drive. I would have to learn how eventually, because walking in the heat and humidity of an Iowa summer afternoon was not advisable. I only vaguely remembered what the heat felt like from my youth spent in this area.

The walk took me an hour and when I arrived at 103 West Seventh Street, I was greeted with an unfamiliar two-story brick house. The street was quiet but looked a lot like it probably had when I was young, the only difference from the 1930s was the asphalt and the modern automobiles. I stood out front of the house wondering why, of all places, this was the address Mr. Ame had included on my identification card.

An elderly woman came out from the side yard, walking

carefully and dragging a bag of garbage behind her to a large black can.

"Would you like some help?" I asked, springing into action. It was way too hot for her to be doing work outside at her age, despite the fact that she was a tall and solidly built woman.

"Sure I would. Thank you."

I dropped my duffel bag near the porch and hurried to her side to take the garbage from her. It couldn't have weighed more than a few pounds, but she'd been struggling.

"Place it in the black can, would you? I have a hard time with my right hand after having a stroke last year, and the left just doesn't have the strength it used to. Thank you."

I put the bag in the can and turned to smile at her.

And saw my eyes looking back at me.

She noticed the same thing.

"As of my last doctor's appointment, I've got some stroke damage, mild kidney disease, and my cholesterol is a little high, but there's nothing wrong with my eyes, nor my mental fitness. You hear what I'm saying?"

I nodded slowly.

She held out a hand. "Ellen Alexander, and you are?"

A FEW MINUTES LATER, I found myself sitting at her kitchen table with a glass of lemonade in front of me.

"Suppose I believe you *are* my brother Cal, which, I mean, I've heard wilder notions...what proof have you got?

I opened up that place in my mind that had been the source of the pain that came with each memory I regained.

"The morning Father and I left to walk from Nauvoo to Muscatine, you gave me a paper bag. You told me not to open it until I got to Uncle Norman's." I swallowed back a sob. "It was the paper doll set I'd made for you, one for each member of our family. You'd made a little cradle for Zachariah out of some leaves and it fell apart on the walk over. I kept that paper bag in my room and took you all out to speak to when I missed you. You never spoke back, though."

Ellen put her hands over her face and when she pulled them away, she placed one over mine resting on the table.

"I used to sneak out of my room at night and stand under the stars to talk to you. Father caught me once and started to scold me, but then he sat beside me, and we had a grand time trying to figure out what your life with Uncle Norman was like."

She squeezed my hand. "We didn't get word until years later that Uncle Norman went to Arkansas. The authorities told us that everyone who worked for him was killed in a fire, a fire that was set to hide the crimes of the townsfolk, but there was no death certificate for you. No remains. Couldn't be too angry with them. Uncle Norman never told those people that their family members died in his care and he buried them in a pit out in the middle of a cornfield behind the clinic. They found dozens of bodies there."

"I swear," I said to her, my voice barely above a whisper. "I didn't know. All I did was help in the kitchen and play piano at mealtimes or whenever Uncle Norman said to."

"I know. Mother wrote to you, wrote to him, but we never heard anything from you. She figured it was because of the troubles, you know. That the mail wasn't getting through. It made her despondent. She did the best she could for us, but she was never the same after you left. She took on sewing work, cleaning houses, whatever she could to keep us fed. Father had to leave us to work in Chicago, but he sent her every dime he could. Two years into the war, he could finally come home, but they were never themselves again." She placed a hand on my cheek. "They missed you so. They felt terribly guilty."

"I wish they wouldn't have. I was grown by then. I needed to be out there contributing to the family. But I never received Mother's letters."

"I figured. You weren't one to ignore your family."

I knew I needed to get this over with. "What happened to them?"

Her smile turned down at the corners. "Father died in 1951, and Mother in 1954. Both peacefully in their sleep. Zachariah joined the military as an officer after college. He died in the early years of the Vietnam conflict."

"I'm so sorry. You lost everyone."

She smiled. "I had a good life. I missed my family, but I learned to surround myself with good people. That's why I took in boarders. I've never been alone that wasn't my choice."

I had one other question, though I wasn't sure if she knew. "Uncle Norman told me once that Father had lied about his past and tricked Mother into marrying him."

"Aha. That was the family rumor. Our father did keep his past secret, but I was able to find out after he passed. He came from Greece. Our real family surname is Alexandrou. It was common for people coming from Eastern Europe to Anglicize their names to avoid problems in America. Such hatred for those who are different. I wish that was no more, but it's still a fact of life for many people in this country. To answer your query, yes, Father did conceal his past, but I believe Mother knew. They were so close. I don't believe he kept secrets from her. And she married him because she loved him desperately."

"I believe that. They held each other in such high regard… What about you? Ellen, did you marry for love?"

She inhaled and raised her eyebrows. "I moved back here

and met my husband after going to nursing school in Chicago. I wanted to be here in case you came back."

"Oh, Ellen…"

"It was the right thing to do. And yes, I did love my husband. He was good to me for many years. We talked about moving away a few times, but I insisted we stay. I didn't want you to think we forgot about you."

A few tears slipped out before I could compose myself, but she patted my hand.

"Times have changed, Cal. Even big boys can cry."

"It's Kal, now. Kallos. I think it suits me better."

"I think so too. Kal."

Through her wrinkled skin and her frail frame, the spark that made my parents work to keep her out of mischief shined brightly. I was grateful I'd made this trip for whatever time I could have with my sister.

We talked for hours, eventually turning on the lights after the sun went down. I cooked dinner for her, which she told me I didn't need to do, and when she couldn't keep her eyes open any longer, she showed me to a bedroom.

"Are you sure you're comfortable with me here? I'm happy to go to a hotel."

She rolled her eyes. "Kal," she said. "I had boarders for years after my husband left me. I've lived here alone for at least the last ten. I keep a shotgun under my bed and I sleep with one eye open." She squeezed my arm. "But more than that, you have our father's forehead crinkle and the same mole on your neck that you always had. I know it's you."

I smiled. "You used to always try to pull it off. Hurt like the devil."

"Get some sleep, Brother."

. . .

The next morning, my phone was buzzing on the nightstand and I nearly fell out of bed trying to catch it before it fell to the floor.

"Ryan! I'm sorry—"

"Please tell me you're all right." His voice was calm and other than looking sleep-rumpled, he seemed okay.

"I am. Ryan…I found my sister."

His expression melted into such a warm smile. "Tell me everything."

"I know I promised I would call you when I got here—"

"It's okay. When you didn't, like the stalker I am, I used an app that lets me track your location. I swear I only used it to make sure you were okay. When I saw that you were at the address on your identification—yeah, I snooped in your wallet—I figured you must have found something, or someone you knew."

"I didn't know *what* I was going to find. Mr. Ame at the carnival, he gave me the card but all he said was that I would find answers here."

"And you did. That's great. I can't wait to hear about her."

"I will tell you everything, but how are you?"

He shrugged. "I'm okay. I don't want to keep you. I just wanted to hear your voice and see that you're in one piece. Call me later?"

He seemed off, but I heard Ellen shuffling down the hall outside my bedroom, and I had an idea.

"Hang on a second. I want to introduce you to her."

I set the phone down on the bedside table, pulled on my soft pants, and finger combed my hair before opening the door.

Ellen was dressed and carrying a cup of coffee. "Good morning. Did you sleep okay?"

"I did. Ellen, I'd like for you to meet my boyfriend."

Her smile was confused, and I knew she would have

questions, but I wanted the two people I loved most in this world to meet, even if it was only on a small screen.

"Oh, all right then. Is my hair all right?"

I held up a finger and darted back over to the bedside table to pick up the phone, where Ryan was still smiling at me.

"Ryan Wells, meet my sister, Ellen…"

Ellen took the phone from me and smiled into the camera. "It's Brown now. Ellen Alexander Brown. Nice to meet you."

# CHAPTER 28

**Ryan**

Whatever I was expecting when Kal's sister picked up the phone, it was not a ninety-year-old woman. I put on my best smile, but inside I was freaking out.

"It's lovely to meet you, Mrs. Brown."

She smiled kindly at me and then lovingly at Kal. "Wonderful to meet you, too. I can't wait to hear about how the two of you met. Kal, dear, I'm going to go make some breakfast."

"I'll be down to help in a minute."

*What the fuck is happening?*

"I can't believe she was here. I had no idea what I would find."

"Um, Kal? I thought you said Ellen was your *younger* sister."

My beautiful man—his expression fell, and the sad look

he gave me when I walked away from him the first time was back.

"Ryan, do you remember when you said you didn't care who I was before? That you liked the now me?"

"Of course I do."

"And when I told you that I was with the carnival for one year?" I nodded, and Kal took a deep breath before he spoke again. "That year started in nineteen thirty-three."

I opened my mouth to speak and closed it again. *Come again?*

"I told you my family left me with my uncle, and you didn't understand why. It was the Depression. My family was starving, and I was another mouth to feed. My uncle told them he would give me a job in his new business, and I told him to send all of my paychecks to my parents, only...he didn't do that. And he didn't give me any of their letters. Ellen was six years old when I left home. I was sixteen. I worked for him for four years before...before he left me at the hands of an angry mob, only returning to find the others who worked for him dead, and me, well, near death. He left me with Mr. Ame. That's all Mr. Ame would tell me."

"But Kal...you said you were twenty-one. If this is true, you're—"

He exhaled a long breath and nodded before looking away from the screen. "I understand, Ryan. It's okay. Thank you...for everything—"

"Wait! Kal! Don't hang up. Help me understand."

"How can I do that when *I* don't understand it either?"

We stared at each other, the thousands of miles between us seeming two small a number as I thought about this distance. Was he mentally ill? Had I chosen to ignore the signs? Because if I were to actually believe him, that he was over a hundred years old, what did that say about my mental state? This wasn't possible!

"I've got to hang up now. I'll leave it up to you if you want to speak to me again."

"Wait! Baby—"

"Goodbye, Ryan."

His face disappeared.

"No! No, no, no, dammit!" I pressed my fists against my forehead and took a few deep breaths. What the fuck was happening?

I broke out in a cold sweat and my legs decided that gravity was a fun thing to play with, giving out and landing me on my ass, which made my still-healing ribs scream. I held the phone in both hands, trying to figure out what to do, when there was a knock on my cottage door.

"Rye? Honey, it's Robin." She opened the door and came inside.

"What? Did you feel a disturbance in the force?"

"Don't pull that shit with me, pretty boy. But yes, I knew something was wrong. What can I do?"

I laughed. Of all the people I could have called at this moment… My therapist would have said, "Ryan, it's time to talk about medication, maybe an inpatient treatment center." My sponsor would have said, "Sweetheart, it's bound to happen, falling off the wagon, but hallucinogenics are not the way to go." But thankfully I was with the two women who might have an actual clue as to what kind of fuckery was going on.

"I'm gonna need…something that isn't booze or drugs, because I feel like I'm in the motherfucking *Twilight Zone* right now and I just broke my damn glasses."

Robin tapped her fingers on the doorjamb and then nodded once. "This calls for cinnamon rolls."

Exasperated, I dropped my hands to the floor. "But I can make those on my own."

She winked at me. "And who taught you how to make

them, darling? Come on. I'll make my special tea you like and we'll get Cassandra out of her sewing room. I think this is going to take both of us."

She pulled me up from the floor where I'd collapsed in my SpongeBob pajama pants and dragged me out of my cottage, through their overgrown garden, and into the sunroom on the back of the house.

"Cassandra! Get down here," Robin shouted. "We need you."

She plopped me down at the table, pulled a tub out of the fridge and flopped it on her counter in a pile of flour that was already sitting there. When I gave her a puzzled look, she grabbed her rolling pin and pointed it at me.

"Told you. Something was off this morning."

Cassandra came flying down the stairs and slid into the archway from the dining room.

"Is it time?"

"What the fuck?"

Robin got to rolling the dough. "Yes it is, Sister Mine. Make us some of the clarity blend and add in some of the lion's mane extract with the citrus-infused honey."

"I'm on it."

"Will one of you…oh come on, I'm trying so hard not to use those words."

"Crazy? Batshit? Yes, remove them from your vocabulary, my darling," Cassandra said. "As someone who is under the care of a mental health professional, I would think you'd know to be more sensitive by now."

"But how else can I describe this current level of ludicrousity?" I dropped my head onto my arms on the table, feeling as if my skin was covered with biting ants. Everything hurt, especially my wildly overtaxed brain, and my stomach was off.

"Start from the beginning."

I blew out a breath and sat upright, albeit slouched like an insouciant teenager. "Kal was playing an organ in the staging area. I'd never seen him before, so I went over to find out why he was touching Roxanne's stuff, but then he looked at me…and when I touched him, holy cow, it was like the world got knocked off its axis, you know? Or like when you're getting your eyes checked and they flick the little wheels until all of a sudden everything is crystal clear like you've never seen it before."

"Mmm-hmm, go on," Robin said, then she whisper-shouted at Cassandra. "The tea! Hurry up!"

The Beaumonts' house was organized chaos on a good day. There were always random books lying around, bundles of dried herbs, candles, and that wasn't even including the supplies for Cassandra's various sewing projects—she made felt dolls that she sold on Etsy and at a local metaphysical store. She also did blends of essential oils, made spell candles, and sewed gorgeous flowy dresses. Creation was Cassandra's gig, and if she wasn't creating something, she was a mess.

Robin, on the other hand, had had a law practice in town for many years, but sold it and now only did occasional consulting work to pay the few bills they had. Gavin had long ago paid off their property, which included a large Craftsman-style house with two cottages and a large detached garage and greenhouse, where Robin spent most of her time.

Gavin's mother had been the straight-laced one in the family and turned her back on the Beaumonts' occult-based practices. When Gavin learned the truth about the Beaumont sisters, he fell in love with his aunts and the life they lived. At sixty and fifty-eight, Robin and Cassandra had a great life. They took no shit from anyone and were kind and generous to me and the guys in Hush. While I hated being so far away from Kal—and so damned far from a major airport—I knew their home was the perfect place for me to recuperate. There were healing vibes here that came from the lush redwood forests and permeated the walls of Beaumont Manor.

Cassandra placed a hand-made ceramic mug in front of me that smelled...kind of gross, but I didn't care. Whatever I consumed in their kitchen was bound to be good for me. They'd long ago removed the alcohol from sight. I knew they still had it for their spell work and rituals, but I knew better than to snoop.

"Thank you," I said, taking a slow sip, immediately feeling more at ease. The buzzing on my skin dissipated and I felt like oxygen was finally traveling to all of my cells.

"We hit it off. I tried to push him away, figuring my bullshit would tarnish anyone else who chose to walk on the path with me—"

"Wait a minute, did you say walk on the path?"

"Yeah. You know. The path I'm on? My life? But we kept getting thrown together. First he was working at my stage, then we ran into each other at lunch, and then Silas and Krish practically played matchmaker, making me come with them and Kal to thc carnival that was on the same grounds as the festival."

"A carnival, you say?" Robin stopped rolling the dough and turned to face me. She had flour all over her sporty black dress and some smudged on her cheek. Her silver-streaked honey-colored hair was pulled up in a messy bun. "Tell me what you remember about the entrance."

"The entrance?" I thought for a minute. "I'm not sure. It was one of those old-timey carnivals, like one I went to when I was a kid. It had one of those big-top kind of banners on it. Something about wanderers...no. Travelers. 'Welcome, Traveler.'"

Cassandra put a hand on my arm but she looked up at her big sister with hopeful eyes. "Do you think?"

Robin sat down on the other side of me. "Tell us the rest."

So I did. I told them the whole story, leaving nothing out. About his memory loss and how he seemed out of place, from another time. I told them about our first kiss, grateful to finally be getting this out of my head. It felt more real as I spoke, but then I remembered some of the awkward moments.

"We used Gavin's Ouija board because he was having trouble speaking at first, but then, it all seemed to come back to him. He could talk, he told me about his uncle and some cancer place…he said his uncle did bad things to people with cancer. I figured maybe he ran a home or something and did some unethical shit. Kal was so worried I was going to not want him anymore if I knew the truth about his past, but I didn't care. I still don't, but… How could I have ignored the signs? What if he really is mentally ill, and I led him on and then left him?"

"Drink more of the tea, you're not making sense. What do you mean, mentally ill?"

"He thinks he's from the nineteen-thirties! He put his sister on the phone with me this morning, his *little* sister, and she was an old lady! Like pushing a century old!"

They looked to each other and something unspoken passed between them.

"Ryan?" Robin finally said. "Do you trust us? Like, are you willing to go someplace you'll feel a little out of control, out of your element?"

"I mean, yeah. Why not? All I've got to lose is the man I'm totally in love with and my freedom, probably, because if I go telling anyone else about this, my parole officer is going to reconsider my release."

Robin put her hand on mine and patted it like she would a child. "Dial down the drama, Wells. This will all make sense in a minute. Go get the Ouija board and bring it here."

I moved my hand from under hers. "I don't have it. Silas had it on their bus, I'm assuming it's back at their place—"

"It's in your bag, go get it." She leaned back and began picking dough out from under her fingernails.

"Look, Robin, I don't mean to be—"

"Rude much? Yeah, whatever, go get the board."

Robin had always been no-nonsense, but I'd never seen her angry or frustrated before and I didn't want to be the cause of it. Little Ryan had a moment of tail-between-the-legs as he stood from the table and hurried out the door to his cottage to appease the woman who meant so much to him.

"Okay, lady," I muttered to myself as I pulled my duffel bag out from under the bed. "Don't believe me? Well here—"

As I unzipped the bag, the Ouija box appeared on top of my performance clothes, which I didn't want to look at again for a long while.

The board. Was in my bag. *How in the fuck?*

I carried it back to the house and into the kitchen in a daze and set it down on the table.

"There it is. This board goes where it's needed, Ryan. I knew after you said you two had used it together that it was here. Now, get it set up. We're going to show you the truth."

But instead of us using the planchette to contact spirits or get answers, Robin had me place my hands on the planchette alone.

"I want you to move the planchette in a figure eight around the board. A light touch is fine, relax your arms, there you go. Breathe in a count of three, hold a count of three, then breathe out a count of three, there you go. Around and around, try to relax your whole body. That's good."

I focused on her voice, my breath, and the movement of the planchette. My vision began to blur and soon, instead of seeing the planchette, there was a pool of swirling colors, and from those colors, an image appeared.

The calliope from the carnival. A much younger Robin and Cassandra stood watching as a man with blond hair played song after song. On a calliaphone. Just like Kal's.

"He's wonderful," Cassandra said to Robin. "I love this music."

"He *is* wonderful. We are lucky to have him."

The man who spoke stood beside Cassandra in a top hat and finery. Like a circus ringmaster. He bowed to them. "Forgive me, I overheard you complimenting our musician. He's new to the carnival, but he plays brilliantly, doesn't he?"

"He does," Robin said, smiling flirtatiously. "He certainly knows how to use his hands."

Cassandra chuckled with her hand over her mouth, but the ringmaster smiled as if he were in on the joke.

"He is a man of many talents, but he's led a tragic life. In time he will find the right path, but tell me, do you two believe in…magic?"

Cassandra laughed again and Robin rolled her eyes, just as they'd done to me so many times.

"Please. I know you know the answer to that. There's magic all over this place. That's why we came."

"Indeed. Well, if that is the case, what would you say if I told you that you were drawn here to fulfill a purpose?"

"What kind of a purpose?" Cassandra asked, her hands on her hips as she mustered up a little attitude.

"You'll have no awareness of your role until the purpose has been achieved. All you must do is follow the path your heart tells you is right, and, when it is time, help another to follow the path of *their* heart."

Robin and Cassandra looked at each other, they each pulled off a piece of cotton candy from the bundle Cassandra was holding, and they both shrugged.

“That’s a given. Of course we would. What’s the catch?”

The man’s smile faded and his eyes became moist with tears. “You will suffer a painful loss, but with it, you will gain immeasurable wealth and happiness. And the service you perform will bring love to two very deserving souls.”

“Then yes,” Cassandra said. “Love is the most important thing!”

“Cassandra,” Robin scolded. “Be careful.”

“Your sister is correct,” the man said. “It’s dangerous to love without wisdom and caution. Therefore, as a gift, I give to you the necessary ingredients.”

Before the sisters could react, he’d reached into his pocket, pulled out his hand, and when he opened it, he blew a fine powder into their faces.

The image swirled once more, and before it disappeared, the calliope player turned around and—

“It’s him! It was him! When was this? What happened? What did you do?”

“Nothing,” Robin said. “Honestly. We went home and never talked about it. We didn’t know what had happened—”

“Until Gavin’s mother left us. Losing her was awful. We’d lost our parents already, and we thought the three of us would face the world together. But then she met Gavin’s stepfather, and he convinced her that she should give up her wicked ways.”

“She left us, and then she died. And we thought we knew pain.”

“We spoke of that night at the carnival for the first time, as if losing her had unlocked that memory.” Robin sighed, taking a sip of her own tea. “We assumed it was done. Nothing could be more painful than losing a sister. But then we met you, and for a while we thought…mission accomplished. We’d brought you and Gavin together.”

“But Gavin was with Mel.” *And he didn’t love me.*

"I never believed Gavin was meant to leave us," Cassandra said with tears in her eyes. "But he chose to ignore the path of his heart. His place was with his found family and his music, but he always wanted more. It was never enough."

The three of us were crying, and at this point I was really wishing for a bottle of something stronger than witches' brew.

"So you're telling me that my Kal was there, playing his calliaphone machine, and this was when?"

"Before you were born." Robin stared at me over her mug as she sipped. "We were in our early twenties. After we left the carnival? Our powers—boom. Way stronger. My business? Boom. Took off. I made stupid money practicing law. I retired at forty-five and I honestly could have been done a long time before, but it was nice to have my fingers in local politics." She raised an eyebrow, and I barked out a laugh.

"Why aren't you telling me this is all fiction? That there is no way my boyfriend, who I am desperately in love with, is over a hundred years old?"

"You know it's true. You knew it the moment you touched, didn't you?"

I *did* know. I knew all I needed to know.

Kal was good, he was wonderful...and he was mine. *My* purpose. Meant to walk the path with *me*.

"So what do I do?"

They grinned at each other. "It's Grand Gesture Time!"

# CHAPTER 29

## Kal

I had so much time I wanted to make up with my sister, so much to learn about the years I'd missed, but it was nearly the date I was expected to meet Hush and fly to London for the tour. Krish had suggested we meet in Oakland so I wouldn't have to fly alone, so after a week with Ellen, I boarded another bus.

"I will come back. I want to take care of you."

Ellen had patted my arm. "You've already done so much." In the week I was there, I painted walls, fixed broken appliances, repaired leaky faucets… all things she'd meant to get around to but since she was moving slower these days, she hadn't had the energy. She also confessed that she was holding on to her meager finances in case she needed long-term care.

"I will make sure you have what you need." I left her all of the cash I had in my bottomless billfold, and by the time I arrived at the bus station it had replenished itself.

"You are always welcome in my home, Kal. And I am grateful to finally have answers to the mystery of my missing brother."

We hugged before I left and I promised to write. This time there would be no one to interfere in my correspondence.

Besides the work I had done for her, I asked her to show me where Uncle Norman's clinic had been. I wanted to see it. She took me to the site, but there was a warehouse complex there now. I hoped it was a better place, that none of the evil my uncle had done still tainted the soil it was built on.

The bus ride took nearly three days this time, though I had more to keep myself occupied. I bought a journal and tried to write down everything I remembered, everything my sister had told me, and everything I still wanted to do with this extra time I'd been given. For example, I wanted to track down the people my uncle had hurt and perhaps find a way to make reparations. It would have to be anonymous, but doing good for those who'd suffered such torture would give me some peace. It was all I could think to do.

But the most important thing to me was to see Ryan again. I needed to thank him for believing in me enough to give me the confidence to go on. We hadn't spoken again since that morning I'd rushed in head first without considering the shock he'd experience being introduced to my sister. He'd tried to call me, but I didn't know what to say to him. I couldn't take his pity yet, not until I was strong enough to walk on my own.

It took me several days to work out in my head what I would say. It came down to gratitude. That I could make him understand.

Love? I didn't think he would believe me capable of it,

since he must have thought I was a troubled person to believe what I believed.

Krish and Silas picked me up from the bus station in Oakland and I'd nearly gotten down and kissed the ground, I was that happy to be off the bus. The band's house was across town in the Dimond District and they were excited to show me my place. They didn't mention Ryan, and neither did I.

Krish parked on the street as there were already two vehicles in the driveway. Being on tour, I hadn't seen how most people lived, didn't understand what the function of the paved area next to a house was for. During my time with Ellen, she did a lot of educating.

"Your place is in back," Silas said, pulling out a key. "It's got a bed, dresser, hot plate and fridge, but if you want to cook, you can always use the kitchen in the main house. We won't have a lot of time to get you settled in before we have to leave, but, you know, when we come back from Europe, we want you to know this place is yours."

"I missed you both." I think my candid confession surprised Silas, but he and Krish both hugged me enthusiastically.

"We totally missed you. Now, go on inside. Everything you should need is there. Get some sleep. We can deal with the rest tomorrow."

"Thank you."

I wanted to say more, but the thought of being horizontal on a soft surface was so appealing, I couldn't wait another minute.

I fumbled with the key and went to open the door, only to realize the two of them were still standing there.

"Was there something—"

I smelled something burning. I quickly pushed the door open, afraid my new home was already destroyed—

"Hi."

Ryan was there, in the flesh, sitting on a couch with candles burning on the table next to him. He was wearing a navy sweater that was stretched out around the neck and a pair of torn tan trousers with holes in the knees.

He took my breath away.

"We'll see you two in the morning," Silas said. "Or…later. Whenever. Basically you're good for forty-eight hours, when we need to leave for the airport."

"Thank you, sweetheart," Ryan said. He stood gingerly from the couch and walked toward me, his gaze never leaving mine. He took my bag from me, gently took my arm, pulled me inside, and shut the door. He set the bag down and placed his hands on my arms, which seemed to have forgotten how to move.

"Hi."

"Ry-an."

"Uh-huh."

"But…how?"

"It's a long story, kind of a wild one, but first… Do you need something to drink? Some food? A shower?"

"I need a hug."

Ryan grinned and held his arms out.

I wrapped him in mine, freezing when he sucked in a breath.

"I'm better, but still sore."

I buried my face in his shoulder and exhaled, almost afraid he wasn't real. Perhaps I was hallucinating after the many hours I'd spent awake on the bus. I hadn't been able to sleep more than a few minutes at a time. It didn't rock gently as it drove along the highways. I wasn't surrounded by my friends. There was no bunk, no Ryan…

Ryan, who was now smoothing down my hair and shushing me as I fought for composure.

"I made them promise not to tell you I was here. I needed to see you for myself before—"

I pulled back and bit down on my lip. "Before you say goodbye?"

"No." He shook his head and took my hands in his. "That wasn't part of my plan at all. I needed to see you before you leave for Europe. I needed to touch you and see you. I needed to tell you...I believe you."

Once his words sank in, I sagged in relief.

"Okay. Then I *would* really like to take a shower before we say any more."

He smiled brightly and clicked his heels together. "Let me give you a tour of your new apartment."

I laughed when the tour ended a few steps away.

"That's it. You've got your living space with a kitchenette in here, and in here," he said, gesturing with his arms, "a miniscule bathroom, which to be honest is about the size of the one on the bus. But...you've got a whole queen-sized bed!"

"I've never been so grateful to see a bed in my life. I want to lay on it right now, but I don't want to get it dirty."

Ryan clapped his hands together. "Then I'll let you shower. Everything you need is in there. I made sure—"

"Are you staying?"

He crossed his arms over his chest and looked...small. Unsure. Tired. His mouth moved like it wasn't quite healed.

"If you want me to stay, then yes. I'd like that very much." He walked over to the couch and sat back down. "I'll wait for you."

There was so much I wanted to say, but just like when we first met, I couldn't get the words to come out right. I nodded and turned for the bathroom, taking one last look at Ryan's smiling, hopeful face before I went into the bathroom.

Which was indeed miniscule. It was difficult to crouch down enough to get under the showerhead, and I kept smacking my elbows on the wall, but the warm water felt wonderful after the long bus ride. I wasn't sure if I was meant for bus life in the long run. I would do it as long as I needed to, but perhaps there was still a way for me to be with Ryan and work around music without sleeping in a tiny bunk.

I finished my shower, brushed my teeth, and used the razor left for me to shave. I realized I hadn't brought any clothes in with me, but I honestly didn't want anything between me and Ryan if he was going to stay.

I came out of the bathroom wrapped in a towel, and I spotted Ryan's bag tucked in the corner of the bedroom. I hated knowing we had only a limited time to be together.

"Feel better?"

He blew the candles out on the table and moved toward me, slowly, as if he didn't want to spook me. The soft light coming from the bedside table cast shadows across his face.

"What smells so good?"

"Hmm? Oh, I burned some sage and palo santo before you came home. Supposed to cleanse the space. The candle is one of Cassandra's creations. It's spelled for clarity, protection, and…love."

He stood before me at the threshold to the bedroom.

"A love spell? I told you, Ry-an, you don't need a love spell with me. I already love you."

He laughed, and I saw the tears collect in the corners of his eyes. He rolled them and crossed his arms in front of him again.

"I thought I might need a little help, you know, in case…" He didn't finish his thought, but I understood. He was as afraid as I was.

I reached for his arms and gently pulled them apart. "No. Come here. Please, Ry-an."

He came to me, pressing his face into my chest and circling my waist with his arms. "I missed you, Kal. I'm sorry."

"Sorry for what? I'm the one who… I couldn't talk to you. I was afraid, and you called and I didn't pick up. I'm the one who's sorry."

"You needed time. I did, too. But I had the Beaumont sisters to set me straight. I was okay."

"Good. Now, do you mind if we get into this bed? I don't think I can stand up any longer."

Ryan stepped back and for the first time ever, he looked shy. "I don't want to crowd you. If you want me to sleep on the couch—"

I stared pointedly at him…and dropped my towel on the floor.

"Or, I could get in bed with you. Sure. I could do that."

I went around the far side and pulled the blankets back, feeling his eyes on me. I lay down, and whatever the bed was made out of was the most blissful thing my body had ever experienced. Well, besides my encounters with Ryan.

"I…um. Okay."

Ryan unfastened his trousers and slid them down his legs. He wore tight black undergarments that accentuated his attributes. He reached for the sweater, but then he turned his back and sat carefully down on the bed. He pulled it off, sucked in a breath, and then panted for a few moments.

"It's getting better, I swear. I saw a doctor up in Fortuna and he said the fractures were healing pretty well. It's going to take some time. Can't sing for a couple more weeks, though, which sucks. I've never not been able to sing, you know. Never blew out my voice, never had any issues with my vocal cords or got sick like a lot of guys."

He turned slightly to smile at me, and I got a load of the extent of his injury.

"Baby," I whispered. His stiff movements showed how much pain he must still be enduring.

"Hey, that's my word," he said. He grabbed a pillow, hugged it to his chest, and then blew out a breath as he lowered himself to his side and then rolled onto his back. "Fuck, that hurts."

"What did the dentist say about your teeth?"

He grinned widely, showing all of his teeth. The front one was missing the inside corner and his upper lip pulled slightly. "Only chipped two of them. None fell out, thank goodness. I'm holding off on having the chipped ones capped. I kind of like how it sullies my pretty boy looks."

I rested my chin in my hand and shook my head. "You need to take care of your teeth, Ryan."

"I know. It's okay, really. Doc says I'm fine, it's just cosmetic. I can live with that. What I can't live with?" He lost his smile. "This space between us."

"Where can I touch you without hurting you?"

He blinked up at me and touched his finger to his bottom lip. "Here. But gently. Stitches are gone inside the top lip, but it's still a little tender."

"Ryan." My hands balled into fists. "I'm—"

"I know, it sucks. He sucks. But he can't hurt me anymore, baby. Now come here, I'm not done showing you where it's safe to touch me." He put his hand on my face and smiled. "I love you, too. My beautiful man."

Our reunion turned out to be less heated than I think Ryan was hoping for, as most of what we tried to do caused him pain, however we did find ways to gently love each other. In the end he was able to lay partially on top of me and let me cradle him in my arms. He said it was easier to breathe that way, right before he fell asleep.

I was exhausted and overwhelmed by everything that had happened, it meant everything to hold him close like that after four weeks apart. I was finally able to shut my brain down and relax.

No matter what happened next, Ryan was here. He believed me. And most importantly, he loved me.

# CHAPTER 30

**Ryan**

I woke up before Kal and refused to move. I wanted to soak up all of the time I had with him, skin to skin, before we had to go back to FaceTime calls for the next two months.

Hush had invited me to open for them as a solo act, but my attorney said no way, not until the legal matters with Backdrop were settled. Without a job, my parole officer wouldn't give me permission to galivant off to Europe, especially seeing as I was currently in legal hot water with the band and the label, and there was the whole altercation that got us thrown off of Warped Tour. I'd been absolved of any wrongdoing, thankfully, so the court date in January to terminate my parole was still on, but I had to be on my best behavior until then.

I hadn't told Kal any of this yet. We had more important

matters to cover first, like whether I was forgiven, that I believed him, which side of the bed the other liked, etc.

Oh God, being in a real bed with him was fabulous. But not being able to get all up in his beautiful body with no restrictions had been infuriating. Having any sort of sexual relations always involves the muscles around the ribs, did you know that? Or the mouth, which was still a little fucked up. Guess I should have paid closer attention to anatomy in school. I'd be patient, but I was already mentally counting down the days until he came back in November, when one way or another, I'd have all of him.

As the sun began to fill the room with light, I thought of all that had happened to bring me to Kal's new home, which I hoped would be temporary.

After the Beaumont sisters' big reveal, they shoved food in my face, made me get cleaned up, and then they drove me to Oregon without telling me what I was in for. A few hours later, when the sun had gone down, they finally parked. I'd been snoozing with headphones on and when Cassandra shook me awake, I nearly had a heart attack.

It was the carnival.

Kal's carnival.

"How did you know where to find it?"

"Have we proven nothing to you yet?" Robin said with an exaggerated sigh.

Walking under the Welcome, Traveler banner felt bizarre. Not like it had with Kal. It felt uneasy.

The sisters walked arm in arm directly up to a tall man with dark hair, the sleeves of his white, puffy shirt pushed up to the elbows. They tapped him on the shoulder, he bowed to them, and then he saw me.

They approached together, a gleam in his eye, and I had to fight the urge not to back up.

"Ryan Michael Wells. Welcome," he said with another

bow. "I understand you have questions for me, that is to be understood, but I warn you that there's very little I can tell you. Think hard on what you ask."

His eyes seemed to swirl with colors until…they were blue? Like Kal's.

"I want to know…how can I help Kal? How can I make sure he has a good life?"

The man tilted his head and his expression softened. "So selfless. People underestimate you. You underestimate yourself. You have almost everything you need to make him happy. There is but one thing I can share with you that will help him on his path."

He gestured for me to come with him and that déjà vu feeling hit hard.

I remembered the tents, the same path I'd taken as a child, the night with Kal and Krish and Silas. The place hadn't changed at all. But I had.

The man led me past the populated area and toward the back where Kal had shown me his most prized possession.

"The calliaphone."

"Mmm. Kallos has had so much taken from him. We did what we could to aid in his rehabilitation process, but a piece of him resides in his creation. Would you take possession of it? Keep it safe until Kallos is able to possess it himself?"

"Of course. What do I need to do?"

His expression turned eerie, the color shifting in his eyes to deep amber, and once again I felt the urge to flee.

"You must be willing, when the time comes, to aid a fellow traveler. Just as your life has been touched by this carnival, there are others, and one of them will come to you in need. Will you vow to help them find their path?"

"Yes, yes. Of course I will. I'll do anything to have Kal in my life."

"Then so be it. I will have the calliaphone delivered to

your friends. It will be safe with them. You may never know when the one who walks the path beside you is a man out of time, nor will you anticipate the magic he is capable of, unless you keep your eyes open to the possibilities. As for you, you must prepare for your rocky journey ahead. Your path is littered with obstacles. Take care with how you travel beyond them."

"I will."

Sure enough, two days after I returned to the Beaumonts' from the visit to the carnival, I got a call from Silas.

"We got a big fucking package for you, and Kal is on his way. You better get down here."

I'd driven my truck the five hours it took to get to Oakland from Fortuna and arrived a few hours before Silas and Krish were scheduled to pick up Kal from the bus station. They helped me load the calliaphone into their garage, Los volunteering to park his Mercedes on the street until I could figure out what to do with this priceless piece of Kal's history.

"How the hell did you find it? Wasn't this the one he showed us at that carnival?"

"It is," I told them, but I wouldn't tell them the whole story. That was for Kal. "The Beaumont sisters tracked it down. I bought it for Kal."

Bought. Sure, there hadn't been any money exchanged, but the weird fucking guy blew some powder in my face and the next thing I knew, Cassandra was loading me back into the car for the trip back to their house. All I could remember was that I'd agreed to do…something. Help someone. It didn't matter as long as I got Kal back.

I had plans that involved finding a place for the both of us to live once my lawyer and I had negotiated the terms of my contract with Wreckage, Hush's label. They wanted to work with me on the stuff I wrote with Gavin, and on my first solo album. Depending on how that all panned out, well, things were in motion and I needed to be patient, yada yada. For now, the only things in my control were writing songs, continuing my therapy and recovery, and loving this man in my arms.

Forty hours later, it was time to say goodbye. I drove the band and Kal to SFO in Silas's Suburban. Brains and his Navy man were meeting them there. Brains was going as the band's manager as Jessica had resigned as their manager. I would have to get the full story later. Navy man—he insisted I call him Paul from now on, since he'd retired. Whatever—was going as muscle and to sell merch or something. The band's other tech had already traveled over with the group's gear and planned to meet them there with their European tour manager.

Silas assured me that Kal would be taken care of, promised he'd be with them at all times, that they'd watch out for him, but it killed me that I couldn't go.

"I wish I could take you to my favorite places over there," I said to him as we embraced for our goodbye. "I hate that once again my fuck-up is keeping me from what I want."

"It's almost over, baby," he whispered, kissing my temple. He'd taken to stealing my term of affection, and I didn't hate it.

"What I wouldn't give for a tight space and your strong arms right about now," I mused, and he laughed.

We'd spent most of our time in his bed, in between doing laundry and packing and discussing our hopes and dreams for the future, but I could never get enough of his touch.

"I'm going to be home before you know it. By then your ribs will be fully healed and I can, how did you put it? 'Fuck you into the mattress'?"

I burst out laughing and squeezed him a little tighter,

chest pain be damned. "You can try. We can both try and see what feels best."

"You can have anything, Ryan. I told you that."

I smiled at him, grateful for what we'd found in each other, grateful for what was in store. I needed to be patient. I sucked at being patient.

He kissed me deeply, pulling me as tightly to him as I could stand. He made it count, this last kiss, and when we came up for air, he whimpered.

"Go see the world," I told him. "Do your magic. I'll be waiting for you."

His smile told me he'd be counting the days as well until we were together once more.

"Come on, Kal," Los said, pulling him away. "I call dibs on sitting next to you. You make a damn good pillow and it's a long-ass flight."

Kal glanced back over his shoulder, and I barked out a laugh at the worry in his gaze. I'd assured him the flight wouldn't be too awful. He had the best travel buddies to keep his mind off of his fear. If I couldn't be with him, my adopted brothers in Hush were the next best bet.

I waved as they entered the sliding doors and allowed myself to cry all the way back to their house in Oakland, which I'd be staying in while they were gone. I looked forward to the solitude, to the plethora of instruments and their home studio, and the time to plot the next part of the path.

Ryan Wells was reinventing himself once more, and this time, he was in love.

# EPILOGUE

**Ryan**

*Two months and two days later...*

"You are a dream, Kal. You pose beautifully. Knew you would, my beautiful man."

"Your beautiful man is going to need to eat soon, or else you're going to have to listen to my stomach growl."

I was on my third drawing of Kal since he'd returned from Europe. The first one had been of him in a Thinker-type pose. That session ended when I fell to my knees and sucked him off until he claimed he was seeing double. For the second, I'd positioned him on his stomach across the back of the fainting couch I'd found at an estate sale in nearby Eureka. That one ended with me giving him his first proper rimming—which he loved, I should add.

This time, he lay on my bed with his arms over his head,

grasping the iron headboard. His biceps were taut, the veins in his forearms stood at attention. He was delectable.

"I'll feed you some snacks. Cassandra and Robin will kill me if I ruin your appetite for the feast they're cooking." I looked down at the charcoal drawing I'd been working on for the past hour. "These pieces draw themselves. You are fucking gorgeous."

He grinned at me and rubbed his feet together. They were crossed at the ankle, giving me nice long lines. I knelt at the foot of the bed with my giant sketch pad and was covered with smudges from the charcoal. I was truly living my best life, but I was craving a different sort of expression at the moment.

"Hold that pose just for a bit." I crawled off the bed and trotted over to the fridge in my silk robe. I grabbed a bowl of grapes and a plate of cheese and crackers the sisters had left for us. They stocked my fridge when I told them I was bringing Kal home with me, and they added a few touches to my already cool-as-hell cottage.

It was a bit bigger than Kal's apartment in Oakland, with a larger bathroom that included a giant claw-foot tub. It also had these fantastic huge windows and glass panels in the roof that let in light and shadows from the giant redwood trees surrounding the property. I'd enjoyed them immensely, but since I planned to be naked with Kal as much as possible, Cassandra had made some gauzy window dressings for the place and she'd built a lovely canopy for the bed out of driftwood pieces and matching gauze material in blues and purples. She'd also made a bedspread of mismatched pieces of velvet in jewel tones and covered the bed in loads of pillows. It was luxurious, especially with naked Kal draped on top.

I was grateful to the goddess for these phenomenal women every day. The two months I spent by myself in

Oakland, however, were incredibly productive. In fact, my new agent, who repped my music as well as my art, was able to book me a gallery show in Oakland with the drawings I'd done while I was down there, and I had another one scheduled for the spring, since all of my pieces sold. In the past, I'd only drawn for fun, but now it felt like a genuine way to express myself and make a little money to rebuild my nest egg.

My attorney said I could sell all the visual art I wanted while the legal matters with the band dragged on.

During that time, I also recorded a demo of all the music Gavin and I had written together, as well as an album full of stuff I'd been working on over the years for myself. I'd never been this productive in my entire life, and I blamed it all on the fact that I'd fallen love. Such a sap.

I brought the food back to the bed and I straddled Kal's hips. "Let me feed you."

The first few bites I gave him were meant to ease his hunger, but then I began to get handsy, sliding a finger between his lips along with the grape, and feeding him from my lips, and I succeeded at awakening my favorite kind of hunger.

Kal let go of the bars at the head of the bed and grabbed my hips. He shifted so I could feel his erection between the globes of my ass.

"*Oh*," I breathed and shuddered as a jolt of pleasure ran through me. I'd planned ahead for this exact moment.

"Oh? Are you all right?" He reached for the curve of my ass and I intercepted his hand.

"I'm great." I guided his hand around so he could discover the source of my delight.

"What is this?" He tried to sit up, but I held him down with a hand to his chest.

"This," I said, pressing my hips into his touch, which

brought out a gasp. "This is a little something I thought I'd use so I'd be prepared."

He ran his fingers over the glass jewel top of the plug I'd inserted before I started drawing.

"Does it hurt?"

"No, baby. I wanted to be…ready for you. I'm ready to let you fuck me."

This time Kal *did* sit up, and he wrapped his arms around me. "I told you, I don't need that. I love how we are together."

"And I love it, too. I've never let anyone have me like this. Not willingly. But I want to try with you. They say when you're in love, everything feels good, so we're going to go with that."

Kal gazed up at me, his blue eyes filled with worry. He ran his fingers around the jewel and touched my opening, which made me jerk in his arms.

"Oooo it feels good, better than I imagined."

Gently, *so* gently, he twisted it in little strokes, and I moaned, pushing back against his touch.

"Take it out, baby. Fill me with you."

He blinked and licked his lips as he slowly removed the plug, his breaths coming faster now than even mine. "Show me."

I helped him roll on a condom and coated it with a generous amount of lube. Then I pushed him back into the sea of pillows.

"Let me." That was the last thing I said that sounded like actual words. I sat back slowly, taking him in, enjoying the burn, and not feeling invaded or hurt or any of the negative connotations I'd given this act in the past. It was no longer something to endure, but another way to love my lover.

And I loved him so much.

His grip on my thighs was firm, but he let me control the movements. It was a shame that it was impossible to ride him like the wantonly mindless heathen I was and draw him at the same time, because the expression on his face of wonder and bliss was my favorite of all.

"Ry-an, I feel…you're so much, I can't…I have to…"

His body curled up and he hugged my torso for dear life as his orgasm took over. He jerked and moaned and held me tight. I was right back in those snug spaces with him. The friction of my cock caught between us, rubbing over his hot skin, sent me careening toward the edge. Just like that. My legs shook as I continued to rock with Kal inside me, moving on instinct.

I put my hands on his neck and pressed our foreheads together as we tried to collect our breath.

"That was so much more than I thought it would be."

I grinned. "And despite what I said before, I'm pretty sure I fucked *you* into the mattress."

He burst out laughing and crushed me with his arms. "I think you're right. That means I still get a turn, right?"

"You get whatever you want, baby."

AN HOUR LATER, after we'd soaked together in the tub and dressed for dinner with the Beaumonts and their local coven, we took a leisurely stroll through the garden to the big house.

"It's beautiful here. I've never seen such big trees. I think it's my favorite place I've been so far."

"Even more beautiful than Spain? I loved the pictures you sent me."

Kal had taken pictures of all the places he went, and he had quite an eye. He made a list of all the places he wanted to go with me when I was able to travel again, including to Iowa to meet his sister. I would do whatever it took to make him happy.

"Even more beautiful. Because you're here. I've never seen you as at peace as you are in this place."

I tugged on his hand. "Has a lot to do with you being here."

We kissed in the moonlight as if we had no place to be, that is, until Cassandra started to rap on the window to get our attention and then began gesturing wildly for us to get our asses inside.

Dinner was a wild and raucous occasion. Kal remained quiet with a perpetual blush on his cheeks at the outrageous comments from the sisters and the witches in their coven. I loved the feminine energy, and being allowed to share in it as a man was something I treasured.

"I could eat this one up." Sheka Kincaid, a hilarious Black woman who was the friendliest one in the group, made her fingers into claws near Kal's arm. He smiled politely but his expression when he turned to me said he thought she meant it literally.

"He *is* quite tasty, but I'm afraid I don't share, darlin'."

She wrinkled her nose at me. "You're no fun. Hey, what about your friends in that other band, Hush? Cassandra, isn't the one you used for your virility spell in that band?"

Cassandra placed a hand over her mouth and giggled. "Los. Shhh, don't tell him. He only knows about the love spell."

"Use him for whatever you need. The dude needs some love magic and soon. He's been using my boyfriend as a pillow for the past two months, so he's probably jonesin' right about now with Kal back in my bed, where I intend for him to stay."

The whole table roared with laughter at poor Kal's embarrassment.

"You good, baby?" I whispered in his ear. "Is this too much?"

His smile was warm, happy…He was at peace. And that's how I intended to keep him.

"It's good. I'm good."

"Speaking of love magic," Sheka said. "Is everything set up for tonight?"

Cassandra giggled and clapped her hands together. "We are all set. We will solve the conundrums of our love lives. All we need is the board—"

"And some chocolate—"

"And those special candles—"

"And some good wine—"

"And that's our cue," I said. I took Kal's hand and helped him up from his seat. "You ladies have a wonderful night, and thank you for dinner."

I speed-walked us out the back door and Kal laughed as he tried to keep up.

"What's the rush?"

"You do *not* want to see what these women do with that board."

Kal laughed and put his arms around me. "That board helped bring us together. Maybe it really *is* magic."

"I already told you. *You're* magic. Now, what do you say we open up the windows in *our* cottage and sleep under the stars again?"

That was exactly what we did, and when I dreamed, I was that little boy back at the carnival listening to the blond man make magical music on his calliaphone, only this time, the little boy was safe. He was at peace.

*The spirit cracked his knuckles and wiggled his fingers over the board. "Three down, one to go." If he couldn't be with the ones he loved the most—Silas, Brains, Ryan, and Los—he could certainly work a little magic. "But first, let's see what these witches are looking for."*

*The spirit watched from the shadows as the women gathered around his board, tipsy from wine, sated from good food, sweets, and sisterhood. The scents of bergamot, peppermint, and lemon wafted from the candles burning around the room and the women began chanting their spell.*

*"If love magic is what they seek, love magic is what they'll find."*

*It was too late for him, but with his board, he would do all in his limited power to bring happiness to the worthy.*

*He flicked his long blond hair over his shoulder and stroked his beard.*

*Let the fun begin.*

***The End...***

For more Warped Tour hijinks, check out:

Summer of Hush (MM)
Brains and Brawn (MM)
Got You Covered – A Hush Short (MM) (Coming Soon)

For more Music-Inspired queer romance, check out:

I Want, More (MM)
Love and Pride (FF)
All I Wanna Do (Coming Soon) (FFM)
Hurricane Reese (MM)
Typhoon Toby (MM)
Earthquake Ethan (Coming Soon) (MM)
Pinups and Puppies (FF)

# ACKNOWLEDGMENTS

As always, I could not have finished this book without the support of my family. I swear, kids, we'll get all of your off-to-college shopping done on time! And to my husband who continues to hold my hand through my post-teaching life and caring-for-parents phase of life, I couldn't do it without you.

To my beloved editor Kelli, thank you for pushing me all of these years and giving me the tools to write this story. This might have been a record LOL/ROFL edit.

To Ari and Rachel, THANK YOU for sharing your world with us! I absolutely loved playing in your sandbox and look forward to future collaborations. And to Ander, Phyllis, and TA, THANK YOU for letting me bounce ideas off of you. Ander, your hatred and disgust over certain folks in the book fueled me on! Thank you all so much.

Thanks to my college friend Eric S. Juhnke for your book *Quacks and Crusaders,* which was a great resource for learning more about the real Norman Baker. This was my favorite research find ever!

To Scott and Mark, Gloria and the PRG crew, and the Gay Romance Reviews folks THANK you so much for helping me get the word out.

My pals in the SBC, I love you and treasure your friendship. You inspire me always.

And to all of you! Thank you so much for coming along on this journey with me. I hope you'll stick around for more shivers and swoons! Please sign up for my newsletter-y thingie at www.rlmerrillauthor.com and follow me on BookBub for the latest news!

# ABOUT THE AUTHOR

Whether she's writing contemporary romance featuring quirky and relatable characters or diving deep into the paranormal and supernatural to give readers a shiver, R.L. Merrill (she/her) loves creating compelling, diverse, and inclusive stories that will stay with readers long after. Winner of the Kathryn Hayes "When Sparks Fly" Best Contemporary award for *Hurricane Reese,* a Foreword INDIES finalist for *Summer of Hush,* and a Daphne DuMaurier finalist for *Connection,* Ro spends every spare moment improving her writing craft and striving to find that perfect balance between real-life and happily ever after. She contributes paranormal hilarity to Robyn Peterman's Magic and Mayhem Universe, recently joined the Carnival of Mysteries shared world project with fellow queer romance authors, and participates in various charity projects by donating her time as a newbie author coach or her stories. You can find her connecting with readers on social media, advocating for America's youth, cruising around town with Great Dane Velma, cuddling with twin black cat familiars Frankenstein and Dracula, or headbanging at a rock show near her home in the San Francisco Bay Area! ***Stay Tuned for More...***

# CARNIVAL OF MYSTERIES

Welcome, Traveler! Join us for a series of M/M fantasies by a talented group of both new and established authors. Whether you enjoy mystery, action, danger, or just sweet romance, there is something for everyone at the Carnival of Mysteries!

Kim Fielding * L. A. Witt * Kaje Harper

Megan Derr * Ander C. Lark * E. J. Russell

Morgan Brice * Kayleigh Sky

Nicole Dennis * Elizabeth Silver * R. L. Merrill

TA Moore * Z. A. Maxfield

Sara Ellis * Rachel Langella

## COMING SOON!

**Pre-Order R.L. Merrill's follow-up to *You Can Do Magic*, Winner of The Paranormal Romance Guild's Reviewers Choice Award and Finalist in the North Texas Romance Writers' Carolyn contest.**

Sixties folk singer Dane Donovan vanished from a desolate highway rest area in 1979. Forty years later, he's found hitchhiking in the California desert on a cold winter's night. He hasn't aged a day, but the roadmap of scars he wears tells a chilling tale.

Veteran detective Walter Muse took over Dane's missing persons case twenty years ago. Still, his haunting connection to Dane Donovan goes back to a peculiar run-in as a child with The Troubadour and his Talking Board at a traveling carnival. He receives a late-night call with Dane's whereabouts and races to Laurel Canyon to see for himself whether Dane is real—or a ghost meant to taunt Walter and his somewhat precarious hold on his sanity. Walter's carefully honed detective instincts are thrown out the window, however, when his obsession with the case develops into an undeniable attraction to the mysterious singer.

Dane is on a mission to stop a new killer hell-bent on picking up where Dane's kidnapper left off, and Walter is determined to protect him, no matter the personal and psychological cost. They'll have to rely on new friends and trusted colleagues as well as the power of a mystical spirit board to stop the killing and have a chance at a real future together.

*You Can Save Me* is part of the multi-author Carnival of Mysteries Series. Each book stands alone, but each one includes at least one visit to Errante Ame's Carnival of Mysteries, a magical, multiverse traveling show full of unusual acts, games, and rides. The Carnival changes to suit the world it's on, so each visit is unique and special.

*You Can Save Me* may be read as a standalone, however, it is a continuation of the tale told in *You Can Do Magic.* Recommended 18 and up. TW for mentions of violence and suicide of a family member.



*You Can Save Me* will also be available on Kindle Unlimited starting August 21, 2024

www.ingramcontent.com/pod-product-compliance
Ingram Content Group UK Ltd.
Pitfield, Milton Keynes, MK11 3LW, UK
UKHW040005200726
13854UKWH00001B/40

9 781953 433176